sweetness

followed

A NOVEL

JAMES MORLEY III

Sweetness Followed

Published by
64 Slices, LLC

ISBN: 978-1-7327196-0-6
eISBN: 978-1-7327196-1-3

Cover and Interior Design: GKS Creative

FOR THREE TWO AND ONE

MY DEEPEST THANKS

TO LIBBY AND TRAVIS.

AND ANYONE ELSE

WHO MAKES IT TO THE END.

november

one

Before she had even begun to flutter her
eyes open, she sensed their presence.
Sitting there all smug and complacent.

She knew because the smell of shoe polish had invaded her dream, promptly altering what had been the sweet citrus aroma of her mother's lemon cake to that of lanolin and turpentine. She now needed only to hang her head over the side of the bed to have visual confirmation. Shifting positions in a single bed was one thing. Doing it in early November in upstate New York was an entirely different ordeal. For one, the covers were exactly the same size as the mattress. She concluded these had been her blankets as a toddler and, rather than upgrade, her mother would wait until she complained enough. Further, her parents had long ago decided that a woodburning stove placed strategically in the kitchen would be sufficient to heat the entire home. They were mistaken. So now the trick became to roll oneself over in such a way as to not allow a waft of cold air to penetrate the covers. Just the smallest bite was enough to ruin an entire night's sleep. It was a nuisance, to be sure, but one that Erin Cook was particularly adept at dealing with. After all, Erin was eleven. And Erin was clever.

Pinching the edge of the comforter with her toes and securing the top corner with her elbow, Erin smoothly orchestrated the transition from back to belly. And there they were. Resting comfortably underneath a floral print dress hung on the doorknob were two black leather shoes. All-terrain eveningwear was perhaps a more accurate description, freshly waxed and polished. Ready for all the required walking that a trip to church on a cold Sunday morning required. Erin let out a sigh that was partially muffled with her faced pressed firmly against the mattress. It wasn't so much that she found church pedantic or duplicitous. That assessment would need to wait. No, her angst was exclusively based on the long-established church appropriate attire. Specifically, the thick-soled boots that met her mother's definition of "a perfect marriage between form and function."

Although she wasn't able to analyze it in such concrete terms, Erin knew she was entering an awkward time in her life. She wanted to behave in a gender appropriate way but couldn't bring herself to make the transition. She preferred *Mad Magazine* to *Teen Beat*. Her closet-sized bedroom displayed posters of Pelé and Mike Bossy in lieu of John Schneider and Donny Osmond. At recess, she opted to play with the boys rather than sit on the sidelines debating which one was cuter. However, one area that she was willing to give it a shot was her wardrobe. That was an easy one. It required minimal participation and seemed—to her, anyway—to be the least intrusive on her character. And Erin's mother wasn't aiding her noble cause with those deceitful clogs. The dress didn't smack of style, but the flowers were girly enough to minimize the tomboy commentary from her older brothers.

Without lifting her head in the slightest, Erin gave a glance to her clock on the nightstand. A three-inch by three-inch white travel clock.

She suspected her father stole it from a hotel room but never called him on it. The hands read six-thirty. Services didn't start for another three and a half hours, which gave her ample time to shift her gaze to the left of her shoes. Leaning against the doorway were a pair of ice hockey skates. The mesh webbing on the toe was worn all the way down to the hard, plastic shell underneath. The blades had been skated to less than a centimeter and were speckled with dots of rust. But they were hers. And they didn't come in a floral pattern.

Erin's wool sock touched down on the cracked wood flooring of the upstairs hallway. She had forgone her mother's suggested attire and was now sporting snow pants and turtle-necked long underwear for her upper half. The skates dangled in her left hand. A cheap orange nightlight was stuck in the outlet next to the bathroom door. It was so encrusted with dust that she wondered what purpose it was serving at this point. The windows in the hallway weren't giving much in the way of illumination, either, as it was still before seven.

Erin arrived at the doorway at the end of the hall, giving the door a few short taps. Then leaning in with as low a voice as she could while still registering an octave: "Ian, I'm going outside. You wanna come?"

A mild thump came from behind the closed door. Erin continued, "Ian, are you up yet?"

Inside the organized chaos of a teenage boy's room, Ian lay face down on his bed, grinding his pelvis into a pillow. A magazine, the pornography kind, just below his head was the focus of his concentration. He closed his eyes to shut out the muffled calls of his sister while he continued with his act, awkwardly trying to simulate what he assumed sex with the nameless girl in the magazine would be like. Slowing down his rhythm, he nervously flipped to an alternate section of the periodical, perhaps hoping a more graphic depiction of lovemaking would speed up the business at hand. His brow furrowed and eyes tightened as if he were inspecting the financial section of the newspaper and found the outlook was grim.

From outside the door, Erin attempted one more plea. "I'm all dressed. Will you meet me out there?" Now although Ian was sweating profusely and giving it the good college try, the innocent request of his eleven-year-old sister had successfully decimated whatever erotic scenario the magazine had conjured up. Ian rolled over in a fit of frustration and hurled his stimuli at door, yelling, "Jesus! Go away!"

Erin stepped back. Startled, hurt, and more than a little confused, she took another look at the door and decided it was best to count this one a loss. Ian, meanwhile, hiked up his pants and sat on the bed, staring at the door. Still panting from the effort, he pondered what to try next. Ian was at a crossroads in his life, as well. He was soon to become the second of his family to attend college and the first to be accepted early. This made it painfully clear to him that the world, and the academic community in particular, found him to be exceptional. Ian had progressed beyond his family. Beyond his older brother, Eli, his sister, Michele, and far beyond his parents, who had ceased their formal education at high school. Ian would be attending the State University of New York at Plattsburg in the coming fall. He would finally be around peers of similar intellect. Currently, however, he was still pulsating with resentment from a masturbation ritual gone awry and wide awake at seven on a Sunday morning. Recognizing that there was little alternative, Ian reached for his long underwear.

⌁

Erin and Ian made their way across the field in the back of their house. They brought with them their Great Dane puppy, Harley. Short for Harlequin, although their father would insist it was short for Harley Davidson. The lanky beast bounded up and down in the snow, his oversized paws too clumsy to maneuver properly. He would occasionally spot a deer or small mammal in the distance and attempt to flop after it for a few futile seconds, quickly remembering that Great Danes are not fond of physical labor. In the springtime, the field would be used to grow corn, peas, and tomatoes—and if the summer were unseasonably warm, garlic and basil. It had snowed that morning, blanketing the field and woods beyond them with fresh powder. Snow was falling still, although it was the kind that was more irritating than enchanting. If it had been a heavier snow, the walk to the pond would have filled Erin with a sense of collective calm, savoring the bonding with her brother. Today it was that cold, wispy kind of snow that never quite got itself going. She ultimately decided that this was for the best, as it meant less shoveling when they finally arrived. And Ian would be in a better mood because of it.

Hockey was the last thing they had in common. They were lucky to have anything in common, actually. When you're eleven, five years in either direction is a huge gap to fill. Erin was bright enough to know that these early morning skates with Ian at the pond would soon be gone. It wouldn't be long before she would make the walk alone, and it made her heart ache to think of it. No one else in the family could skate and her girl acquaintances would never participate in such a preposterous endeavor as walking a quarter mile into the woods to shovel snow and bat a puck around. Harley, she could probably talk into it.

When they reached the edge of the field, they began to push through a wooded area. As they also carried with them their own assigned shovel, stick, and skates, it made the whole endeavor a bit unwieldy. Each time they brushed past a new-growth sapling, it would shake fresh accumulation down their necks. The shovels dragged and caught on small shrubbery, and the skates would occasionally slip out of their hands and fill up with snow. But that wasn't the point. It was all about the final destination. When they reached a clearing, Ian moved to an edge and dropped his gear. Erin promptly ran out to a makeshift goal that had been cobbled together from scraps of wood and old chicken wire. She picked it up as best she could and shook it clean. Erin loved to be the first one on the ice. She likened it to crawling into fresh linens that had dried in an early April breeze. Ian had moved beyond simple pleasures, now that he was part of the cultural and academic elite. Erin jumped up and down, hearing the ice creak and pop below her as it settled in.

"Quit screwin' around. You gotta be back in an hour," Ian shot over at her. Erin stopped jumping for moment and stood with her hands at her side. She considered jumping more simply because it annoyed him but let it go. Ian had already begun clearing the pond, pushing up the edges of the embankment and rounding off the corners.

⌒

The area brightened ever so slightly as the morning went on. The two skated around, passing and shooting the puck while the white mist danced around them. The disc would bounce off the chicken wire, releasing another puff of freshly fallen snow. Harley trotted around the perimeter of the surface, carrying a puck that he'd collected. The frozen pond squeaked and sent ice chips skittering across the surface with each awkward turn. Neither of them were particularly gifted skaters but it scarcely mattered. They didn't participate in leagues and they didn't seek to improve. They also rarely spoke. Ian preferred it this way and although Erin would have welcomed the occasional quip, she was just happy to have the company. Ian had other things on his mind and Erin was too immature to understand his emotional needs. Or so he assumed. It wasn't until Ian had his own interests at heart that he broke the silence.

"Did you water the chickens?"

"No." Erin fished the puck out of the net. She sensed a scolding on the horizon and made a deliberate pass back to him to keep whatever was coming at bay.

"What about the horses?"

"No."

"You know that's gonna piss Mom off. I told you to do that before we left."

"Why do I have to do it? They aren't my stupid pets. I can't even lift the thing when it's water, much less when it's frozen solid."

"Well, you'd better fuckin' do it before we get back, or I'll pop you upside the head." Erin was confused by his aggressive tone. Older brothers were always threatening one form of physical abuse of another, but the course language made it less playful. Rather than confront his tone, Erin opted for a different approach.

"I'm gonna tell Mom you swore," she sheepishly returned, with her chin in her neck.

"Go for it."

"So then you'll get in trouble too."

"No, I won't."

"Why not?" Their light game of pass and catch seemed to get progressively harder as the conversation wore on.

"Because she'll ask you what I said, and then you'll have to say "fuck," and then *you'll* get in trouble for swearing."

"That doesn't make any sense." Erin threw her hands to her sides in protest. Her stick in one hand struck the pond, sending up flakes of ice.

"Well, welcome to real life. That's the way things work, I'm sorry to say. Ready to go in?" Ian had succeeded in sucking the fun out of her morning. She almost wished she had come alone.

"No. I don't want to go in. Stay here with me."

"Sorry. I'll leave the dog with you. Later." Ian plopped down in the snow and began taking his skates off. Erin followed, slowly pushing off with one leg.

"Like fifteen more minutes."

"Nah, I'm getting cold. I've got shit to do."

"What shit?"

"Don't swear."

"Please just stay a little bit more."

"Nah, I'm not gonna be doing that." Ian picked up his gear and started to make his way through the wooded path. Erin watched him go and then noticed the shovels sticking out of the embankment.

"Hey, Ian! You forget your shovel!"

"Oh yeah, can you bring mine in for me? Thanks!" he said without turning around.

"I can't carry all this by myself!" Erin cried back, with a stomp of her skate to extenuate her frustration.

"Ian!" Erin moved her blades back and forth, realizing the futility of further dialogue. In only a matter of seconds, Ian had disappeared around a turn and she was alone. She stood motionless for a moment, hoping perhaps he was just executing some hilarious joke. But the punch line never came. Erin turned to face Harley as he dropped a puck at her feet. She lightly batted it with one hand into the goal as the dog raced after it. The snowflakes were getting a little bigger by this point. She longed for someone to share the moment with. Harley returned with the rubber disc and Erin reached down with her mitten-covered hand and patted him on the head. The two played an extended game of passing the puck into the goal while Harley went and got it. In no short time this became tiresome for both parties and the two just stood there examining each other, Erin wishing Harley would somehow miraculously evolve the ability to speak. And Harley perhaps wishing Erin would go chase the puck for a change.

Erin awkwardly made her way through the woods, trying to carry two large shovels, her stick, skates, and a small bag. With each clumsy step the shafts banged together, causing her to fall off balance, which in turn caused her hat to fall into her face. Harley jumped around her, assuming this was some sort of playtime thing. It was certainly the most entertaining one in quite a while. Much more so than the previous diversion. As Erin tried to pull her way through a maze of small trees, the shovels caught on the foliage, sending everything to the soft powder on the ground. At her wits end, she unleashed for the first time in her eleven years, "Fuck!"

The sharpness of the profanity stopped her. It also gave her an inflated sense of self-esteem. The problem was, there was no one to hear. And thusly, no one to help. She tried again, this time opting to make it a two-syllable word. "I said fuck! F-UCK!" Her voice cracked with stress, as if to say, *I'm eleven years old and I'm saying "fuck!" Does someone want to come scold me! And in the process, help me?* But no one was there. Just Harley waiting for her to keep the game going. Erin stared at him for a brief moment, trying to decide if there were any way to get the dog to carry the shovels for her.

Erin and Harley emerged from the woods into the vast expanse of fields that was the family farm. The creek that served as a natural fence for unwanted critters trickled quietly as Harley jumped through it. Erin had begun to successfully navigate through the rocks with her belongings when her boot hit a slick patch of moss. Her left foot shot forward, sending her right knee cracking against a boulder and her entire bottom half promptly submerged in the stream. This time, no profanity came. Only the sound of water moving through rocks. She closed her eyes as she felt ice water cling to her legs and begin to fill up her snowsuit like a sponge. Erin had begun to pull herself out of the creek when she spotted a small figure bouncing through the fields of snow. About twenty yards in front of her, plumes of powder billowed up around it. It picked its head up to reveal it was a weasel carrying a chicken in its mouth. The fowl hung limp, its neck broken and wings roughly stripped of their feathers. Erin almost made a move to go after it and then promptly realized the futility of such action. She moved her gaze to Harley, who just watched it take off into the woods. Erin looked down at him with a festering glare as if to ask, *Why aren't you doing your dog job?*

⌐

Erin stumbled in through the back door of the house leading up to the kitchen. It was a spacious family kitchen complete with a large woodstove and an even larger kitchen table. Tragically, though, from wall to wall was an atrocious brown utility carpet accented with yellow cabinets. She opened her hands and spilled the shovels, sticks, and skates onto the floor. Her father, Lyle, and mother, Helen, were seated at the table at opposite ends. They both looked up at the disturbance with the same expression of quiet disinterest. Lyle's reading glasses resting on the edge of his nose. Both of them in their church clothes and finishing up breakfast. Erin returned the stare with her hands on her hips. Her parents could instantly tell Erin was hoping that ruining their serenity would serve as a fine form of nonviolent protest. Of what, they had no idea.

⌐

The local Episcopal Church was surprisingly well appointed for such a small town. The Cooks had arrived late and were seated in the very front row. Erin suspected this was some form of punishment. She sat quietly at the edge of the church pew, her floral pattern dress and steel-toed shoes showcasing her fashion sense as predicted. Helen was seated next to her, both she and Lyle listening intently the sermon. Erin flipped through the handout and had already begun to fold in the corners and see what kinds of shapes came out. These days it was only the three of them making the spiritual commitment. Erin had slowly watched each of her older siblings abandon the concept of prayer and belief in God in general. Sunday morning mass used to be a family outing. Now it was strictly for those under sixteen. Erin hadn't yet made up her mind about organized religion or a higher power, but she did resent the notion that everyone else had somehow gotten out of it. The incident at the pond had raised her blood pressure, making her more ornery than usual. She seized upon the sensation.

"How come Ian doesn't have to go to church anymore?" Erin whispered to her mother.

Lyle looked down and gave her a glance and a headshake signaling, *Not now.*

Helen leaned into her and whispered back, "Now is not the time for this, Erin."

"No, I wanna know."

Helen was hoping to quell the curiosity right there so she assumed a little redirection would do the trick. "Maybe because he knows the kitchen floor isn't the right place for your toys."

"Ian left me out there to carry all that crap in all by myself!" Erin whisper-yelled back into her mother's ear. The redirection had failed. Helen put her hand on Erin's leg and gripped tightly around her upper portion of her knee.

"When we get back, I'll help you take it to the porch," Helen returned, still managing to keep her voice in a whisper. And still trying to kill this line of thought before it spread.

"I can take it to the porch myself. I left it there to make a point."

Helen turned and looked Erin right in the eye and reached deep down into her Victorian upbringing to deliver, "And what, pray tell, was your point, Erin?"

"Ian is an asshole!" Erin shouted back with her arms outstretched and palms facing upward. *Wasn't it obvious?* It was to her. The sermon stopped. The congregation turned. And Lyle shot lightning bolts out of his eyes at his daughter.

Helen promptly grabbed Erin by the wrist, tucked her elbow into her midsection, and bent her hand forward. The pain was excruciating and even worse, restricting. Lyle had brought that trick home from his job as a prison guard and used it as a form of light resistance on the boys when they outgrew him. Erin winced and clenched her legs together to keep from crying out. Helen pulled her in close, hissing at her in a whisper that those seated nearby could easily hear: "You mind yourself, young lady. Don't test me. Afterwards you'll apologize to everyone."

She released Erin from her grip and returned to her perfectly aligned posture within seconds. Erin's eyes were watering as she brought her hand close to her lap, massaging the strained area. She was despondent. Her wrist throbbed with pain, yes, but moreover it was that she had chosen to finally speak up for herself at the most inopportune time. The outburst was to be remembered not for her biting commentary about the family structure but because it occurred on the Lord's acreage. On the Lord's time. Erin hated herself for wasting the opportunity. Helen, meanwhile, leaned in to her and casually said, "If you're up for it, we can stop by the bakery on the way home. Get some donuts. Sound good?"

Erin just scowled. *Nearly snap my wrist then try to offset it with the promise of junk food? How typical of Mother,* she thought.

Sweetness always followed.

two

Ian was staring at the cracked plaster in his
ceiling. He could do this for hours on end,
finding new shapes and patterns in the
random lines and jagged edges that spread
out from a water stain in the middle.

Over the years, he had the pleasure of watching the spot mature from off-white to a yellow before finally settling in on its present hue, that of a mustard brown. Their house was old, even by upstate New York standards. The home was built in the 1700s, and his mother liked to elaborate to neighbors and relatives that it was part of the Underground Railroad. Ian wasn't so sure he believed that anymore and suspected this was her way of justifying why nothing was ever modernized. The roof would never be fixed so as not disturb an important piece of American history. The outlets would remain two-pronged and the windows single-paned. Ian had often tried to apply the same thesis to cutting the grass. "Former slaves probably walked on this grass and we shouldn't tarnish their memory by tampering with it," he would say. For some reason, such logic never seemed to connect with his parents.

The "shit" he needed to do consisted of sitting on his beanbag chair smoking a cigarette. The windows were opened so as to hide the aroma of burning tar from Lyle and Helen. All this really served to do was to allow what little heat there was to escape while his clothes and fabrics absorbed the smell of cigarettes.

Taking as long a drag as his lungs would allow, Ian lamented on how he was born in the wrong decade. He still carried the wounds of how the formidable pairing of Mondale-Ferraro could garner only fifteen electoral votes to the other guy's five hundred and twenty-five. *How could the majority be so ignorant yet he so enlightened? Six more months,* he thought. Nineteen eighty-five was only a few weeks away and would be the year he graduated from high school.

The screeching hiss of hydraulic brakes interrupted his meandering thoughts enough to allow him to lift his head up. Ian struggled with deciphering a way to look out his window while expending the least amount of effort. This seemed to be a common trait among the Cooks. Unable to concoct such a scenario, he reluctantly got up and sat on the windowsill. In the summer, he wouldn't have been able to see through the natural boundary separating the two houses, but the trees had long since dropped their leaves. A large moving van had pulled into the driveway next door. Ian instantly thought it was a curious time of year to relocate. The crunching of ice over gravel gave way to an Audi station wagon. Which in turn was followed by a Volvo sedan.

He wasn't accustomed to such fine automobiles in his neighborhood. Their four-bedroom house was several miles from the main interstate and this was strictly a blue-collar neighborhood. He watched as a family of four exited the cars. A teenage boy who looked about his age ran awkwardly up to steps of their new house. He watched curiously as the mother quickly followed. As if to protect him. Ian gave this an odd glance but was promptly diverted by the sight of the girl stepping out of the sedan. She was short, but Ian could tell right away that she had everything where it was supposed to be. A dirty blonde ponytail hung out from beneath a wool cap and her jeans were perfectly worn. Ian quickly deduced her personality. Athletic, perhaps a skier, which would lend one to tattered jeans in the winter. Her lengthy stride suggested confidence, as did her lack of concern with her appearance. He couldn't make out any breast shape from this vantage point, but that was the least of his concerns. He was a leg man, anyway. Ian had already played out the scenario in his head.

New girl in town meets moderately popular local boy. He charms her with his free spirit philosophy and gets her to hate her parents and all her material possessions. The courting procedure would include such guaranteed winners as woodland trail walks, buying Swedish fish at the penny candy store, and demonstrating how he could flip Vanguard on the Atari. All the while enlightening her on their obligation—nay, their ethical duty—to wage a steady conflict against conformity. Then they have sex in his car like all the other kids were doing.

Or whatever. Some variation thereof. Details subject to change.

All told, Ian had yet to experience intercourse with a real live girl. This frustrated him to no end. He considered himself attractive enough, although he observed that looks were of little consideration as far as adolescent copulation was concerned. He concluded that his biggest flaw was that he was average across the board. In every way that one's worth can be measured, Ian came up right in the middle. He had neither the bad boy appeal of a true lower-class rebel nor the chiseled, all-American, gated community quality of the rich kids. And girls found him decidedly boring as a result. He had no reason to think this new girl would be any different. But if her backside were high enough, he would certainly make a concerted effort to find out.

Erin sat on her bed, flipping through an issue of *Fangoria*. It was issue
#7 with Jack Nicholson on the cover from *The Shining*. She had read
this issue before but still found the articles intriguing. A concept that
concerned her parents and baffled her classmates. Her acquaintances
at school were starting to question what she found so appealing in
those magazines. She dare not refer to them as "friends." When a
knock finally came at her door, Erin gave the quintessential "What?"
without turning around.

"Hey, Erin, can I come in?" came Lyle's voice from outside the door.
It was 4:30 on Sunday. This was daddy-daughter time. Each Sunday,
Lyle and Erin would talk for thirty minutes. It didn't matter about
what nor was it relegated to them being at home. Lyle had seen the
direction other little girls had taken whose fathers didn't make an
effort to be a part of their lives. And he was determined to not allow
this to happen to him.

Erin looked away from the magazine but still didn't turn around.
"I'm not over the shame of what I did yet."

"That's okay. I just wanna see how you're doing. It's four-thirty.
Daddy-Erin time, you know?"

"It's not locked," she called out. Lyle opened the door and closed
it behind him. Erin stayed seated at the window while Lyle made his
way over to the bed and sat down.

"What's going on?" Erin didn't respond and instead looked out at
the window. Lyle was fascinated by his youngest daughter. She didn't
turn out the way they expected and that was a beautiful thing, as far as

he was concerned. He loved that she followed her own path. Despite the unrelenting pressure at school to think and act and look a certain way, Erin was Erin. The only facet of her personality that gave him pause was that she never cried. It's not that Lyle enjoyed seeing his daughter in tears or derived some sick pleasure from her misery, but he just couldn't get his head around how nothing seemed to connect with her enough emotionally. He had seen her shed tears as an infant, of course. And later on when she would run into the coffee table in the living room or skin her knee bike riding, but that was all.

When Lyle's mother died two years earlier, he was certain he would get tears from her. But it never came. And Erin was close with her grandmother. It hurt Lyle in a weird way that she didn't cry. He recalled being secretly bitter during their Sunday talk that week. He attributed her lack of sentiment at the funeral to Erin being uncomfortable with an outpouring of emotion in front of strangers. But this was their special time together. Where their private feelings were supposed to be openly exchanged. And she gave him nothing. She spoke of her grandmother and the great times they had had and memories she'd cherish, but her delivery was so matter-of-fact that it frightened him. It was like she was reading a book report and was concentrating on getting all the facts out but with the sentiment purposely omitted. He worried that if he were to ever pass on, he would receive the same unemotional treatment.

"So, you wanna come sit by me or do you prefer the window?" her father finally said. Erin continued with her pouting expression but still moved over to the bed. After a few swings of her feet she leaned into him and gave him a side hug. Lyle never got tired of the way his daughter felt. Her smell and the way her little elbow would press up

21

against his rib cage. She had such a way of resting her body against his that he knew she felt safe around him. He cherished the idea that he was her protector and that she thought, however inaccurately, that her father could save her from anything.

And in an instant his thoughts raced to Erin's death.

He couldn't get the idea out of his head. He pictured how it might happen and how he might react. How it would affect their lives and whether he could go on after. Would he go about his motions to put food on the table for the rest of the family or would he curl up in the fetal position in some corner of the house and sob until he withered away? Lyle had done this from the moment she was born and he knew why he did it. He was so frightened by the notion of his children passing that the only way to combat it would be to play it out in his head. He viewed it as some sort of macabre defense mechanism to guard himself in case something was to really happen to Erin. *If she ever does come down with a terminal disease or gets hit by a car, I'll have gone through it so many times that I'll be ready for it*, he thought. He knew it was selfish and twisted and would undoubtedly prove futile if something ever did happen to Erin. Yet that's where his mind went, nonetheless. He put his arm around her and glanced over at the magazine, picking it up.

"Yuck. How can you read this?"

"I think it's cool. What's wrong with it?"

"I'm surprised it doesn't give you nightmares."

"I know it's fake. It's the real stuff that gives me nightmares. Besides, it's better than the girly stuff my friends read."

"Where'd you get it?"

"One of Ian's friends. Am I in trouble again?"

"No." Lyle flipped through the magazine, curiously. His face wrinkled at the graphic photos depicting Tom Savini's handiwork in *Martin*. "Huh. You know your mother would probably want me to take this away from you."

"Would I make a better daughter if I were into boys?"

Lyle gave her a look as if to say: *You certainly didn't get this wisdom from me. Or your mother.* "Of course not. Your mother and I just want to make sure everything's going ok. Sometimes it's pretty rotten being a kid."

"Why doesn't Mom like me?"

"That's ridiculous. Why would you say that?"

"I can just tell."

"Well, I can tell you that's ridiculous. She loves all you kids."

"But why Ian?"

"Well, we don't play favorites. You, Ian, Michele, and Eli all get an even distribution of parental love. And when we start to love you too much, we send you to your room because we just can't take it anymore." He squeezed her and kissed her on the head. She forced a smile and leaned into him. "So, what else?"

"Harley and I saw a weasel running off with one of the chickens this morning."

"Really? Have you ever seen a weasel before?"

"No."

"They can be pretty nasty. Well, we better get rid of it or your sister's gonna have a fit."

"You mean she's gonna have to get rid of it." No response from Lyle, just a look. The eldest of the children, Michele, had already left the house. When Michele was in middle school, she decided she wanted horses, and then chickens, and before they knew it, the Cooks had a makeshift farm on their hands. The kind that produced all of the labor and odors but none of the scant financial upside. But like many adolescent endeavors, her passion for animal caretaking proved more romantic than concrete and was fleeting. And Erin was stuck with all of the actual, real-life chores involving them.

"Why me again? None of these animals are mine! I'm not doing it anymore." Lyle knew she was completely justified in her protest, but there wasn't any alternative. They were stuck with these beasts and they couldn't just let them starve. Plus, the fresh eggs were pretty nice.

"I'll let you use the .22."

Erin gave him a reluctant look that said: *Really?* Lyle had always taught his children the proper care and handling of firearms, but he knew this particular bargaining chip was sure to cause friction. On the other hand, there was always the chance it would be interpreted as clever parenting on his part. He hoped for the latter. Erin looked up at him and gave a slow and deliberate, "Okay."

"There you go. You remember what we talked about." Lyle knew Helen had a more progressive take on gun ownership. She believed that if there ever were an intruder in the house, the police would arrive in time to quell the situation. Either that or she could charm them with conversation or kindness. Being that he dealt with criminals on a daily basis, Lyle knew that neither of these techniques was likely to be particularly effective. Helen would rattle off talking points such as, "A gun is two hundred percent more likely to be used against a family member than on a criminal and I won't have them in this house!" Lyle wasn't sure from what source she was accumulating this specious data, but it seemed a bit reactionary to him. He wanted to remind her that even if accurate, it was because the overwhelming percentage of crimes are committed by one family member against another. *Thusly, one could also state that a knife is 200 percent more likely to be used on a family member, as would be a baseball bat, a golf club.* He could have gone on.

"Just try to keep it low key around your mother," Lyle quickly followed. He wasn't sure to what extent such advice would prove to be helpful, but it seemed like a responsible way to conclude the exchange.

Erin nodded in a confident *Sure* kind of way.

Swish, he thought with a fatherly grin. Issue resolved.

three

Helen sat in the kitchen by herself, staring at
the needlepoint in front of her. She picked
up her tea and took a long, deliberate sip.
Then, just as delicately, set it down.

She had been working on this particular design for several months
and then one day in late September, she just stopped. She would
take out the circular ring and her thread and always have the best
intentions, but the will just wasn't there. She analyzed this, as she
did all insignificant minutia in her life, and found it pathetic that she
didn't even possess the required stamina to complete a needlepoint
design. Next on the pitiable inventory was analyzing the whole thing
in the first place.

Although she had a husband and four children, Helen still found
a way to be lonely. In her youth, she always thought of herself as
having creativity, although her parents never encouraged it. Helen
thought she had a unique take on modern life and spent her
post–high school days trying to craft her own cartoon strip. She
took a day job to support her creativity after high school. Yet, like
so many others, her day job was slowly transformed into her real
job. When the reality of this subtle shift finally hit her, she was

emotionally deflated. She now pictured her life as that of a butterfly larva transposed. She started out with beauty and grace and wrapped herself up in the chrysalis commonly referred to as the traditional American family. At some point she had nibbled her way out to reveal a wriggling worm sporting a conservative wool skirt from Talbots. It was perhaps the visualization of such self-depreciating reflection that had stifled her sex drive.

Helen had tortuously watched so many other young cartoonists of her generation achieve their dream while she just got older. Sarcastic animals, cats in particular, seemed to be what the comic reading public couldn't get enough of these days. It had even reached the point where she would read only the strips of artists who were older than her. And *Peanuts* just about summed that list up. She had married a young prison guard to support her and he in turn got her pregnant to keep her from running off. At least that's the card they each played when arguments ensued. She assumed she still loved Lyle and was confident he loved her. Although at this point in their marriage, it seemed akin to one's love of warm sheets out of the dryer. Convenient but then it quickly fades when room temperature creeps in.

So, when Erin darted through the kitchen with a small bolt-action rifle in her tiny arms, she almost didn't notice.

"Stop, please," Helen said without looking up. "Explain this." She grabbed the barrel of the gun and instantly loathed the coldness of it.

"Dad said."

"Said what?"

"Said I could. Something's killing the chickens."

"This makes me nervous. I don't like it." Helen was choosing her words carefully. She actually despised the idea of having a gun in the house, and the notion that her eleven-year-old daughter was about to engage in some form of domicile security bordered on offensive. Helen wondered whether there was any issue of the day that she and Lyle agreed on anymore. She supported the notion of unlimited reproductive rights while Lyle found the concept a mournful euphemism. Lyle embraced the idea of capital punishment for the worst human beings while Helen felt no good Christian could in good conscious support such barbarism. Yet they still had their faith. Although they often used their faith as a justification for whatever position they held. Jesus wouldn't do this, or Jesus would have hated that. A well-studied follower could easily find some collection of wording in the Bible to explain away pretty much anything. Their belief in the Lord was firm and that could make up for any superficial difference they might have. But how to raise their youngest daughter didn't quite fall under the banner of "superficial difference."

The youngest child is often a surprise. "Surprise" being code for "accident," of course. Helen could already sense a power struggle over whose mold Erin was to be cut from.

"Dad said!"

Helen looked at Erin and then nodded. "Back in an hour."

Erin pulled Harley up from his comfortable spot on the floor and bounded out the back door. When the door slammed shut, Helen found herself once again staring at the needlepoint in front of her with the empty ticking of the grandfather clock. Seconds later Ian ran through and grabbed his coat from the back of a chair.

"Wanna go the mall with me, Ian?" Now here was the child that she understood. She and Ian had been cut from the same cloth. *I'm the reason he's soon to be a college boy*, she told herself regularly. Helen had pushed Ian to take his schoolwork seriously and the results had paid off handsomely.

"Nah, I'm going with Eli."

"Maybe I can take both of you. How's lunch on me sound?"

"Nah, we're cool," he said on his way out.

When the door slammed shut for the second time, Helen picked up her tea and took another long, deliberate sip. The liquid rattling against the roof of her mouth competed with the ticking of the old clock for most depressing sound of the afternoon. Both accentuated her isolation. She gazed at the settled tea leaves slowly forming an emerald sludge at the bottom of her cup, then turned her attention to the muted exterior. The faded words from hundreds of washings still read *Who Wants to Cuddle?* with an equally weathered cartoon bear sipping cocoa. Helen wondered what it would feel like to smash the thing against the table but then remembered she'd be stuck cleaning it up.

Then she just as delicately set it down.

four

Ian was letting the engine run on his 1978
Chevy wagon. He got it used as soon as
he passed his driver's test and at the time it
seemed like the ideal purchase.

It had one of those new cassette decks and a wide backseat just in case he managed to find a young lady who was willing. That was until Josh Standish, the town loser, pulled into the high school parking lot with the same car. Standish was known throughout the community as being the kind of kid his parents should be embarrassed to have spawned. One time he was said to have gotten whiplash taking riding lessons and spent two weeks at school walking around with a puffy, white neck brace. His thinning hair and full face only served to make him look like a giant uncircumcised penis in corduroys. And Ian detested the notion that he and the resident douchebag had the same taste in cars. Every afternoon the girls at school would see Ian Cook and Josh Standish getting into the same '78 wagon and that made Ian guilty by association. He now hated his wagon and half hoped it would die so he'd have an excuse to get something else. Or maybe leave the door unlocked with the keys in the ignition so it would be stolen.

When Ian's brother, Eli, hopped in the car, he had already thought up four other ways to off his car. "Where you been?" Ian asked. Eli just pulled his collar up and the wagon pulled off. Eli recently had moved a few miles down the road into a basement apartment. It was a big step, but he still came home frequently for free food and laundry. His formal education was behind him but dependency was still front and center. Eli had flirted with the thought of joining the military, but the recent bombing of the Marine Corps barracks in Lebanon had caused him to reconsider. The administration also didn't seem too interested in initiating any form of revenge for the attack, which frustrated him further. The lack of focus had him working part-time at the local plumbing supply warehouse. *Pick your frustration*, he surmised.

Ian had just pulled around the corner when they saw Erin and Harley seated in the snow. She appeared to be fixing her boot and had shoved the rifle into a snow bank like a Revolutionary soldier would have before crossing the Delaware. Eli let out a breath of laughter as he motioned to Ian. "Check it out. I wonder which of the parents sanctioned this action." His tone indicated that it was an obvious call. Ian slowed the car down and leaned out the window.

"What the hell is this? Dad let you use the .22?"

"Would you rather he gave her the Mosberg?" Eli chimed back.

Ian leaned back in the car seat, lamenting, "Dude, Dad is messed up."

"See ya, Erin." Eli waved from the passenger seat. "Watch you don't shoot yourself in the foot."

The two pulled away with the exhaust pipe gargling and the tires crunching over the snow. Erin stood up and grabbed the gun from the snowbank and once again she was left alone with the dog. She gave them a curious look as they drove away and slung the gun over her shoulder. She turned toward the chicken coop and Harley followed suit.

_⟟_

Lyle had requested the Sunday evening shift close to three years ago. By this point in his week, he'd had enough of Helen's temperament and couldn't sit through another episode of *Murder, She Wrote*. As he made the twenty-minute backwoods drive to the Adirondack Correctional Facility, he thought briefly of Erin's solo hunting expedition. He couldn't help but think that a healthy portion of his rationale was simply to irritate Helen. The only time they would have sex in the current decade was after an argument. Agitation and mild insults seemed to get the blood moving better than traditional foreplay. And Lyle was running out of ways to get under her skin. He suspected she had figured out his little routine and was becoming more resistant to common annoyances. She could ignore someone so beautifully it was almost an art. So he had to up the ante. *Let Erin use the gun on her own. Yeah, that was a clever play.* He wasn't too concerned over Erin. She'd been around firearms most of her life and had a healthy respect for them, as opposed to fear. But Helen was a different bird. There was no telling how this one would play out when he returned home.

He really could have gone for some snow at this point. A lonely drive in the winter always seemed more inviting if there was some flurry for the headlights to cut through. His gloved hands were slick on the steering wheel. He had left his watch cap in the lockers at work so the tips of his ears were starting to sting. Rubbing them only made them burn more. The car slowed to a stop at the intersection of Route 12 and Oak. Lyle glanced up at the rearview mirror and caught a glimpse of himself. He wasn't a handsome man and he knew it. Lyle had tried to cover what part of his face he could with a dated mustache, but this was only moderately successful. He wasn't particularly gifted either. Handsome, gifted men didn't become prison guards. At least he had never seen any come through his prison. They all pretty much looked like him. He wished he had been better looking, if only for Erin's sake. Michele got her mother's looks. Erin, regretfully, had gotten his.

The chicken coop was perhaps better described as a functional outhouse that exceeded all local building codes. A small shack built to hold maybe fifteen to twenty birds, with a small door leading to an outside enclosure. The whole thing was clearly made by people who were not carpenters. It had taken over a year to build it from whatever scrap of wood they found in the bargain bin at the local hardware store.

Erin approached it slowly. Not because she was afraid of an impending weasel attack, but she dreaded what she might find inside. This was one of those "real things" that gave her nightmares. Erin stood awkwardly outside the enclosure. The barrel of the rifle dipped into the snow as she clutched it with her pink mittens. The wind wafted the stench of spoiled food across her face. There were feathers all over the compost heap of a floor and the blood had caused some of the plumage to cling unceremoniously to the fencing. One feather in particular was vibrating against the wind, frozen in place courtesy of the deep purple coagulate that had formed at the root. Erin wrinkled her nose at the sight of it. It was certain to get worse inside.

Harley sniffed around the perimeter while Erin moved over to the door. She opened the door to the chicken coop to reveal a bloody mess. Feathers and chicken carcasses lay everywhere. Only four chickens had survived the slaughter, perched on various overhangs throughout the shack. She pushed open the fence with the barrel of her rifle, the rusty spring hinge creaking with ominous resistance. Erin formed a guilty look at the carnage, as if her delay in reporting the intruder had led to further deaths. Harley trotted into the coop, causing the scant surviving birds to go berserk. Flapping and clucking all over Erin, erupting in a maroon cloud of what could only be called frozen blood dust.

"Harley, no! Get out!" Erin screamed. She set her gun down as she forced the Great Dane out by his hindquarters and latched the door. Harley put his paws up on the outside of the fence and peered in. Newly molted feathers rained down over Erin as she stood there holding the rifle at her side while taking in the mess around her. She hadn't the slightest idea where to begin. And perhaps most vexing of all, had yet to fire a shot.

⌐

The razor wire fixated atop the steel fencing wobbled as the sedan made its way through the ice-encrusted tracks of the security gate. Lyle pulled his Chevy Citation past the spike strips and into the spacious parking lot. The Adirondack Correctional Facility claimed to be maximum security due to the viciousness of its residents. The walls and bars, however, suggested it was "maximum" in name only.

Lyle pulled the car into a spot and turned off the engine. This time of year, it wouldn't be long before the sun went down and the windows began to frost over. Lyle now wished he had gone with Erin or at least given her something that resembled responsible parenting. As opposed the *Go Kill The Damn Thing!* approach he had taken.

The parking lot lights turned on with a sharp clang and began to cut through the approaching dusk. *Must be five o'clock*, he thought. Lyle had taken the job at the prison when he found out Helen was pregnant. He wasn't college educated, but he knew enough to accept responsibility for having such a potent set of testicles. And prison guards had the best retirement plan within a hundred-mile radius of their house. Twenty years and he'd be set. The children would always have a house they owned to come back to and who knows—maybe then he'd go to school. Ian had made the family proud by being the first Cook to pursue and achieve secondary education, and Lyle was ashamed that he could only afford to send him to a state school. Ian deserved better. Perhaps by the time Erin was of age, she'd be good enough at something to earn a scholarship.

Lyle could go over the regrets in his life ad nauseam before pitying himself into an apoplectic stare. He needed this time alone in the car before making the lonely walk to the guard tower. He couldn't let his coworkers see him like this and would never allow this bitterness to seep into "Daddy-Erin" time. Not that he condoned placating his daughter, but it was important for Erin to believe that her father was the confident shining light in her life. Helen had staked the claim as being Ian's moral compass and had pushed Michele into the starving artist lifestyle that she had found so glamorous as a teenager. *There's one kid we can count on moving back home before too long*, he thought.

Helen had already encouraged the children to grow and feel, just so long as they grew and felt as she did. He found it frustrating that Helen's notion of critical thinking meant to apply it to everything Lyle felt had merit. This more than any other reason was why he pushed himself to be stronger around his youngest. He would play the role of the all-American dad for Erin. Even if it left him tortured when he was alone.

⟵

Erin had spent the last thirty minutes walking around the coop, picking up dead chickens and dropping them in a large green garbage bag. She resented that this was how she would end up spending her Sunday afternoon. When Erin's mother first romanticized having farm fresh eggs at the house, Erin, too, thought it sounded wonderful. They had even begun to name the chickens that developed unique feather colorations or a distinct personality, which essentially meant either "sheepish" or "ornery." Chickens don't come in "pensive." Yet as Erin held the limp feet of her third grade teacher's namesake, "Mrs. Lange," Erin deemed the whole concept ghastly. She dropped Mrs. Lange into the garbage bag, which had now become so full it required two hands to drag it outside. Harley's interest in the bag increased with each dead fowl she laid into it.

Erin retuned to the coop and swept up the remaining mass of feathers and chicken parts into a pile while Harley pawed at the gate. He didn't enjoy being in such proximity to fresh game and not being able to act upon it. When Erin returned moments later, she found the bag ripped open and its contents spilled over. Erin quickly surveyed the area near the coop. The remnants of the massacre took an even grislier tone now that they'd been scattered over the white snow. Her eyes went to a blood trail leading around the backside of the shack and into the field she'd crossed earlier that morning.

Erin retrieved the rifle from inside and patted her leg, thinking this was an effective technique to call Harley to her side. As his obedience lay mysteriously elsewhere, he trotted off into the snow on his own. She looked down at the bag and kicked a few spilled chickens back into it. With the rifle slipping in her pink mittens, Erin walked out into the field, following the tiny trail of blood.

Harley bounded through the snow, sniffing and pushing his nose into the fresh powder. Dusk had fallen, giving the field a bluish tinge. Fifteen more minutes and there would be no tinge at all. Just dark. Erin followed him as he awkwardly clomped toward a row of trees and shrubs that separated the two properties. The dog stopped and headed back to her side. Erin looked through the bushes and dropped the gun to her side. She reached into her pocket and pulled out a handful of .22 shells. They clinked together softly, clinging to the small threads of loose wool on her mitten. She reluctantly put them back in her pocket and took her mittens off. Luckily they dangled securely, as they were the kind that attached to one's jacket. She dropped out the small clip on the gun and loaded them into it. She popped the clip back in and cycled the rifle with the bolt action. Erin pulled the weapon to her shoulder and looked down the sight, scanning the area in front of her.

Initially she saw nothing but snow-covered shrubs and the beginnings of the forest. Suddenly clumps of snow had begun to drop from their resting place until she saw it. Her weasel poked its head up out of a bush, carrying a mangled chicken in its mouth. Erin's eyes tightened.

She couldn't believe she was actually going to get to shoot something. *Wouldn't Daddy be proud?* Her mother, less so.

Pop! She released a round on the rifle, sending snow flying and the weasel darting off into the woods. Erin immediately recycled the weapon and fired another round at the critter. This one crackled through the bushes and nestled somewhere in the dense foliage that lay beyond. Clumps of snow fell to the ground while the faint crack of the .22 echoed through the woods. Erin ejected the used shell out again and brought the rifle down. Her pink cheeks were flushed red from where the cold stock had touched her face. She knew she had missed her target but felt oddly satisfied. It was an exhilarating moment. She loved the way the rifle felt when it released a round and the sharp crack it made when it fled the barrel. Even the satisfying "cha-click" of cycling the bolt gave her a comfort and security that, thus far, related to nothing else in her life.

Erin arrived at the spot moments later to find her chicken lying in the snow where the weasel once staked its claim. She approached it with a girlish frown and picked it up by its feet. No sign of any weasel. Nor any sign that she may have inflicted mortal damage upon it. Erin looked across the field and saw the sunlight begin to silhouette the fir trees and turn the horizon a golden orange. Her hour was up. *No matter*, she thought. She decided this was to be her quest and would make her father proud because of it. Erin still had the mystical desire to make her parents happy. She wanted desperately to be accepted. She was an average student and a below average athlete and would never be entered in a beauty contest. If she could kill this animal, bring harmony back to the family farm, then perhaps it would raise her stature in her parents' eyes. She had always been told that she was meant for great things. That there was nothing undeniably special about her was a minor hiccup. None of the customary childhood accomplishments had materialized, but it was possible that this was her secret calling. She would kill the weasel. She would shoot it and bring it back to her parents the way she had seen barn cats offer a slain mouse as a gift. *Now,* she thought as she looked out over the wooded expanse, *I have given myself purpose.*

December

five

Monday morning found Ian slouched back in his driver's seat, letting the engine run. This was the last week of classes before Christmas break so the cigarette he was slowly enjoying gave an even greater sense of euphoria.

Although it was possible the carbon dioxide from his idling engine was the catalyst for his lofty sprits, he was confident the approaching week would be a solid one. Teachers typically let up on the workflow this time of year, giving Ian time to work his angle on the new neighbor. In his head, the whole thing was to play out like a John Hughes movie. His initial assessment of her appearance was admittedly mottled from his bedroom view, so he was hoping she wasn't waiting for the New Year to start school. Ian's lack of progress on the sexual baseball diamond of life was starting to frustrate him to no end.

He tossed the cigarette into the driveway and pulled his car to the road. Standing at the end of the driveway was Erin, bundled up to her face with her weighty backpack titling her torso a good twenty degrees. Ian smirked at her and rolled down the window.

"Miss your bus?"

"I don't think so."

"Come on. I'll give you a ride."

Ian looked down the road to see the new girl standing outside her driveway with someone he presumed was her brother. *Oh, this could be good*, he thought. Erin looked through the window to decipher his gaze and had already pieced together what the gears in his head were churning on. Ian looked at Erin and motioned to them. "Go ask them if they want a ride."

"Can you let me in first?"

"Would you just . . . ?" Ian returned, but Erin had already realized the quicker she got it done, the quicker she'd be in the car. While the car shook, Ian leaned over to roll up the passenger side window. He watched Erin's precise little steps across the crusty snow. He couldn't place why he felt the need to antagonize her constantly. Perhaps it was because he felt her turning into his father. And one redneck in the family was enough.

Erin stopped and motioned over to the wagon. The girl seemed to nod and then motioned to her brother. Erin just shrugged and had already started back. Ian wondered if she put in a good word for him but doubted that's where Erin's mind was. When he saw the girl and her brother start to walk toward the car, he felt a bolt of anxiousness race across his chest. For some reason, he didn't actually think they'd accept Erin's carefully worded offer, but it was happening. As she walked closer, his mind raced. She went from passably cute to a drop-dead knockout in an instant. Her walk miraculously developed a confident and deliciously sexy twitch to it. Even the way she wore her wool cap was suddenly a statement of coolness. From this point on, whenever he rolled into the high school parking lot, he would be known as "Ian Cook who drove the hot new girl to school" instead of "Joe Average with the same car as the cock monkey." So long as her brother wasn't a total dick, all would be right with the world.

Erin opened the front door, to which Ian snapped, "In the back!"

"But the heater's up here!"

"Erin!"

Ian gave her a sharp glare, to which Erin responded with her now patented throw the arms at her side routine. She flung the rear door open. The new girl was now seconds away from being seated within kissing distance. Again, his mind galloped ahead. He prayed, in the secular sense, of course, that she was a liberal. Liberal girls always put out more promptly and with more gusto than conservative ones. But not too liberal. Too liberal and you found yourself in militant feminist territory where they're taught to hate men and consider any form of physical contact to be rape. The doors to the right and behind him clicked opened. Ian watched her leg take a graceful step over his cracked leather seat. Lands' End snow shoes. *Practical and stylish.* Jeans on the bottom half. *Nice and thin.* Perhaps some hamstring definition was detectable, but that could have been a shadow.

She was in and opened with a firm but noncommittal, "Hey, I'm Beth. Thanks for the ride."

And just as quickly, the fantasy faded. She was no longer hot, no longer cute, and in fact turned out to be essentially the female equivalent of him. *Jesus Fucking Christ*, he thought. Although he despised Christianity, he found its derived profanity to be the most expressive. Ian spent the next seconds of his life taking inventory on all the areas on her face that were in need of improvement. Eyes too close together and a muddy mix of green and brown. Some acne scars. Dirty nondescript hairstyle and color. He could have gone on.

Ian tried to form as masculine a smile as he could. "What's up? I'm Ian. That's Erin." So much for being the class stud. He had, in a moment, been relegated back to class nobody.

"This is my brother, Edward," were the next words to escape Beth's mouth. Ian glanced up and adjusted his rearview mirror to reveal said brother. Greasy, matted bowl cut. Flat facial features. Enlarged tongue. *Wait a goddamn second. The fucking kid is retarded* flooded callously into his brain. In his mind, he was assessing the whole situation with the eye rolling of a lifetime.

"Hey, what's up?" said Ian, in an attempt to make it seem like he dealt with this kind of thing all the time.

"YEAH!" said Edward. Both responses were equally aloof in their sincerity.

So now Ian was driving the Plain Jane, her retarded kin, and his annoying sister to school. He wanted to tell them all to just get the hell out of his car so he could go back to the way his morning started. But is that how the tolerant college bound behaved? He thought not. Either way, Ian could forget about being labeled the class nobody. When he pulled into school that morning, Ian would unwittingly stage a coup over the reigning king douchebag.

Erin, meanwhile, had taken it all in. She could read her brother's face well enough to know his little scheme had backfired to an epic degree. And a smile crept across her lips. She looked over at Edward and gave a genuine "Hi." She had never met anyone with a handicap before, but seeing Ian so completely out of his element had somehow given her renewed poise.

"YEAH!" said Edward.

Beth had been smiling at Ian the whole time. She had mistaken his monosyllabic repartee with Edward to be acceptance. "Appreciate it. Freakin' cold out there," Beth said, to keep things moving.

"Yeah, it gets that way." Ian pulled the car out of the driveway and started down the road. Perhaps if he really looked like he was concentrating on the road, that would keep conversation to an absolute minimum.

"HE HE YEAH!" said Edward. It was not to be.

Ian relented. "So you just moved here then, yeah?"

"Yeah, our dad's a professor so we move around a lot. He'll do a couple years at SUNY and then we'll probably move again."

"Sounds annoying."

"You get used to it."

"Oh yeah?"

"I'm good at talking to strangers," Beth delivered with a hint of flirtation. Ian was still intent on getting everyone to school safely and refused to allow even a glance in her direction. In the backseat, Erin was watching Edward. His eyes never seemed to focus on anything, but they rarely moved either. She longed for him to close his mouth but suspected that was his easiest way of breathing. His hands also never left his crotch, and not in a relaxed kind of way. He had a mechanical-like grip on either a healthy portion of his slacks or his actual scrotum. Erin was familiar with the male anatomy. That is, as far as the general arrangement of it all was concerned. This was courtesy of both a progressive state-funded education and sharing a bathroom with two boys. Neither of which prepared her for the manner in which Edward tended to his package. When they drove past something that piqued his curiosity, the grip became more intense. For the ten seconds that it took them to pass the Ferrils' cattle farm, Erin watched as his fingers contorted and the skin across his knuckles pulled as tight as a snare drum. It seemed to provide him with a sense of comfort, so Erin decided it couldn't be a bad thing.

Ian was getting close to Erin's elementary school and considered asking Beth and Edward to walk the extra mile and half to the high school. "So, is Edward getting out here or . . . ?" Ian asked as the school appeared around the corner.

Beth let out a breath of coy laughter. "That's the elementary school."

"Right, I know."

"Oh, I get it."

"Get what?"

"He's older than me, actually. What grade are you?"

"I'm ah . . . a senior."

"Yeah, he's your age."

"All right."

"You think because he's handicapped that he should be in a class with third graders? That's pretty offensive."

Ian could see where this conversation was headed and found himself praying for a ten-point buck to dart in front of them and impale her through the windshield. He refused to give her the satisfaction of an apology and then thought perhaps his verbal gaff was a blessing. If Beth thought him to be dick, then he could put an immediate halt to chauffeuring the short-bus gang.

By the time Erin hopped out of the car, not another word had been exchanged. The drive to the high school was silent, as well. Ian did his best to make the act of taking the keys out of the ignition a good two-minute ordeal. This was an adequate enough signal for her. When Beth finally exited the car, she grabbed Edward by the hand

and briskly headed toward the front office. Ian leaned up against the car and watched them go. He let out a contented sigh and for the first time since he could remember was looking forward to sitting through his first period calculus class, solely because those two wouldn't be in it. There was something remotely cute about her but not enough to regret pissing her off. And certainly not enough to pursue the relationship any further.

SIX

Helen stood at the doorway of her bedroom,
watching Lyle sleep. *Christ, could he snore,*
she thought. Helen wondered just how it was
possible such a noise didn't wake him.

She pictured the inside of his esophagus, jagged and worn like that of a tailpipe that had succumbed to oxidation. It had come close to ending their engagement a number of times. Helen would spend hours staring at his vibrating larynx, expecting a multi-engine turboprop to come flying over their apartment at any second. And when he wasn't snoring, he was grinding his teeth or passing gas or displaying any number of vexing behaviors that served to push her into a sort of calculated madness. Still, the faithful woman in her loved that he worked so hard for the family. That he worked a job he certainly would have preferred not to do so that she could be home with the children won her over. Granted, all the children were either out, on their way out, or settled in with school, but there was always housework to be done. And he believed in the Lord.

Each of her children had gone through an atheist phase, and none had yet to return. Erin was the only one who still acknowledged that Christmas was, for the most part, about the birth of Christ. Ian and

Eli were fully entrenched in labeling Christmas a product of multinational corporate propaganda whose roots lay somewhere in a pagan solstice festival. Helen certainly had done her part to nudge them in that direction, but the wheels had been greased too effectively and they kept gliding. Yet oddly enough, neither sought to return the Atari 2600 they received on Christ's birthday a few years prior.

There were a number of men who sought Helen's company when she was single and living in Milburn, New Jersey. She would take the subway into Manhattan every day for her aforementioned day job and, if the opportunity presented itself, pitch her comic strip.

It seldom presented itself.

When she accepted Lyle's marriage proposal, part of her couldn't help but see it as the ultimate sign she was giving up. Her independence now waving the white flag of surrender in the symbolic form of a discounted wedding band. With her eldest daughter, Michele, on the verge on embarking down a similar path, Helen debated whether to encourage her to marry. *It's wrong to have dreams. They only lead to disappointment,* she should tell her. It's unlikely she would soon grace the pages of *Parenting* magazine with sage guidance such as that. As a schoolgirl, her teachers would laboriously recite such uplifting fodder as, "If you believe in yourself and try hard, you can achieve anything!" But as she got older she realized this just wasn't true. Particularly if your goals are founded in a high-risk, low-reward pursuit such as comic strip writing.

Artistic talent is subjective. If her material never reached the desk of the right person, the world would forever be deprived of her comedic dexterity. She came to the conclusion that there were likely millions of never-to-be-discovered talents out there from a variety of disciplines, and she just happened to be one of them. For her own sanity, it was comforting to blame her failures on simple bad luck. It just wasn't possible that every unique talent gets discovered and lives the dream life of financial independence. And there were other womanly matters to consider—namely that Helen's ovaries were starting to sag and she was running out of time to land herself a security blanket. And the concept of time was a continual source of aggravation for her.

For as long as she could remember, she visualized her place on the traditional calendar. And she saw this calendar as a square, broken up in sides dictated by the school year. January through May would occupy the top, June on the right all its own, July and August running along the bottom and the rest going up the left side. She was always at one spot in the square, going around and around. Within the square, each week had her pining for the weekend. Just two more days. Then one more day. Then before she knew it, she'd be wishing for those five days to hurry up and end. It was here she realized that she was, in essence, simply waiting for her life to be over. A concept so utterly depressing that she hoped being a mother would give her life renewed purpose.

She had known since she was a little girl that she wanted a family, and the church always spoke so highly of those who passed on their faith to the next generation. She wanted to do her part, and she ultimately decided that finding a man of faith was more important to her than finding the man of her dreams. Men of great social stature or financial means seemed to skip church anyway these days. The handsome ones sure as hell did, that was for certain.

The corners of her mouth curled down as she starred resentfully at Lyle. She raised her cup of tea to her mouth and took a deliberately loud drink, hoping the popping gurgle of her sip would be enough to disrupt his snoring. His strenuous inhalation had sucked his tongue back into his throat, causing him to gag. He then stirred, kicking his leg out of the sheets and rolling over to face her. She studied how the hair had mysteriously vanished from some parts of his leg and resurfaced unmercifully to plague others. His skin color was only two shades by this point—white and red—thanks to his polyester prison uniform. *He was like the goddamn Swiss flag,* she would say.

And there he lay in their bed. The man that she picked—nay, settled with—to fulfill her Christian responsibilities, chief among these obligations being to repopulate the Earth with more Christians. Overweight and reeking of that godforsaken prison. And where did all that leave her? Four children later and her breasts resembled compressed tennis ball cans. Her upper thighs rippled with the denting of cellulose while her calves looked less like they were courtesy of Bally's Fitness and more like courtesy of Rand McNally. Helen began their marriage a svelte size 2, yet before her youngest child was even out of middle school she was struggling to stay in a size 8. He was the one who wanted so many kids. She would have been happy with two. But he wasn't the one who had to suffer through the pregnancy, the birth, and its unequivocally cruel aftereffects. He didn't have to cry through migraines and vomiting only to eventually have the walls of his vagina require surgical stitches.

Helen thought she could have returned to her original shape, or at least gotten close, and then came Erin. She never wanted a fourth, and when she returned from the doctor that day, she asked Lyle if an abortion was out of the question. *What I am even asking him for, anyway? It's my body,* she thought. Her hips that would be forced out an additional three inches. Her midsection that would have permanent tire tracks across it. Plus, they couldn't afford it, anyway. Maybe the financial incentives would speak to him if her own private choice wasn't enough. Lyle told her that even thinking such a thought was blasphemous. That God wanted them to have this child and they should feel blessed. *Then how about I shove this embryo up your ass and you see it through to delivery. Don't you dare make me feel guilty for my emotions. You aren't a woman. Don't pretend you can empathize. You will never, EVER understand!*

They had the child. Lyle wore her down. He spoke of the church, and he spoke of morality, and he spoke of the love they would share when she was born. And Helen knew that whenever Erin did something precious when she was a toddler, she would pay for her words. Helen would get a hug from Erin or watch her adorable little attempt at dancing or a baby-spoken "I love you, Mommy," and she couldn't help but be charmed. Lyle, meanwhile, would give her a look. A glare that sardonically stated, *Don't you wish we'd had that abortion now?* She hating being the bitter woman, but he drove her there. She hated what four children had done to her and she hated that he held her own words against her. Even though he never once spoke it, she knew. And then she looked down at her body once again.

You did this to me, you pathetic loser. You corn-fed white bread hick. What do you do? You guard criminals. How the hell did I settle for you? I was gorgeous. I had talent. I had potential. You and your stupid dick. You gun-toting conservative piece of shit cocksucker!

Lyle then opened his eyes to see his Helen staring at him.

"Hmmm . . . morning," said Lyle.

"Good morning, my love," she said.

seven

Mrs. Lange was wearing a long blue skirt
with white stockings. Her sandy blonde hair
was cropped just above the shoulder.

The white belt across her waist pulled her top in just enough to cause the boys in the class to stare at her. They weren't really sure why, but they couldn't take their eyes off Mrs. Lange on days like today. Nor could Erin. But it wasn't due to some dormant homosexuality waiting to spring forth. It was because Erin now saw her fourth-grade teacher as the slaughtered chicken she failed to protect. Protruding out of her polyester suit were brown feathers caked with blood. They rustled each time Mrs. Lange wrote another line detailing the day's agenda on the chalkboard. When she turned around to address the class, Erin saw that her top beak had been cracked off, causing the bottom half to jet out, most assuredly the product of a losing battle with the weasel the day before.

"We're going to have a light schedule this week. Figure you guys have earned a break," Mrs. Lange said, with her broken neck hanging limp to one side. "We're going to start off with some fun stuff. A little holiday decorating you can take home to Mom."

And with that, Erin felt a wave of nausea wash over her. Mrs. Lange had returned to being a late-thirties elementary school teacher, and Erin had to returned to being the quiet little outsider. With the amusement of the morning's events coupled with the vision of a slain farm animal in front of the class, she had forgotten all about what the weeks before Christmas break typically entailed—namely, holiday themed arts and crafts. This ritual had included but was not limited to the construction of garbage bag wreaths, tin can mobiles, and perhaps most daunting of all, the feed sack stockings. Erin couldn't place how or when it started, but she was so terrified of failing to complete the assignment or having it displayed on the schoolroom window that she was overcome with anxiety whenever the idea was even presented. Today was no exception. Her eyes felt the faint pressure of impending tears that, of course, would never come. She quickly rubbed her fingers against her palm to stifle the clammy sensation growing on her hands.

"This will be very simple and I think you'll find it quite easy," said Mrs. Lange. And right on cue, the two boys behind Erin snickered. John Campbell and Derrick Macaskill like to fashion themselves the class jokesters. Their latest bid of comedic genius was to assign the nickname "It" to Erin. Thusly, whenever the word "it" was said aloud in class, hilarity ensued. Erin was used to getting picked on from her older siblings, but for some reason, being the brunt of a joke from the class hicks really stung. They were the kind of kids who seem to have mustard surgically implanted into the corners of their mouths. The grotesque stains were always there, regardless of the season or what they actually had to eat that day.

Mrs. Lange brought out various colors of construction paper and a little steel basket that contained red and green safety scissors. When she was done detailing the Santa Claus door hanging they were about to tackle, she cheerfully summarized with, "And that's about it," to which John and Derrick responded with a hearty chortle. Clearly, whether the word "it" was used as a noun was of little concern to these two prodigies. The kind of kids that couldn't blow their nose without checking to see if anything worthwhile came out and then had to show it to everyone.

To the casual observer, Erin was no more or less attractive than any other eleven-year-old in her class. Yet her posture and lack of confidence helped to shuffle her down a few social pegs. She wasn't blessed with a perfect set of teeth either. She had something of an imposing overbite. Too many teeth in some areas, not enough in others. Perhaps it was that she was more of a loner. Or it's possible it was her penchant for reverting to tomboy characteristics when the going got tough. Whatever the reason, Erin had been singled out for torment. The little tendons in the back of her eye socket began to ache as she struggled to keep her emotions in check. She clenched her knees together and locked her head in a fixated position, finding a benign spot on the floor to plant her gaze. Little green dots began to form off the sides of her field of vision and coagulate in the middle of her line of sight like amoeba in a petri dish. For most little girls, this is likely where the tears would come. It didn't happen for Erin. Instead, her body did the next closest thing.

Erin sucked in her bottom lip as a wet spot began to form in the seat of her pants. She leaned forward and pulled her chair as close to her desk as she could, making a biting screech in the process. Wet jeans were a terrible thing. They immediately sealed to one's thigh as if possessing the same chemically adhesive properties as surgical glue and in no time would begin to rub and chafe said area. *If I could cry like a normal person, this wouldn't happen,* she thought. Erin wondered if the morning could get much worse. Mrs. Lange then asked the students to form groups. So, yes, evidently it could.

She began writing the assigned groups on the chalkboard. Erin watched with terror as the names were scribbled down. Her hand began to ache. Erin had never quite learned how to hold a pencil properly. She gripped it in the way an infant might hold a spoon, thumb tucked inside the index finger with the astriction of a battle-field tourniquet. She couldn't write more than two words before her hand would cramp and require massaging. This made the task of essay writing excruciating. Her penmanship was wretched. All the other girls in her class had greeting card quality writing. Uniform and bubbly with the dots over the Is and the Js near perfect circles. When Susie Macintyre inched next to her, her notes looked like they were straight off the "My Little Pony" packaging. Erin's were closer to Egyptian hieroglyphics.

"Your group's over there," Susie snapped, with the obnoxious self-assurance that only a PTA board member's child could produce. As her luck would dictate, Erin's group was forming on the other side of the classroom. While others were getting up and trading seats, Erin remained fixed in hers. Erin's brow furled and she let out a forlorn sigh, knowing what was ahead of her. She began to inch her desk and chair combination across the room. There may have been a good three seconds of her journey that went unnoticed until all the other students had settled in their respective places. The remaining minute was spent with the rest of the class staring at Erin. *Screech. Pause. Screech. Pause.* Twenty feet to the other side of the room. The snickering had already begun by the time Erin reached her circle. This she could tolerate. The torment that would be unleashed if she were to reveal that she'd peed herself would be more than she could withstand.

She began the monumental task of squeezing her desk into what remained of a space, all with the grace and ease of parking a cruise ship with a standard transmission. The incident did little to quell the perception amongst her classmates that Erin was an odd duck. No one spoke to her as the assignment progressed. At least Campbell and Macaskill weren't in her group. Cherish the small blessings. As the construction paper was passed out, Erin stared at it briefly, thinking that perhaps it might make an ideal urine blotter. And indeed, it would. But she would need to wait until recess was called before putting it to the test. When the bell finally rang, the students collected their things. Erin remained, having convinced Mrs. Lange that she required more time to make this project meet her already established high standards.

Mrs. Lange wasn't buying it but also felt there was no point in challenging her. Besides, she could already smell the piss coming from group number three.

⌐

Ian wore loafers, even in the winter. He had replaced the pennies in the leather folds with bus tokens. This was originally meant to be a statement on embracing the public transit system, until he realized how much public transportation ate into one's cool factor. It was much more important to be seen as hip than conscious to traffic snarls. It didn't matter that driving his own car required him to work a job stocking frozen foods at the supermarket, wearing a maroon vest.

Congested roads had yet to reach the upstate areas, so very few people road the buses, anyway. This, coupled with the fact that not a single person had noticed that they were bus tokens, had him rethinking the whole proclamation.

Still, he loved the way gravel sounded underneath the thin rubber soles. He sat on the curb in the back of the school. This was the parking lot that the delivery trucks, maintenance trucks, and the occasional police car used when coming to school. None of which was likely to be pulling in there today. He ran his shoe across the pavement slowly, listening to the soft crackle of chipped pavement rolling against itself. He looked up when he heard the light click of cheap metal coming toward him.

"Hey, man," said the wearer of all this metal. Doug Vaughn was a bona fide rocker and needed to make sure everyone he came across knew it. The consequences of someone thinking that he wasn't prepared to rock out at any minute would be disastrous. He was also as emaciated as a teenage boy could be while still qualifying as severely out of shape. His tight black jeans gave way to the slightest of potbellies. This was covered up by an equally tight black t-shirt bearing the iconic images of Iron Maiden, Black Sabbath, Ozzy Osbourne, or some similar ilk. He and Ian had been friends in middle school and didn't have much in common anymore. Except smoking—and as it happened, that was sufficient. Doug reached into the breast pocket of his jacket to pull out a package of Camel non-filters.

"Four more days," Doug said as he shook one out for Ian.

"Uh-huh," was as thoughtful a response as Ian could give at the moment.

"What's your story?"

"I don't know. I drove this new girl to school today. Can't figure out if I like her."

"You think she'll put out?"

"I don't know. Maybe. Probably."

"Then I'm confused."

"I'm just not sure if she's really my type."

"She has a twat, right?"

"Pretty sure."

"Then I'm confused."

"It's just, I thought she was super hot right away, but then it was like, she came close and starting talking and . . ."

"And what?"

"And her brother's a retard. It's weird."

Doug sat down next to Ian and gave him a good stare in a way that suggested he'd like his cigarette back.

Ian continued, "It's like this. If I made the effort I probably could get with her. We probably could have sex. Relatively soon. But if she wants to go out, like boyfriend-girlfriend go out, I just don't know if I could handle being around that kid. It makes me uncomfortable. I'd be as if I were settling just to hook up." Ian extended his cigarette after a good inhale. The way an English professor extends his coffee mug when completing an eloquent summation. The similarities obvious.

"My advice is to get over it. You can't graduate from high school a virgin, man. That would be so gay."

"Why? You're about to."

"I got prospects, though. And this is the first girl I've heard you talk about in six months."

Doug did have prospects. He was always going to concerts and meeting the sort of trashy low-standard girls who would find Doug appealing. Ian never went out. He would read the newspaper and listen to NPR and think about how much he wanted to distance himself from his father. He had the lifestyle of someone twice his age. Only he still lived at home and his greatest accomplishment was getting into state school.

"You at least need to get yourself an orgasm. From someone else, I mean. A girl."

"I get it, Doug."

"For real. If this new girl can come up with a load using her hand or mouth, you know what? That's good enough for me. I'd count it, man."

Doug patted Ian on his back in the sort of condescending manner that a coach would after you were the last one cut.

"Thanks for that."

Ian stepped out his cigarette on the pavement and pulled his collar up around his neck. From a distance the two of them couldn't have looked more different. A passerby might assume Doug was trying to accost Ian for money. Or they had had some weird agreement where one would provide protection for the other's essay writing skills. The dilemma being neither was very good at either. Ian knew this relationship wouldn't last the next six months. Doug already had plans to move out west and try to get on some band's stage crew. A hair band, naturally. If James Taylor was the only one hiring, he might as well kill himself. Ian felt like suggesting that they should keep in touch over the summer and beyond, but every wording that played out in his head just sounded gay. And there would be no homoerotic behavior on display between these two.

"You wanna go get a Ding Dong or something?" said Doug.
"Cool," said Ian.

Beth extended her hand to Edward, his stunted fingers maladroitly grasping her slender ones. Having an older brother whose mental capacity would never outreach that of a five-year-old was something she never got used to. Her father, being a professor of classics, didn't exactly exude masculinity, and Beth sorely needed a manly man in her life. She always hoped that Edward's affliction was temporary, like chicken pox or bed-wetting, and he'd eventually grow out it. She wanted the feel and security of an older male protector, and neither of the adjacent men in her life qualified. She loved her brother and wanted the best for him, but at a certain point she wondered what that would entail. He wasn't going to change. For normal brothers, you can hope that they'll study harder, land that perfect job, beat that drinking problem, or dump that cunt of a girlfriend. They'll grow, learn, fail, succeed, fall in love, fall out of love. Something. Edward would not. He was as smart as he was ever going to be. He was as attractive as he was ever going to be. He was as capable as he was ever going to be. And Beth wondered how long Edward would be her burden.

She hated thinking in those terms, but that was reality. She knew he brought her down a peg on the social ladder. It was unavoidable. Most people, particularly the nuanced cliques of public schooling, are uncomfortable around the handicapped. It takes a special kind of person to see past the speech abnormalities, facial deformities, and sporadic cock wailing that encompassed her brother. And Beth was confident such a person was not going to be found in a logging town a short drive from the Canadian border.

She felt the judging eyes of her newly anointed classmates, each one with a specific agenda. The girls sizing her up to see if she was a potential threat to their popularity. The guys feeling out what sort of lay she might be. The sort of self-protective scrutiny one does to decide if they were amongst friend or foe. Yet each one layered with a hint of pity that Beth was stuck standing in line for the school bus in 30-degree weather while holding the hand of her enfeebled relative. While the rest of the kids were spilling out into the senior parking lot, laughing and chatting and smoking, Beth stood silently. Her eyes fixed on the approaching line of school buses, as if deciphering which one was theirs required maximum concentration. This was the hardest part about being the new kid. She just needed to make it through the first week. Then people would see how cool she really was.

When the doors swung open, Beth moved her gaze to the parking lot. Ian was leaning casually against the hood of his car, although it was the sort of pose that someone with little self-esteem strikes while trying to exude false confidence. He didn't look in her direction, but she could tell he wanted to be seen. And by her. It was too cold to make prolonged small talk outside, so his motivations were obvious. *I'll stand here looking awesome so that new girl sees that I'm most assuredly not giving her a ride home. Even though I could.*

Edward made the first cautious step onto the bus. He was still unsure of his surroundings but would never ask why they were taking a different way home. Edward never concerned himself with such petty concepts as social status. In this regard, Beth was wholly envious. That old saying, "Ignorance is bliss"? Well, it was never more applicable than in high school. How wondrous would it be to walk around completely unaware how others were incessantly judging you? *Pretty freakin' great,* Beth decided.

Beth guided Edward into a seat in the front of the bus. Secure under the mask of slush spattered windows, Beth was free to openly look in Ian's direction. He wasn't the cutest guy she'd seen all day, but his callousness in the morning was something of a turn-on. Her misguided rationale was that any guy that much of a prick must have something going for him. Such validation was certainly common amongst women of all ages. This is why violent felons in prison receive fan mail from female admirers.

Beth was sure she saw Ian give a head nod toward the bus. And the lanky headbanger he was with shifted his look accordingly. He was talking about her. Now good or bad, it didn't matter. Beth decided that she was in his thoughts in some capacity. As to whether they were the romantic kind, well, that she would need to work on.

eight

Wednesday nights were hardest on Lyle.
Technically, though, they would qualify as
Thursday mornings.

Thursday and Friday were his nights off, but it always took him a
day to get back on normal schedule. He would sit in his stitched
plaid recliner with his leg resting on Harley lying prone at his feet.
Listening to the woodstove crack and hiss would make the incessant
sounds of steel and concrete dissolve away. It was a jet-black monolith
that rested on a bed of brick. A stain in a perfect circle marked the
top. This is where Helen would put her pots of water to keep the air
from becoming too arid. The stove would run virtually nonstop from
October to April, thus the faint smell of ash was always present. Lyle
would justify the work, smell, and heat by saying they just couldn't
afford to upgrade to gas or electric. That was partially true. He could
have made sacrifices if he really wanted. The reality was he loved the
way it made him feel. A man felt more like a man in front of his own
fire. A coil steel grill just didn't have the same allure.

Lyle was content in his life. He had made mistakes in his youth.
Things he would have done differently. Bad luck that he wished had

gone the other way. But his home was almost paid for. The last of the children was getting along fine in school, and soon she would be on her way. Starting her own life. A family somewhere. Lyle smiled to himself at the thought of Erin with children. He pictured her coming home from some faraway place doing great things. Picking her up at the airport in his truck and the family piling into his car. Her handsome, well-adjusted husband and their children. Lyle decided he was made to be a grandfather. And looked forward to the day when it might happen. But he was certainly in no hurry.

He picked up his thick-bottomed glass off the coffee table and took a contented sip. He had felt it best to stop drinking when his oldest daughter reached kindergarten, but he still loved the feel of a heavy glass and the sound of rough ice cubes clinking together. It was just tonic water. Not even a lime. It wasn't until he set the glass down that he noticed someone else in the room with him. He turned his head upward to see Helen standing in her bathrobe.

"Hi," he said.

Helen smiled, although it was a cartoonish "We need to talk" kind of forced smile. The kind where the edges of her mouth curled up but the eyes remained stagnant. She shuffled her bare feet across the coarse orange carpet and sat down on the bricks.

"Can't sleep?" Lyle followed.

Helen shook her head. Twenty years together and she still had trouble starting conversations with him. She had long abandoned the concept of soul mates. Bunkmates was better, maybe. Joint checking account mates.

"Did you let your youngest daughter go hunting alone?"

"I did."

Helen nodded and brought her hands to her face. Rubbing her temples and then pausing to cover her eyes briefly. Lyle was anticipating this conversation and was not going to be intimidated. "What's your concern?" he followed.

"The fact that I would even have to list them is disturbing, Lyle."

"Okay, then. You let her ride her bike alone."

"So?"

"You let her go swimming and fishing alone."

"Yes."

"You let her go sledding alone."

"Yes, I do. So what?"

"So she's just as likely to get hurt doing any of those things."

"That is utter nonsense. Only a complete idiot would equate hunting with sledding."

"It didn't take long for the name-calling. More children die from drowning every year, Helen."

"But I taught Erin how to swim, Lyle!"

"That's right. And I taught her how to use a gun."

Helen threw up her hands. "Ugh! You are such a redneck I can't even stand it. There's no point in continuing this."

"You aren't going to continue this because you can't argue based on emotions. You have some deep-seated emotional problem with guns. I don't know why. But the fact remains there's a greater chance she will drown or get hit by a car than get injured by her own gun. If we allow Erin to run around swimming, biking, ice-skating, or whatever all by herself, then there's no reason why she can't go hunting alone. If she wants to. And she wanted to."

"I don't want it in my house. Is that clear?"

"What if you come across some creep threatening to molest your daughter? Or worse."

"As of this moment, your carelessness is her biggest threat."

"That's really sick, Helen. I'm a good man."

"I'm putting a stop to this. I'll tell her in the morning." Helen straightened out her nightgown and got up. "You think you're some calculating, rational man. But you're not. You are inviting disaster by allowing this to continue. It's just a matter of time before your little stunt goes awry. Don't say I didn't warn you."

Lyle didn't say a word and let her go. This was how all serious conversations ended. With one of them getting frustrated, dropping a personal insult, and leaving. Nothing was resolved and there weren't going to be any minds changed. They were just coming from two different worlds. Lyle's world was that it was better to educate, inform, and instruct children on as many things as possible. His thesis on parenting was that all of his children would learn how to ride a bike, change a tire, swim, and handle a gun. Other parents could do what they wanted. But he always believed that sheltering children from any of those things would only hurt them in the long run. He looked at guns the way Jack Fowler looked at snakes. If you understand them, respect them, and know their tendencies, then you quickly realize that there's not much to be afraid of.

Helen, on the other hand, viewed a loaded rifle floating around the house like a poison-laced spring. A rattlesnake stuffed in a kitchen drawer. You were just welcoming chaos and increasing your chances of tragedy exponentially.

When he heard the creaking of the stairs, he stood up, glass in hand. Reaching into the glass, he grabbed the last ice cube and tossed it on the top of the stove. The cube reduced to liquid instantly, then boiled, then evaporated. The hissing caused Harley to pick his head up, but only for a short while. Lyle stared at the stove for a moment. He then bent down to close the vents, his knees and hips popping all the way down.

He got up slowly, ligaments popping in protest once again, and walked over to the kitchen. Setting his glass in the sink, all he could hear was the ticking of Helen's grandfather clock. She actually called the thing "Grandfather," which really creeped him out. "Time to wind Grandfather," she would say. Which made him wonder if her grandfather's ashes were stored somewhere inside. He'd dared not open it up to investigate. Instead, he looked out the window into the field behind their house.

The weather had turned cold early this year and frost had already built up around the windows over the kitchen sink. Lyle knew this meant in a few weeks he'd have to go down into the basement with the kerosene blowtorch and defrost the pipes. He'd much prefer Erin to do it but had to assume Helen would have a thing about fire accelerants, as well. The family had made it through Thanksgiving without much incident, apparently because Helen was internalizing her anger with him. He'd much rather have a subdued Christmas and didn't want anything boiling over at the wrong time. For a working man, family holidays are everything. And you only get so many. Each year is one less to experience, and Lyle was determined to ensure there were no blotches on the Cooks' holiday resume.

⌒

Lyle pushed open the door to their bedroom with one hand. The door was never closed all the way so that they could always keep one ear open for the cries of children. They hadn't awakened to any cries since Erin was a toddler, but such habits are hard to break. And now it was more to monitor when Ian was returning from a late night. Lyle looked over to Ian's room and saw that the light was still peeking out from underneath the door. He assumed he'd fallen asleep with the light on.

Helen was curled up facing away from him. He knew she was still awake. When she hit full sleep mode, her breathing would settle in. So precise you could set it with a metronome. She wasn't breathing at all now. He walked over to her side of the bed and saw her eyes staring straight ahead. He sat down on the edge, his weight forcing her to roll slightly towards him as he put his hand on her hip. The springs in the mattress ached, releasing a strained squeak.

"I'm sorry," he whispered.

"Do you even know what you are sorry for?" Helen did not whisper.

"That you're upset."

Helen pushed his hand off her hip and pulled the pillow in tighter. She was good at pushing his buttons.

Christ, he's such a sap, she thought. "So, in other words, you aren't sorry. You just don't want to go to bed angry." That she said out loud.

"Okay. I'm sorry we have trouble communicating. But you're right. I can't be sorry that I upset you, because I was decent. We simply disagree."

"Fine."

"Helen, I'm trying to be civil. You're the one who got personal down there."

"How?"

"You called me a redneck. Remember?"

"Oh, stop it. You wear that as a badge of honor."

That was only half true. Lyle grew up thinking that redneck was a complimentary moniker that epitomized strength, knowledge of the natural world, and skills that were actually useful to society. The difference between knowing how to change a tire and being able to recite *The Canterbury Tales*, for example. Lyle coped with his internal struggles the only way he knew how. To give off even the slightest hint of anger would only confirm Helen's decision to label him the archetypical angry white male. What happened instead was that it forced his normal persona, that of a mild mannered white male, into retreat. He actually had real world knowledge and a charmingly dry sense of humor that would often surface in the most inopportune times. He feared when it might come out.

"Erin is not yours to shape into another you," Lyle said. His tone was that of an exhausted man who had long since used up his nuanced A-material. "Let her find her own way."

"Nor is she yours," Helen hissed at him. Her face scrunched against the pillow.

"But she isn't happy."

"Have you asked her?"

"Yes. We talk, Hel. I make time for her."

"She's fine. When's the last time you heard her cry?"

"When's the last time you heard her laugh?"

Lyle paused. *Damn, is Helen right?* He couldn't recall. He hated to think of his little girl going through life in silence. Muted from all emotion, for whatever reason he couldn't place.

"Is that your measure of happiness?"

"For little girls? Yes, it is."

Lyle got up from his position next to Helen and stood up. Helen shuffled the covers back to their original spot with a satisfied grin on her face. He walked over to his side of the bed and lay down. Pulling the covers over him, he stared up at the ceiling. If his daughter had become an emotionless monster, what was the point? She was the reason why he did things. Why he got up in the morning to go to that prison. Why he pushed through his marriage, thick or thin. He turned his head to the left to glance into the hallway. Feeling something but seeing nothing.

As it happened, sitting outside the bedroom in the hallway was Erin. This was the first time she had heard noise coming from her parent's bedroom in the middle of the night. She had returned from a trip to the bathroom to hear her parents inside talking about her as if she had already passed on. She had never considered for an instant that her demeanor affected her parents in such a way. That their happiness was contingent upon hers. That they derived some form of cathartic emotion from seeing a smile on her face or hearing her giggle at something absurd.

Erin stood outside their door for a while longer as this burden went through her head. Her stance and posture reflecting that of a wounded soul. Her hips planted awkwardly to one side, her head hanging low, the left side of her bottom lip tucked in. Her face stoic. *I'm failing them. They're miserable because I don't laugh enough* is what first rushed through her head. But as the night wore on and Erin returned slowly to her bedroom, her thoughts changed. Her thoughts changed to bitterness because she was happy. She was content. She was confused about some things and didn't feel comfortable with irrational emotions the way many of her classmates did. But that did not make her a miscreant. If there was such a thing as emotional blackmail, Erin decided her parents were guilty of it. But not directly so. After all, they never confronted her with their feelings, and she was spying on them. Still, with the covers heavy against her chest, she felt a new burden well up inside her. Erin wanted so badly to make her parents happy, to have the children at school like her and invite her over to play. But it seemed as if the more she was herself, the more she succeeded in being the girl who had to eat lunch alone.

nine

There was a distinct smell to the plastic
chairs. That aching smell of stale urine. The
floor was stained from the sweat of older
men feigning exercise the night before.

Surrounding the space were those portable room dividers. The thick
green fabric kind with folds that had worn through, revealing the
cheap corrugated paper underneath. They had smelled of cigarettes.
Cigars. Pipes. They were used when the Red Cross would set up their
blood drives. On weekdays when the auditorium would be used as an
adult learning center. On evenings when there were adult basketball
teams using the courts for their intended purpose. And today. Where
the under-twelve children would spend the remaining half hour of
church. Sunday school.

Erin stared at the folded walls in the same hatred as when she stared
at her dress. For they had a virtually identical floral pattern, their respective manufacturers' naïve assessment that adding flowers to something
would miraculously lift them up from the doldrums in which they
rightfully belonged. Or they just didn't care. For all Erin knew, her
mother had made her dress from portable wall leftovers. Or the walls
were made from dress fabric leftovers. Neither would have surprised her.

Heather Moss was Erin's Sunday school teacher. She was a recently married young woman of twenty-five, although her colleagues in the church would say she married too late. Heather was one of the few people in town who was doing exactly what she wanted to be doing. She had gone to school for philosophy. One of those fake majors the college bound always chose when they didn't have to rely on degrees to get the jobs they wanted. Heather was also the first girl in town in to be in an interracial marriage. Her husband, Thomas, was black. And not the light-skinned, *maybe he's just a dark Italian* kind of black—like, Nigeria black. And since there weren't too many blacks in upstate New York anyway, it was the primary gossip at the supermarket and the local hair salon for months. Until everyone realized that it really didn't affect their life in any way and they were happier than most other couples in town.

It may have been Heather's confidence in herself that bothered people. She was happy in her job as a legal secretary. She was happy using her Sunday morning to pass God's words along to the next generation. And she was happy riding what many believed to be the most superior example of unconstrained manhood in town.

As this was the first Sunday in December, the little partitioned room was decorated with all things Christmas. Although the Christian version of Christmas, not the shopping mall version of Christmas. There were white lights along the top, which were pleasant enough, but the decorations that covered the walls were all nativity in nature. Wise men. Stars. Crowns of thorns. And Heather would waste no time in reminding her class why they were here.

Heather clapped her hands lightly to settle the kids down. Erin, naturally, needed no settling down. Heather spoke in a calm and healing voice. She should have been singing slow jazz at two in the morning on a rainy night. "Now I know you're all excited. You see the lights we have here. Maybe some of you already have a tree at home. You're going to get presents, you'll eat yummy food, and you'll get a few weeks off of school. But do you remember why we do this every year?"

"Christmas," one boy said.

"That's right. And what is Christmas?" Heather asked.

"When Jesus gave himself for our sins," said the same boy.

"No, that's Easter. Christmas is when Jesus was born. Given to us by God as a gift."

"Some gift," another little girl said. And others laughed.

"I know, huh? You'd rather have an Atari, right?" Heather's tone playful. She knew how to talk to kids. Especially those on the cusp of being teenagers. The teenage years are when most kids break away from religion. They begin to question everything. And Christianity inherently raises questions. If she was going to keep even half of these kids going to church, she would need to reach them now. And the less preachy, the better.

"Yeah. Or new skeeth. Something," said the kid with the loose-fitting retainer.

"Yeah, new skis could be good," Heather added. "But then what?"

"What do you mean?"

"I mean, skis break. They chip. Some rust. Grow old. New styles and shapes come and go. But the gift of Jesus that God gave to us—well, that is the gift of happiness."

And Erin broke her stare. She raised her head from her fixated spot on the floor and looked at Heather. As if she had never heard anything so bizarre. Foolish. Inane. Heather couldn't read her. But she did notice. She had watched Erin for some time. A faithful student of Sunday school in attendance only. She rarely spoke and didn't seem to have made friends with any of the other kids in class. She recognized in her the type of lonely girl that could go on to great things, if only the right person touched her in the right way. So when Erin actually broke off to make eye contact with her, Heather didn't want to waste it. She wanted so badly to address Erin personally on the issue but knew that would only force her into retreat.

"See, happiness is what makes us human. This great joy that we feel for others and ourselves. That's an example of what a gift Jesus was."

"Pffttt," the same kid said.

"No, it was, actually. When God gave us his son as a man, he was showing us and teaching how we all can be better people. See, human beings, left to their own, are lost. We very easily succumb to anger and selfishness and all sorts of bad things if we have nothing to guide us. But when we're given guidance and we know right from wrong and up from down, that's the secret to a fulfilled life. The secret to being loved and, in the end, the secret to happiness."

"What if I'm not happy?" said Erin. Her knees knocked together and her shoes pointed inward, toes touching. Her dress hung off her shoulders like lawn tarp. "I'm not saying I'm not, but what if I weren't? Does that mean Jesus doesn't love me?"

Heather bit her lip. She saw in Erin's eyes that something was about to break. She wanted desperately to grab this child and rush her off to the garden and hug her and hold her, talk with her for hours. But this wasn't the place. And society generally locked up grown-ups who did similar things to children. Instead she gave her the most nondescript, benign response she could think of.

"No."

"Or maybe Jesus doesn't exist and that's why I'm not happy," Erin said with a purse of her lips. Followed by a shrug of her shoulders.

The room stopped. A few ohs and ahs were heard around the room. Heather was not expecting today's class to take such a direction. *What the hell?* she thought. *I figured I'd just pass out these plastic mangers and that would be it.*

"Jesus exists, Erin."

"Where?"

"In your heart."

"That doesn't make sense."

"It does if you have faith."

"Which is the same as saying he doesn't exist."

"Jesus does exist."

"Then where? Where is he?"

"He's in here," Heather said, as she tapped her chest.

"No, that's where your heart literally is. Where is he now?"

"Well, he died."

"But I thought he came back."

"Yes. And then he died again."

"And then what?"

"We'll talk about that come Easter. Today we're talking about his birth."

"This is stupid."

"Erin, please don't talk that way."

Heather knew that she'd better get a hold of the group quick or bedlam would ensue. She didn't want to get personal in class but knew that she had to pull out the stops or risk having class by herself next week.

"All right, Erin. Let's put it this way. Who do you love the most in your life?"

Erin looked at her. She'd never been asked such a question before. It made her head hurt to think of it. People in her family didn't verbalize the word "love." The tone of each letter vibrated through her as if strung from a deep bass note. She wanted to tear. But could not. So once again, her eyes began to ache.

"What do you mean?"

"You know, your parents, probably?"

Erin focused in on her. *Was that the case? Do I have to pick both? Of course, I love both. But that's what they're expecting. And my mom loves my brother more, I just know it. Say something. Hurry!*

"I love my dad."

Heather noticed that she didn't mention her mom but wouldn't dare press her on it in front of others. She could tell this youngster was in a fragile state and just wanted the conversation to be over with. Truth be told, Heather had met both Erin's parents and that's whom she would have picked, as well.

"Okay, you love your dad. Now, how do you know you love your dad?"

"What do you mean? I just know."

"But how do you know?"

"'Cause I can feel it."

"Where?"

"Her—"

Erin had made a half motion to her chest as she cut herself off. She looked up at Heather. Heather wasn't about to say "gotcha" to an eleven-year-old girl at church school, but it sure would have put a nice exclamation point on the morning. Instead, the two just looked at each other. Erin with a bitter scowl that little girls do when they realize they've been had. And Heather with a calm sense of concern. The questions Erin was asking were healthy, but the anger that oozed from her voice was enough to force Heather to catch her breath.

"All right. So, I'm sure you've heard this story before, but Jesus was born in a manger under the Christmas star to the Virgin Mary. Virgin meaning that she was not with a man. The baby was placed in her by God. That has never happened before or since. And it was such an important day, such an important birth, that . . ." Heather's voice began to crack. She raised her hand to her mouth to catch herself and tried to continue.

"Excuse me." She cleared her throat. She stared at Erin's furrowed brow. Her bottom lip that stuck out. Her big round eyes on the verge of tears that would never come.

"It was such an important day that the three wise men gave gifts. You remember. Gold. Frankincense." Heather sniffed. Her eyes were watering.

What the hell is going on? raced into her head. She felt something welling up inside her. A sense of mournful love and desperation to communicate a message to Erin. *Keep it simple. Don't preach. You're losing them.* She pushed forward. "And myrrh. This is why we still exchange gifts at Christmas. Not to . . ."

Erin continued to stare at Heather. She couldn't place it. But looking at Erin was filling her with a type of love and emotion that she just didn't know how to process. She kept hoping that a prosaic retelling of the Christmas story would calm her down, but it only made the tears come faster.

"It's why we exchange gifts. Not to see who can spend more or to get whatever piece of plastic crap you think will make you happy. Because Jesus loves you! That's the point! That's why we do this! Because Jesus loves you all so damn much! And this is where he was born!"

Heather pulled a bag out from under her desk and dumped a dozen little plastic mangers across the table. They skittered and bounced all over each other, with a few of them sliding off onto the floor. The class was staring at Heather. None of them had ever witnessed a grown woman in full meltdown mode before, but they would certainly be taking notes for a detailed reenactment on the car ride home.

Heather finally collected herself and wiped her face. Mrs. Stenhouse, the elder woman who ran all the continuing education classes, whipped open one of the folding doors.

"Heather, can I speak to you for a moment, please?" said Mrs. Stenhouse with a voice that was more concerned than angry.

Heather nodded and left the room.

Erin watched her go and looked at the rest of the class.

"Jethuth Chritht," said the kid with the retainer.

In December 1983 the center of Elizabethtown, New York, was like the Old West. In the middle of the night, when the traffic light switched to blinking red, tiny swirls of snow would pass through the sparse streets like tumbleweeds. Instead of the clinking of spurs, one could hear the rumble of a snowplow shaking loose road salt over packed snow. There was a post office and a corner store. Even the local tavern had avoided neon in its windows. The town had somehow managed to recede into the modern age without so much as a blink. So when a Cumberland Farms convenience store opened at the same intersection, it looked distinctly out of place. Brightly lit with distastefully colored advertising in the windows, it was the first step in the demystifying of Elizabethtown. Soon it would be just like any other town. It was around this time when such stores were becoming staples of American life. If you were foresighted enough to get in on the trend early, chances are you could have retired young. If you weren't, and most people weren't, they were a local nuisance and far from convenient. The grown-ups saw them as a spot for young people to congregate and think up mischief while being supplied with cheap, high sugar, low quality food. Nothing good could possibly come from such a combination.

Ian would make the half-mile trek down to the Cumberland Farms most Saturday mornings to try to break the local Ms. Pac-Man record. Pac-Man fever had come and gone, so it only made sense that it was still the hot topic in Elizabethtown. It always took a few years for current trends to migrate that far north. When Ian had decided there would be no record breaking that day, he ventured back out into the cold. He was still pulling his hood tightly around his face when he spotted Beth entering the corner store. And from what he could tell, Edward was not by her side.

Ian darted across the slushy intersection and sloshed through the parking lot of the Country Token. The Token was the brainchild of some recent graduates of Rensselaer. The idea was that they could pick up all the "bread and breakfast" clientele that was passing through town on their way to Whiteface. Selling crafts, penny candy, syrups, cheeses, and assorted produce from local vendors would bring a sort of rustic charm to the community. What it failed to do was bring in any discernable income to the proprietors and thusly was always on the verge of collapse. Yet co-owners Ken and Barbara Metcalfe continued on happily without the slightest hint that their life's savings were similarly on the verge of collapse.

Ian pushed through the solid oak door, knocking against a tiny bell hung from the doorframe. The charming ring, coupled with the solid creak of the old floorboards, was too much even for a cynic like Ian to ignore. Dust pooled in the beams of light and the rustic tones of Benny Goodman, Teddy Stauffer, or Glenn Miller were always emanating out of the back office. The door was kept open surreptitiously to enlighten the younger patrons to a musical world they probably weren't familiar with. Plus, it only added to the atmosphere.

Ian exchanged a brief smile with Ken, who was reading the local newspaper behind the front counter. The counter was beautifully hand-crafted of maple with a glass front to display the dozens of penny candies for sale. And this was legitimate penny candy—as in, each piece cost one cent. When the trend was adopted by movie theaters and supermarkets some years later, it was all done by weight. Here all sweets were created equal. A Swedish fish cost the same as a snowcap which cost the same as a caramel: one cent. It was a great way to get the elementary school kids to come in, but unless you sold a thousand-dollar hand carved grandfather clock once a week, it wasn't smart business.

Ian spotted Beth browsing amongst a shelf of porcelain angels. He didn't figure her the religious type with parents such as hers, but you never knew. He pretended to be really debating whether or not to purchase a wool pot holder when she spotted him.

"Hi, Ian."

He put the item down, but not before she took note of it. "Hey. What are you doing here?" Ian inquired. It was obvious what she was doing there, but still that was the best salutation he could come up with.

Beth held up the figurine. A pasty-colored angel with a cherub-like face. Really ugly stuff. Ian figured he'd forgo his initial contempt for the grotesque heirloom and start with a softball.

"Cute. I didn't figure you for the church going type though."

"I don't buy gifts for myself."

"Grandmother then?"

Beth pointed her finger at him in a mock congratulatory way. "Right you are."

"So, I've been missing you at school the last couple weeks. That first day I gave you a ride just ended kinda weird and ah . . . I just wanted to say I was sorry about that."

Beth smiled. Her eyes relaxed and she lowered her figurine to her waist from the defensive pose up by her chest. "It's cool," she said. "I'm sensitive about my brother. I guess I made that pretty clear."

"Yeah," he said pointedly. She cocked her head while he quickly tried to recover. "But I get that. I mean, you're really great with him. I haven't spent that much time around retarded kids, so I didn't really know what to say."

"And *you* made *that* clear."

"No, but you know how it is. Do I pretend he's not there, do I give you pity—I mean, what?"

"You just act normal. He's harmless. He's a good boy."

"For sure. I just like you and wanted to say I'm sorry that our introduction went so shitty."

Beth's emotions were mixed. On one hand, this boy was making an attempt to be apologetic and charming. On the other, he used words like "retard" and "shitty" in said attempt. Still, it's not like she was getting courted by anyone. "You like me, huh?"

"Yeah, in a friendly nonthreatening neighbor kind of way."

"Oh, is that all?"

Ian laughed. "Oh, no you don't. See, I can't win. If I say no, then I'm coming on too strong. If I say yes, then it's a sign of rejection. I know how this whole thing works." He didn't, of course, but his balls felt heavier saying it.

"Do you?" Beth said, her grade school giggle following suit. She had a great laugh and it hit Ian right in his chest. She wasn't as cute as he made her out to be that first day at the bus stop, but so what? She had this way of blending her laugh perfectly into the last word of her sentence. And a one of those bottom teeth smiles that not too many people can pull off.

"So maybe I could buy you some candy or something and we could forget about that first day?"

"I'd like that."

Ian nodded. He was making progress. It was just a question of how much. There was now little doubt that a smooch was on the horizon. Not today, but if he could manage to dance around the subject of her brother, certainly by the end of the week. If they hung out in the evening, for sure. Then breasts. If alcohol were to enter the equation, then anything was possible.

As the two walked to the front counter, Ian was happily lost in thought. Cataloging all the body parts he hoped to investigate and in what order with the precision of a Wall Street bean counter. Ken, meanwhile, had been watching them from afar and smiled at this budding winter romance. Beth placed the figurine on the counter. "Just this, please."

Ken smiled and started scraping the bottom of the angel with his fingernail to get the sticky little price tag off. It was one of those stickers that looked like it was going to require paint thinner to permanently remove it. But still Ken kept at it. Grinding his finger determinately up under the angel's dress as if trying to bring the poor woman to climax. It wasn't until a few awkward seconds passed that he relented, saying, "You may want to try a little nail polish remover on that one."

To which Beth nodded in agreement and passed him some cash.

"And I'm gonna get some candy too," Ian added. As coolly as one can deliver such a statement. *You should see me order cigarettes*, he thought. *Much more testosterone in those purchases.*

Ken opened the sliding glass door and shook open a tiny bag. "All right, what can I get ya?"

"Just some Swedish fish. Good handful."

Ken counted them out on the counter and finally gave the damages. "That will be thirty-six cents," he concluded.

Ian passed him a dollar and then turned back to Beth. "You had these things before?"

"Not for a while."

Ian popped one in his mouth. "Well, they're pretty great."

Ken stopped with the cash register draw open. "Okay, out of a dollar, and that means you get how much back?"

Ian froze. "What's that?"

"How much do I owe you?"

Ken was notorious for playing this game with the elementary school kids. He liked to think that he was adding to their mathematic skills that clearly went unchallenged in school. In reality he was losing customers. Kids didn't want to be bothered with doing algebra for old-time candy when they could get a Snickers across the street without the pop quiz.

"Huh? Just, you know."

"How much?" Ken continued. Ian couldn't believe he was going to see this through. It wasn't so much that Ian was bad with numbers, but for whatever reason, the pressure to perform basic mathematics in the presence of this girl he was trying to entice was too much to endure. Ian couldn't think. All he could think was that he wanted to dive across the counter and slug this guy for putting him on the spot. *No, I can play his game. This is easy. One hundred minus thirty-six. No problem. Here goes.*

Nothing came out. Ian just continued to stare at Ken. It was as if Ken had asked Ian to summarize the meaning of life in three words or fewer. And there was a gun to his head. And a stopwatch.

Dammit! Why can't I do this?

At this point, Beth looked over at Ian. "Ian? What are you doing right now?"

It had gone beyond simple parlor tricks. This whole thing was now an assessment of his manhood. Get this problem right and he'd get the girl.

"Screw you, man."

"What did you say?" Ken was stunned.

"I said screw you. I'm not your lab rat." Ian was not going to be challenged by this conformist.

"Ian, Jesus. He was just playing around," Beth pleaded.

"Please leave. Do not come back until you've cleaned up your mouth."

Ken took the dollar out of the cash register and pushed it across the glass over to Ian, who immediately snatched it up. Ken gave Beth a look of pity and made that little swirl motion next to his ear. The one that signifies, *This kid's got problems.*

"You can do better," Ken said after her.

Beth brushed him off as she snatched her figurine and quickly raced after Ian, the little bell chime ringing twice in succession. Ken took the bag and shook the little red fish back into their rightful place. He gave a glance at the door that said he pitied this generation of angry young people. He looked through the glass to watch Ian pull his jacket up around his neck and tuck his chin low under his collar. Beth came to his side and Ken could read the poor girl trying to decipher his bizarre behavior while simultaneously trying to help him justify it. He'd gone through enough adolescent romances in his day to know there was one unfolding outside his store. Ken smiled as he pretended to read their lips.

What were you doing in there? Beth would say.

I don't like to have my intellect questioned, Ian would say.

Then why didn't you answer him? Beth would say.

I just don't wanna talk about it, Ian would say.

Beth then put her arm on his back and walked out of his view. He could tell instantly that this was their first physical contact. And further, that it had been sometime since Ian had been touched.

This wasn't how Ken pictured his life when he enrolled at business school. Engaging in subtle voyeurism that admittedly filled him with a kind of meek satisfaction. But the notion of using all his newly acquired knowledge to simply be plugged into a stack of cubicles in Manhattan was out of the question. He would rather struggle and be poor the rest of his life than succumb to that slow tortuous death. Barbara had an identical take on life so they were both perfectly content in their little shop. They would continue to court local merchants for trinkets no one seemed to want. They would continue to burn up their savings on rent and utilities and taxes on a niche shop in a desolate location. But all the while, they would smell the maple, and hear the oak creak, and feel the terrifying independence that only a small business owner in American can feel.

And from the office, Judy Garland continued to sing about some "Fascinating Rhythm."

ten

When the Friday before Christmas vacation finally arrived, Erin's bloodlust for the weasel had not subsided. By this point she was seeing it in her sleep.

While most little girls were eagerly anticipating which monstrous amalgamation of Cabbage Patch Doll they would unwrap, Erin couldn't wait to squint her eye down the barrel of the .22 and initiate a little holiday payback on the marmot.

She sat in the middle of the school bus by herself. Her route got stuck with one of the older buses so her seat had long discarded that sharp putrid smell of pulled rubber. She was staring at a knife wound that had been inflicted on the back of the seat in front of her. The yellow stuffing inside already had years of pen scratches and punch holes through it. Pink seeds of used bubble gum and candy wrappers gave the seat a sort of carnival flair, she decided. Best to look on the bright side.

Running her little nail across the frost on the inside of the window, she started to shape the minute collections of snow into a little circle. Pulling her finger away, she watched the tiny ice crystals slowly melt on her fingertip. She then pressed her finger in the middle of the circle.

The tiny sphere grew bigger from the heat of her touch, smoldering outward like the end of lit cigarette. Erin watched as the water dripped down. Her shape now resembling a star that she deemed familiar. From where, she couldn't place it. The water trickled down further now, making her shape menacing and more like a supernova than some cartoonish bedtime mobile. Erin felt the urge to look away, as if this curious event were mocking her.

It was then that Jamie Peterson sat down beside her. Jamie was the eighth-grade goddess, which is another way of saying she was the first one with tits. She had dirty blonde hair that hung with the perverted density of a cluster of grapes. Trashy but far from intellectually deficient, she just liked to fool around. Early developers are often saddled with the burden of having to be the first to experiment. And be experimented on. As far as Erin was concerned, that simply meant she didn't mind being "it" in a game of tag. And she didn't bother Erin. And anyone who left Erin alone was okay in her book.

Jamie passed her a quick "Hey" and then looked to the front of the bus.

"Do you want to sit with me?" asked Erin. She would have welcomed the conversation for a change. Even if her stop was approaching.

"Nah, I'm on my way to the back."

Erin looked behind her to where the older boys sat. The soccer studs. The hockey gods. The basketball stars. The back of the bus was where all the cool stuff apparently went down. Gum chewing, soda drinking, dirty words, and if things really get out of control, an ass cheek pressed against the window pain.

"See Luke Crossman back there?"

Erin turned to see. He was there.

"Yeah."

"Nikki dared me to blow him on the way home. It's gonna freak him out, but he'll love it." To most, this would have gone beyond the "cool stuff" visualized in Erin's head. But this didn't meet any criteria. Erin looked at Jamie the way a household pet might when you explain to them why crapping on the furniture is a bad thing.

Jamie gave a girlish little laugh and covered her mouth with her hand. "And don't you tell anyone."

Erin shook her head *of course not. Of course not,* meaning that she had no idea what blowing someone entailed. Jamie waited for her next opportunity and hopped back a couple more spaces until she reached the last row. Jamie exchanged a playful pat on the leg and a whisper in the ear of the seemingly blessed Luke Crossman. He put his hand over his mouth that "No way!" kind of way and thumbed his buddy next to him to promptly get the hell out of his seat.

Erin stared ahead. There was a significant part of her that was pretty sure "blowing" someone was vitally more than it appeared. Erin was making fine use of her skills at deciphering context clues. Otherwise, why the secrecy? Why the knowing laugh of getting away with something that the bus driver would deem improper? This was something that required further exploration. Erin inched over in her seat. She paused. It was essential that this task be well under way before she sneaked a glimpse—otherwise Jamie could be scared off. Although it was likely that Jamie wasn't intimidated by much.

When Erin decided enough time had passed, she pressed her head against the back of the seat and slowly moved forward. Although her eyes were no longer obstructed by the seat, she still had trouble deciphering what was going on. She saw Jamie's legs. Her light blue jeans creased across her hip in a half-moon shape while her torso was bent forward across the seat. Erin stuck her head out into the aisle, but this still wasn't sufficient. She would need to get out of her seat to have closure on this investigation.

Erin turned back to face the front of the bus. Her move to the seat behind her would need to be expertly timed. She wasn't known for causing trouble, so if the bus driver saw her acting out of order, he was liable to make a big deal of it. The bus pulled to a stop and a small group of students got out. Erin saw this as her chance. When the bus pulled away, he would need to be watching traffic so there would be no time for a glance in the rearview mirror.

She heard the hiss of the hydraulic brakes. The flap of the rubber sealant on the door slapping shut. Finally, she felt the bus lurch forward and she bolted from her seat. Attempting to make a simple leap across the aisle and back one. Yet unbeknownst to Erin, the driver accelerated to avoid a yellow light. When the engine engaged, the momentum carried Erin back not one seat but several. She shot forward, her arms out instinctively to brace herself. Although the only available brace turned out to be Jamie. Erin grabbed onto Jamie's jacket, pulling her head off of Luke's lower torso, causing his member to slap against the aluminum siding of the bus. The culmination of each of these events caused Erin to do the next logical thing: scream hysterically.

eleven

The creek behind Ian's house had frozen
over early. The immense pines above them
formed a soft canopy that created a false
sense of warmth.

Ian was hoping that taking Beth for a winter wonderland stroll on his
property would fill her with a similar fantasy. The reality was that
Beth's nostrils were sticking together each time she sniffed. Ian's
initial plan was to show her his appreciation for nature, but as the
afternoon wore on, she would have preferred he had waited a few
months. Beth reached a gloved hand for his.

"I wanted to ask you. My parents are having a sort of holiday
slash housewarming party tomorrow night. And I'd like you
to come."

"You would?"

"I would. I've mentioned you once or twice to them and they're
curious to meet you. And . . ."

"And . . ."

"And there will be booze."

"Booze."

"Yeah, alcohol. My dad's pretty cool about that stuff during the holidays so I'll bet we can sneak some and he won't even care. Seventeen is close enough to eighteen."

"Well, yeah. That sounds awesome."

Ian had to confess that it did indeed sound awesome. Few things in life deserved the moniker of *awesome* but getting free alcohol and not having to sneak around about it was up there. And then there was the "play" factor. Ian had read a study somewhere that most girls lose their virginity in their own homes. Their rationale was that they felt safer. So between Beth feeling safer and being half-cocked, Ian was feeling pretty good about things. Yes, the concept of holiday parties and family didn't set well with his antiestablishment mind-set, but Ian conceded that all societal doctrines took a back seat for the potential for him to finally get a hand job from someone other than himself.

⌐

Ian rang the doorbell at Beth's house and instantly felt a wave of nausea. He hated meeting new people, particularly in large quantities. Even though he would have skipped it, he was curious as to why his parents weren't invited. Yet when Beth greeted him at the door, one look around the room satiated his curiosity. He had never seen so many academics in his life. Every male was slender with salt and peppered facial hair. Some had goatees, some had beards, but virtually all wore thin wire spectacles. They all held their respective cocktails with the same precise movements, like they were just concluding some important point. And they were the first ones to think of it.

Beth reached down and grabbed his hand. Her other hand held some holiday cocktail. Eggnog mixed with something, he presumed.

This was the first skin-on-skin contact they had really engaged in. Glove-on-glove just didn't count. Ian was building it up to be some global event and because it took place in a room full of strangers, he felt the evening was off to a tepid start. Beth leaned into his ear to whisper, "I'm happy to see you. I'll get you a drink later." And gave him a peck on the cheek.

Again with the public affection, Ian said to himself. He formed his best fake smile and put his hand on the small of her back. She lit up instantly.

"All right, you need to meet my dad," she said with a smile.

Ian was already on the lookout for Edward. He expected to see him leap around the corner at any minute with a Christmas tree ornament stuck in some orifice. Then Ian would need to pretend that he didn't notice. *Is this normal? Do I laugh? Do I politely suggest that he remove it?* He was playing out all the possible scenarios involving Beth's brother when Beth turned her father around. Richard Kessell was the youngest of the men with beards and glasses, but he certainly fit right in. Ian could picture him with a corduroy jacket with suede patches. Richard was dolling out small portions of liquor from a crystal carafe. Ian couldn't see any signs of a beer keg, but perhaps that was kept in the basement out of sight.

"Dad, this is the boy I was telling you about. We're neighbors actually. Ian."

Ian extended his hand. "It's nice to meet you."

"You, as well. Well, you're not a Reagan guy, are you?"

"No. No way. Mondale. Well, I would have, but you know. Seventeen."

Beth's father extended an inch of amber liquid in a rocks glass. "That's okay, good man. We'll get 'em next time. Care for some cognac?"

"Maybe in a bit. Might be a little heavy for me." Ian liked him instantly.

Beth took the glass from her father with a wry smile. "He'll try some."

Ian took the glass with the same level of trepidation that children do when they're given medicine. A mix of suspicion and guilt with a dash of insecurity. What made the experience even less enticing was the low murmur of polite conversation had evaporated. And all eyes were now trained on Ian. As if the whole room was in on some fraternity prank. Beth had witnessed Ian's pseudo meltdown at the corner store, and for a brief moment she worried he would pursue a similar tactic to weasel his way out of it. Ian put his nose to the glass and got his first fragrant blast of 80-proof nose-hair-singeing elixir.

"Smells good," he forced out amidst watering eyes. The adults in the room gave a polite round of arrogant chuckles. Ian put the glass to his lips and took his first cautious sip. In an instant he was sure he could feel the layers of skin peeling off one by one. *Epidermis, dermis, hypodermis. My lower jaw should be exposed by now*, he thought. The polite chuckles grew into genuine laughter as Ian struggled to force the quarter teaspoon down. Beth stepped in to save him and set her empty glass of dairy-based punch on the hutch.

"Here, let me show you," she offered, taking the glass from his hand and tasting a healthy portion. "Come on. I'll show you around."

Beth grabbed his hand and led him into the next room away from the judging eyes of her father's colleagues. Ian nodded to the crowd as if he has just performed some sort of magic act. In reality he was little more than a court jester. The room was on its way to being a study of some sort but for now was lined with cardboard boxes on top of furniture. Some finely woven rugs lay rolled up in plastic against the walls. Beth passed his glass back to him.

"I'll get you something else," she said, pulling a bottle of wine out of a box.

Ian looked at the glass and saw that it was already empty. She had spared him having to nurse it the rest of the night, but he wondered what that type of concoction would do to a tiny frame such as hers. She of eighty pounds about to embark on her third beverage in the last three minutes. Ian watched as Beth uncorked the top of the wine, gave a glance around, and then shrugged, taking a swig out of the wine bottle as if she were in a Coke commercial. "Here, try this," she said. "Think of it as communion."

Ian took the bottle and did as requested. "Better?" Beth asked.

"Yes. But, any beer?"

"No. My dad's not much of a beer guy."

Ian wasn't surprised. He figured if was going to fit in around these higher society types, he'd better learn to like something else, as well. Beth sat down on the floor amongst the boxes and patted the ground next to her.

"So. Worst memory of childhood. Go."

"Ummm . . ."

"Okay, I'll go first."

Ian noticed how the more she drank the louder her voice became. He wasn't sure if this was because mixing various forms of booze made one deaf or just removed societal filters in general.

"Want to hear about my first period?"

"Um, not so much. What else you got?"

"Really? It's kinda gross. I thought boys liked that stuff."

"Well, it's a scale, sorta." Ian watched as she tossed back another half cup of fermented grape juice. She passed him the bottle.

"In a sec."

"Man, you're a lightweight, aren't you?"

Although Ian appreciated her leading him out of the main entertaining room, he didn't quite get her angle of taking him down to size on his drinking prowess.

"I'm just—I dunno. Taking my time."

Beth took another sip and stood up. She extended her hand to him.

"Let's talk somewhere else."

Ian never imagined he would be hesitant to accept what seemed a clear indication of a run around the bases. As he took her hand and stood up, Beth leaned in to kiss him on the mouth. He closed his eyes, appreciating the female affection. *It had been a while.* But then he was brought back down to earth when all he could taste was this evening's alcoholic blend.

Dammit, he thought. *Why is the fantasy so much better than the reality? Taste and smell,* he concluded.

⌒

Ian stepped into Beth's room, holding his right elbow with his left hand. He knew he did this when he was uncomfortable. Previous girlfriends had even criticized him for it, although he seriously doubted such an assessment was soon to escape Beth's mouth. Her behavior downstairs had pretty much sealed the deal. He had watched, almost remorsefully, how Beth had gone from room to room, sampling each form of alcohol. Wine mixed with cognac mixed with eggnog. Which had already been mixed with brandy. He figured she initially wanted to take the edge off, then to look cool, then to excise all inhibitions. But as her filter decreased, her obnoxiousness increased. Ian observed how in the span of forty minutes, her speech and clothing became loose. And she had forgotten how to use her inside voice. *Ah, this is the difference between sexy and trashy*, he thought. By the time they slipped out of view and she guided him up the stairs, he was no longer interested in anything she had to offer physically. It was a new sensation for him. Here was a relatively cute girl willing to lay down naked with him and he didn't want to. Curious, as this was Ian's first real experience with alcohol. He was certain of one other thing: he could really go for a shot of something himself now. It sucked being the stone cold sober one when your potential bunkmate is Jack Tripper drunk.

Beth closed the door and immediately removed her sweater, revealing a black lace bra. The understatement of the next thirty seconds was that black was not her color. It only served to make her skin seem even more pasty white. One glance at Beth in her new state would be enough to give schoolchildren a rough understanding of how the cardiovascular system is laid out. The haste in which she removed her sweater had pulled her bra out of alignment, highlighting the blue vein that snaked its way along the bottom of her breasts. He had to concede that they did appear perfectly shaped, despite their ostensible translucence. *Christ, I wish I could stop analyzing everything*, raced his brain. This was the rationale for drinking at holiday parties, he concluded. If all attendees were lucid, they'd never get past the obligatory "How's work?" "How's school?" "Cold out there!" "How's little Erin?" line of questioning. He half considered going back downstairs and asking Beth's dad for a shot of that cognac now, but he'd likely missed his chance. She removed her bra promptly, although not in a sexy way like they did in the movies. It was more of a utilitarian way or how he thought the procedure might go down at the school nurse's office when checking for lumps. He saw more veins. They pulled from her rib cage like ivy up a brick wall, disappearing into the fleshy part and then surfacing again closer to the nipple. Ian swore he could see the blood moving through them. This was in contrast to the blood that was most certainly not moving toward his groin.

Beth stumbled forward with a mouth agape. The smell of Martini & Rossi digesting roast beef was near gag inducing. Her tongue sloppily grazed the side of his face before entering his mouth. Darting around and checking his teeth for any signs of left over date nut bread. When she finally pulled away, she gave Ian a wry smile and moved over to her boom box, nimbly snapping open a cassette tape and clicking the trap door closed. Ian shuddered at the thought of whatever unsexy tune would soon be escaping the speakers. Sure enough, the twang ballad of the Oak Ridge Boys' "American Made" began vibrating his eardrums. Ian had already discounted the idea that a higher power watched over him but began questioning if something was testing him. If he was being tested, the person doing the testing had a keen read on what buttons to stomp on. His elbow returned to its soothing place in the palm of his hand. This was his pacifier. His security blanket. His place of refuge while in public.

When the vocals hit, Beth raised her arms above her head, placing her hands on the bookcase. Her shoulders flexed, pulling tight the skin and giving definition to that little indentation in the small of her back. She swayed her hips back the other way and began to undo the fastener on her skirt. Ian felt a pulse of adrenaline shoot across his midsection and down into his crotch. He just might be able to get into this. His eyes darted across the room to the last remaining impediment. The illumination coming from Beth's Pluto lamp on the nightstand. If he could somehow minimize all sources of light, he could feel around and pretend Beth was anyone he wanted. He assumed all the parts felt the same when you're working around inside anyway. He assumed.

Beth put her hands inside her skirt and pulled it down, resting her head flush against her locked knees in the process. When she stood up, Ian's look changed to one of pure incomprehension. To the uncorrupted mind, Beth was a normal girl. But to the mind poisoned by thousands of images of pornographic stimuli, she failed to meet his unrealistic standards. *Where was the flawless this and the perfectly curved that?* For no reason other than his sober narcissism, Ian was able to intellectually demand that others be perfect while he could claim "authenticity." *Don't judge me, but I'm more than free to judge you.*

Beth sauntered away from the cassette player and made her way back to Ian. Her black underwear sagged remorselessly. The way an empty plastic grocery bag might when hung from a doorknob, accentuating her paper-white skin tone and her nonathletic muscle tone. She grabbed Ian's hand and guided him over to the bed. He had been frozen in the same position for so long that the carpet fibers remained stagnant when he finally stepped aside. Pushing him into a seated position on the bed, Beth reached for her hand lotion. Ian crossed his legs awkwardly, hoping this would be a signal that conversation was a more appropriate route. Beth wasn't in any condition to be reading signals and pushed his leg off the other, getting onto her knees and wedging herself between his crotch.

"First things first," she said as her fingers fumbled to undo his belt.

"Beth, I dunno. Everyone's downstairs."

"No one cares about us. Trust me."

Ian heard the soft click of his belt buckle and the soft snap of leather through a waist loop. His mind raced. He had been so busy taking down to size everything about this poor girl that the idea of actually getting physical had been pushed aside. He needed to get erect and quickly. He closed his eyes in a way that he hoped Beth would read as the anticipation of something pleasurable. The truth was that this was his thinking face. Scouring his mental Rolodex of adult talent to find one that most resembled Beth in an attempt to replace the real her with a plastic better version of her. Beth's hand reached under the elastic band in his underwear to feel a rubbery stub. She tugged on it as if her hand were a recent hatchling trying to vacate an earthworm. An earthworm that was surgically imbedded in the topsoil. A sharp, vise-like tug. Ian was certain this wasn't her first sexual encounter but had to wonder if the lawnmower pull-cord method got her previous dates off. He suspected not.

She pushed down on the lotion dispenser, leaving a healthy amount on her left palm. While the awkward tension in the room was now the dominant force, they each stuck to their respective goals. Beth was going to get him off if it killed her while Ian desperately wanted a story to tell. To the outsider they appeared to have a cohesive agenda, but one was deteriorating more rapidly than the other. Ian pleaded for himself to look past his corrupted sense of reality. He thrust his hips forward hoping that would shoot some blood down there. Then his eyes opened and he caught a glimpse. He saw that giant dollop of sour cream and he thought of chili. *Shredded cheese. Scallions.* He heard that awful country music and he thought of Alabama. *Spanish moss. Humidity.* He saw those drooping panties and thought of his grandmother. *Crow's-feet. Harelip.*

Beth put her right hand in his pants, cupping his testicles with the help of half a cup of Neutrogena. But Ian was nowhere to be found. He was busy attending a country fair in Hokes Bluff with his granny. So much for pretending he was skewering Ginger Lynn poolside. Ian's flaccid member, meanwhile, was lost in a sea of lubricant. An oversized Gummi bear enduring some bizarre adolescent interrogation tactic. Ian would have much preferred that scenario. At least then he could have talked and put an end to their misery.

Beth finally relented and pulled away, her hand a sopping mess. Ian's underwear fared no better.

"Just relax, baby," she said, placing her palms on his jeans.

"I am. Sorta."

"Then what's going on down there?"

"I can't, um . . . It's just weird. Your dad's right there. This isn't gonna work," Ian sheepishly whispered as he inched up his pants.

"I don't believe you. You'd do me if you wanted."

"I know I would so . . ."

"You some kinda faggot?"

"Shit no."

"What then? You don't think I'm cute?"

"No, you're fine."

She cocked her head at him. "Just fine?"

Ian threw his head back. "No, cute also. Cute is what I meant. Stay with cute."

Beth finally got to her feet. Her eyelids fluttering while she tried to regain her equilibrium. She was embarrassed. He was embarrassed.

It just sucked all around. And not in the way either had intended. Beth returned to the dresser and began to put her clothes back on. Ian watched her and for the first time really did think she was cute. But with his package now suctioned to his leg, there would be no erections in the discernible future.

Beth turned to face him. "I'm not dumb. I can tell I'm not as pretty as most girls. But I have other qualities, you know."

"I know you do, Beth."

"Ah! Told you! You think I'm homely. I knew it. Get out!"

"Ugh, Christ, I was talking about the other qualities thing you said!"

"You're an ass."

"I'm not gonna do this. There's no point."

"Just go then. Get out of here."

Ian wanted nothing to do with her body, but he certainly didn't want it to end this way. He started to redo his belt. "It's got nothing to do with you. I'm just weird. I'm a weird guy, okay?"

"Yes, you are."

Beth turned and flopped face first on the bed. Ian remained at the doorway.

"I still want to hang out and stuff, just you know . . . away from adults."

"Leave!" Beth screamed, with her face muffled against the pillow. He did.

As Ian made his way downstairs, he could hear Edward laughing. That crazed uncontrollable laugh that only someone without a care in the world could have. Someone who will likely never experience the vehement misery that is a failed attempt at high school coitus. As the staircase bent around, Ian caught Beth's grandfather, wearing a pair of antlers, hobbling through the front hallway. Grunts and labored breathing escaped his mouth, making what one could only assume were reindeer noises. Whatever the Christ they sound like. His posture wretched. More so. Edward then followed with his gauche little steps, shaking a candy cane as if it were a whip. He was sporting a red hat with puffball top. Edward stopped in his pretend sleigh just enough to give Ian a wave of recognition. *Oh, I get it*, Ian said to himself as he watched them trot noisily into the living room. Ian passed them a contented smile. He had to confess that seeing Beth's grandfather so accepting of Edward's chromosome deficiency was charming. If this had been an after-school special, the two of them would be swirling amongst the fellow partygoers in slow motion. The myriad colors of the Christmas lights pulled into a soft focus in the background. Beth's grandfather playing reindeer. Edward playing Santa Claus. There was not a condescending cell in his body. This man was judgment free. It was as if this handicapped child was as handsome, gifted, and noble as the Rhodes Scholar quarterback some other old man got as a grandson.

They're both retards, he thought.

Stepping down onto the hallway tile, Ian made eye contact with Beth's parents, who were just greeting someone at the door. Richard raised his glass of eggnog and brandy in Ian's direction. Their mutual hatred of all things Reagan had successfully cementing a new bond between them. Catherine smiled as her eyes glided down. Her smile dissipating in precise coordination with the wine glass in her hand. Traveling from side of mouth to side of body. Ian dropped his smile concurrently as he looked down to see two perfectly preserved, lotion-streaked handprints. Gleaming in the reflected light of the Christmas bulbs. Labeling him guilty. The paradox, of course, being that he was guilty of being a flaccid epigram but little else. A crooked little smile formed in the corner of Ian's mouth. *Richard would appreciate this delicious irony*, he thought. *I should tell him.*

Ian had been so distracted with not having sex that it looked like he had just had sex. Or at least come pretty damn close. Ian grabbed his coat off the hanger and extended his hand to Richard.

"Thank you very much for dinner. I was nice to meet you."

Richard gave a halfhearted handshake but felt it best to send this boy on his way.

It seemed like a good way to end the evening until Beth came crawling down the stairs in the same outfit Ian had left her passed out in. T-shirt. Panties. Nothing else. Her bare feet slapped against the tile as she made her way over to Ian and Richard. Catherine immediately came to her aid, putting her arm around her.

"Beth, sweetheart, this is not appropriate."

"I'm fine!" Beth snapped back as she stumbled to the doorway, pushing her mother away.

By this point the ambient conversation of the dinner party had lulled to a whisper. Most of which consisted of self-conscious bewilderment while being mindful of the holiday spirit. Such as "Dear Lord, that young lady is trashed." Ian was feeling better about his jeans since Beth had entered the scene. All that was left now was to make a prompt exit and he'd have two weeks over winter vacation to forget about it. Beth had no intention of letting him go quietly. She extended her hand to the gentleman standing next to Richard.

"Hi," she said. It was sharp and girly.

Richard pursed his lips and turned to the older gentleman. "Kurt, this is my daughter, Beth. Beth, Kurt is the dean of our literature department. You can call him Mr. Wheeler."

Beth extended her hand, which was gracelessly taken by Mr. Kurt Wheeler. "Hi. And I'd like you to meet the fucking asshole who wouldn't fuck me."

Even Edward had stopped laughing.

"Him!" Beth pointed her pinky finger at Ian, who in turn gave a nod that signaled, *Yes, I think they're aware of whom you speak.*

In case no one heard it the first time, she repeated, "This is the fucking asshole who wouldn't fuck me." That sealed the deal for Edward.

He erupted into a hearty guffaw, running into the front foyer, wailing on his cock and balls with reckless abandon. Like the school bully who has the resident bookworm in a headlock. Beth walked into living room and began to grab people by the arm, pointing to Ian and reiterating what by now had been accepted as common knowledge. That yes, Ian was a jerk. That no, full penetration was not achieved. And yes, people would be talking about it the next morning.

If asked, Richard would have to confess he was feeling mixed emotions. True, his mutual housewarming slash Christmas party had degenerated quickly, but on the plus side, his daughter was still a virgin—so far as he knew. He opened the front door and nodded to Ian, who was more than relieved to be getting out of there. Pulling his hat around his ears, he felt the warm gush of air pushed out by the door closing. As he started down the brick walkway, he could still hear Edward inside cackling and repeating, the best he could, Beth's newly assigned catchphrase.

twelve

It was Christmas Eve in 1981 that Lyle developed the habit of cleaning his fingernails with a knife. For his entire life up to that point, he would bite and rip and gnaw at his fingernails.

Hangnails were a constant, as were easily transmitted colds, flu, and canker sores. It was a vile addiction. And one that he had been unsuccessful at breaking until he spent Christmas Eve with his ailing mother at the Ridges Retirement Home. This evening, one of the last in the year of our Lord labeled 1983, Lyle sat in his chair by the woodstove, cleaning his fingernails with a knife. Gliding the blade just under the white part, he could collect a tiny spec of grit and calcium and then flick it off into who knows where.

He'd heard the kitchen door open moments before. Ian entered and exchanged a modest hello, then he was off to bed. Erin having nestled in some hours before. Lyle decided he would wait up for Eli and greet him with a beer and smile. Although if he didn't hurry up, it was liable to be just a beer.

The fire popped and hissed in the woodstove next to him. This wasn't how he had imagined spending his evening. But as had become such frequent fare, he and Helen had argued on the way back from

Christmas Eve service. She had gone to bed. He had not. He had attempted to broker a mild sexual exchange. His efforts at being subtle had no longer worked, so he figured perhaps Helen would be in a festive mood with the birth of Christ upon them. This figuring was inaccurate. So, he was left to stare at his hands and marvel at how old they'd become. He held the knife up to his wedding band to see which reflected light better and then analyzed the outcome. And then he thought of where that knife came from. And how he came to never bite his fingernails again.

Lyle's mother had never planned for her later years in life. "What's the point? I don't plan on living that long," she would argue effectively. It seemed to make logical sense until her disposable income and motor skills started to head in similar directions. Her plan was to die in her apartment. When that didn't happen, the burden of caring for his mother lay solely on him since he was an only child. As the husband of a wife who refused to be bothered with such misery, the emotional burden was worse.

Lyle loved the holiday of Christmas as a child and even more so as an adult. The joy of watching his children react with glee when they opened up just the right gift was better than any he felt on the other end. But when his older children began to loathe religion and consumerism, they really sucked the fun right out of the whole thing. *All this greedy spending of money is terrible,* Ian would say. *You're ruining the planet with these nonbiodegradable plastics,* Eli would follow. More than likely, they were repeating whatever rant their teachers had recently spouted off. Lyle found it curious that Ian wasn't terribly opposed to the government greedily spending people's money—only when individuals did it themselves. It was the culmination of these attitudes, his dire financial situation, and the overwhelming sense of guilt that pushed him to his mother's home that evening two years ago.

It was the first holiday Lyle had spent at the retirement home. He stepped out of the elevator that evening to the sight of just what kind of holiday cheer government subsidized retirement care can buy. The tile floor was yellow, although clearly not originally. The walls were a mix of brown and orange. Again, likely not what the architect had intended. A three-foot-tall faux Christmas tree blinked on and off. A black Santa Claus was stapled to the tackboard with care. Tinsel and cotton were applied to the interior windows with the precision of a sand blaster. And then came the sound.

A group of volunteers were singing in the rec room. Their only musical accompaniment was a poorly tuned ukulele. These people needed to be commended. Although for their hearts, not for their gift at music. They were attempting to sing "Jingle Bells" to an audience of nine residents. All ranging in age from eighty to one hundred. All ranging in condition from "passable" to "any minute now." Lyle stepped forward and spotted his mother amongst them. She was seated in the back. Her head hanging low, starring at the lyric sheet in her lap. Her right hand clutching a Styrofoam cup of strawberry ice cream. Her left hand inside her blouse, clutching her breast.

As Lyle tried to take it all in, he made eye contact with another woman in a wheelchair. Her torso lay askew, her hands folded in front of her and her eyes starting a hundred yards into the distance. She was missing both legs. And she wore a bright blue hat with yellow trim that read "World War I Veteran."

He wasn't sure if it was a directive from the administration or a personal one, but many of the employees had opted to wear a piece of Christmas flair. Lyle noted how whatever the intentions were, the sight of a janitor pushing a slop bucket past a deranged senior citizen while wearing a Santa's cap induced feelings of lurid irony rather than holiday cheer. He stared at his mother slumped over in her chair. That thick smell of festering yeast, either from the evening's menu or the dozens of extinct vaginas that darted the hallways. Everything mixed with industrial strength bleach. Carrot puree had as distinct a smell as any after it had passed through ancient bowels only to find refuge in a pair of Depends undergarments. It was a cruel world after all. And no amount of puffball hats and caroling was ever going to change that.

Lyle would scan the faces of the depressed souls and wonder what their lives entailed. It broke his heart to know this would be the fate of most war veterans. The world's most attentive and adoring mothers would likely die alone. Lying prone on steel beds with creaking mattresses, staring at blank walls. A lifetime of memories would be all they had to paint with. Being spoon-fed baby food then waiting for the burly black nurses to flip them over and wipe their anuses. Lyle suddenly had a renewed affection for his line of work.

When he approached his mother, the recognition was faint. She passed a curled smile and then returned to her hunched position. Lyle put his arm on her frail shoulder and pulled her torso to him. "Merry Christmas, Mommy," he whispered into her ear. He distinctly remembered the look on her face as she scanned the waiting room for other visitors she might know. And the dialogue that ensued.

"Did any of the kids come?"

"No, Mom, they couldn't make it."

"Oh."

Of course, they could have made it. It just depressed the hell out of everyone to go there. And this was Christmas. No time for depression. Unless it was someone else's. Lyle was angry at himself for not forcing his children to go. For no other reason than to illustrate the "Honor your father and mother" commandment. He was too easy. And tired of the fight. Lyle remembered how quickly he had to redirect the conversation or risk sobbing himself. He pulled out a pamphlet.

"So, Mom, there's a Lessons and Carols presentation this afternoon in the chapel. I thought you might like to go. I could take you, if you'd like."

"Oh, that would be lovely. Thank you, dear."

So, Lessons and Carols it was. Lyle wheeled his mother into a makeshift chapel on the first floor of the building. It was a conference room that had a wooden altar built on one end. It looked more like the witness stand at any old-timey court house, but throw a wooden cross and a nativity scene by the podium and bam! Instant chapel. Lyle saw that a row of residents had already staked claim to the best seats in the house. Their wheelchairs were aligned inches from where the majestic wood of the alter touched the utilitarian carpet of the conference room. They sat motionless yet attentive. Like a row of infantry guarding Fort Ticonderoga. From outside, Lyle could see a heavy flurry starting to develop, only fueling his analogy.

He pushed his mother to the last spot in the second row. Placing a leaflet of the day's proceedings in her hands, he took a seat in a chair on the wall. Lyle pretended to flip through the leaflet and be interested in what the hour's proceedings might produce. If there was indeed a merciful God watching over them, the proceedings wouldn't go more than forty-five minutes. There was to be an opening by the resident pastor, followed by readings by those residents who could still communicate orally, intermixed with plenty of Christmas music. The religious kind.

Lyle sighed. *Well, I like Christmas music, so how bad can it be?* He watched as more and more residents in wheelchairs were rolled into the conference room. Most by attendants. Very few by family members. They were packed in like cars at a drive-in. As many as could fit within a row and still be within the fire code. Lyle wondered if this was joyful to any of them. Wheel to wheel with your equally feeble neighbor. Did they size each other up like young men did in bars? But instead of *I'll bet I can take that guy in a fight*, it was *His face is decaying quicker than mine*. This had to be the case. Men were still men, right? Lyle was busy dissecting the crowd when a decrepit man was pushed in front of him. There didn't appear to be any space left, but the attendants fit him just the same. His wheelchair was thinner than most. As was the man. He had oxygen tubes taped to his nose with thick white tape. *This must be what nerds look like at the end*, thought Lyle. They always found someone way of out-laming the competition. The man looked over at Lyle, who was biting his fingernails. The man began to copy him, so Lyle looked away.

When the last of the residents had taken position in the far end of the room, a young woman approached the podium. Young in these circles being sixty-four. She introduced herself as Deacon Sandra and proceeded to bless the audience. He remembered the sad faces closing their eyes as if being cooled by a gentle mist. It was no secret why this audience embraced the notion of blessings. When you're so close to the end, you'd better believe in something. Otherwise it can be an even lonelier place. Lyle was a true believer, but even if the whole Bible was just nonsense, it served this purpose. *Giving these lonely souls some form of comfort couldn't be a terrible thing. It just couldn't. If religion had a place in society, this was it.*

When the blessing had ended, it was time for the first carol. Lyle looked up, intrigued as to how this was all going to go down. Then a fat woman stepped up on the podium. The boards creaked with each awkward step. She carried a guitar in her hands, although it looked more like the kind of guitar they sell to kids to see if they're really interested in playing. Before parents drop the coin on the real one.

The woman introduced herself as Dusk. *Hippie parents*, Lyle concluded. Dusk then stated how her parents had died when she was very young, which is why she volunteered so much of her time at the retirement home, and Lyle promptly felt like an ass. He had to confess that no matter this woman's weight or musical ability, she had to have a heart of gold to willingly spend her time amongst this crowd. Still, the cynic in Lyle decided that this woman would need to be the last undiscovered maestro on the planet to make anything resembling Christmas music escape that combination of musical accoutrements.

As it turned out, Dusk was thankfully undiscovered, and the audio that was liberated from both mouth and guitar was something of an anomaly. There were chords and notes and lyrics, but one dare not call it music. Dusk strummed away and sang "We Three Kings of Orient Are" as if it were the last song these men and women might hear. He suspected she sang all her songs with the same enthusiasm. Dusk knew no other way. But Lyle then heard an off-key accompaniment. He at first thought Dusk had brought with her a taped recording of some low stringed instruments. He quickly realized that the sound was the residents. Following along the best they could, reaching all the highs and lows with the musical precision of back-alley cats having intercourse. As a young man living in Troy, New York, Lyle knew exactly what this sounded like. And the similarities were remarkable.

Lyle had begun criticizing the old couple two rows back. Perhaps it was some odd coincidence or perhaps a little intervention from above, but at that moment, his lips formed a smile and his eyes caught those of Deacon Sandra. Lyle had always been intimidated by men and women of the cloth and was convinced they could read minds. The woman knew the callous things he was thinking about these people.

Lyle began to get nervous. So once again, he began to chew on his fingers. It wasn't something that really suited a man of his age, but old habits die hard. Out of the corner of his eye, Lyle saw the Skinny Man next to him put his finger in his mouth. And begin to chew.

Dusk meanwhile had finished her song, and Lyle listened intently as resident Marcy Herr read Matthew 1:18–25. *This woman has to be seconds away from death* raced through his brain. Deacon Sandra was still staring at him. He reached for his mother's hand. Most would see it as a sign of gentle comfort while these words of gospel were spoken. For Lyle, it was a gesture to break his mind from the flood of insensitivity that was pushing through at every sighted nuance. His mother reached over and patted his hand. Her veins were as violet as the scarf the woman in front of her wore wrapped halfway her up face. *Christ, it's hotter than an oven in here and you're dressed like we're outside*, Lyle thought again. And Deacon Sandra looked up from her Bible. And

Lyle tore a thick nail off his middle finger, quickly moving on to the ring finger. There wasn't much there, but he'd find something. And the skinny man in the wheelchair followed suit.

Mandy Herr finished up her passage with a denture chattering "The word of the Lord." And the room of almost dead people gave a collective "Amen." Sounding like a spring breeze pushing through a bagpipe. Lyle was looking around to see if anyone heard that. Deacon Sandra raised her head, but it was blocked by the inescapable ass of the tragically undiscovered artist known only as Dusk. Her next rendition was that of "God Rest Ye Merry Gentlemen." *Oh, thank God*, thought Lyle. *I could use a good cat fucking.* Dusk started strumming. The group started their whining drone of noise. And Lyle jumped to his left hand, searching for a nail. Something his incisors could grab onto. *Give me something*, he pleaded.

"To save us all from Satan's power let nothing you dismay. Oh, tidings of comfort and joy. Comfort and joy. Ohh, tidings of comfort and joy."

Trust me, thought Lyle. *There's nothing on this entire earth less comforting or less joyful than listening to this whale of a diva mangle this music in front of these thirty shriveled up corpses.* "What on God's earth is wrong with you, woman?"

Although that last part he said out loud.

And Dusk stopped singing. And his mother released his hand. And the Skinny Man in the seat behind him tore the entire fingernail off the pinky finger of his left hand. It came loose with a transparent goo that still clung to the moist flesh at the end of his finger. Even while the nail itself crunched away in his mouth. And all of this Lyle did not catch out of the corner of his eye, but dead on. Absorbing every stinging moment of it. It was gag inducing. So powerful was the nausea that Lyle pushed forth his mother's strawberry ice cream onto the cornflower blue carpet. It splattered with the weight of the world upon it, daintily hitting the unsuspecting residents with the delicacy of their make-believe blessing.

And through it all, the residents kept singing. They sang even though Dusk had stopped leading them and even though Lyle's sweater was absorbing the burning odors of stomach acid. And that, he supposed, was just what the whole Christmas spirit was all about. Perhaps what the whole day was to be all about it. And he wept at the sight of himself.

His mother turned to face him, her eyes glassy that her son had befouled the afternoon's festivities. But mostly because they both knew, deep down in their core, where the spinal column connects with the fibrous back tendons, that this was to be their last Christmas memory. Grandma Cook had held Lyle in his sleeper as a toddler and helped him open his first Christmas presents. They would each grab an end and he would run off in the other direction. When he was older, she would go sledding with him. When he was a teenager, she would struggle with his distance from the church. When he was a young man with a wife, Grandma Cook was there to welcome him back, this time holding Eli as a toddler wearing footie pajamas. These were the memories they shared together. But they were all relegated to the back of the line to make place for this latest Christmas Eve memory.

She died that spring, finally succumbing to her bladder cancer that made her rot from the inside out. Alone and scared amongst bare walls and strangers. Lyle was working at the time. And he never did apologize for ruining their last Christmas Eve together. So, on this evening, like all the others since, he sat on his recliner. His eyes glassed over, loathing himself and the memories he forced upon himself. Unable to provide his mother with a gentle time. Unable to provide his children with a reason to cherish Christmas. But on the upside, he never bit his fingernails again.

Erin awoke at 3:30 that Christmas morning. Something had bolted her awake and it wasn't the anticipation of a life altering trinket wrapped underneath the tree. It was another wave of nausea. A pressure on her core that made her abdomen feel like concrete. She wasn't one of those children who raced downstairs to tear open gifts before others. Hard times on the family had been successful in quelling all materialistic expectations at holiday time. It was difficult to say whether this was a calculated action by Lyle and Helen or an inevitable byproduct of phasing out television and trips to the mall. The rationale being that if children aren't exposed to advertising or retail displays, then they won't know what they're missing. If they're fed, clothed, and educated properly, they will turn out to be happy children. Because of all this, Christmas never carried with it the same mystique that it had others. Her immediate relatives didn't come to visit so it was never seen as a gathering in the way that Norman Rockwell might have painted it. There were no warm memories to cling to. It was simply a day to sleep in. Except this time.

Erin had curled her top comforter over her head so that just the side of her face was exposed to the air. She had situated herself so that her clock was perfectly cropped by the covers, staring at her clock for

what felt like most of the night. Until she blinked her stare away to
see it read 3:31. She decided to get up and at least give herself some
quiet time.

⌐

Erin's stocking was hung in the library. And since the fireplace wasn't
functioning, the stocking was simply resting on the mantel. It looked
better when it was empty and could be hung in its traditional locale.
It's what the Cooks called the library, despite that little reading was
ever done there. It was where books and magazines were kept so it's
possible that's what served as sufficient criteria. That and the obligatory
copy of *Encyclopedia Britannica*. This latest collection was still in the
plastic wrap. Ian had outgrown its necessity and Erin had yet to reach
it. So there it sat. The edge of the pages shimmering with that fake
gold masking and the spines stiff like granite. Not a single crease in
them. One could argue that even placing it on the shelf in an easily
accessible location was a huge step.

Erin stepped into the room and saw that the cookies and can of
Budweiser that she had left out for Santa Claus had been polished off.
Her father had convinced her that after having so much milk at other
houses, Santa would appreciate the change of pace and would welcome
a cold beer. This made sense to Erin and ever since, she had seen fit
to oblige. She walked up to the long-frosted windows and could see
the wind whipping snow around in the streetlights. It wasn't snowing
as she had hoped. Just cold. Just a typical, brutally cold December
morning. She put her face against the glass and watched as her breath
created a little spot of mist and then disappeared. She looked up into

the sky to see if the stars were bestowing anything special on her. But they weren't. Not today. A night sky vacant of clouds almost made the cold seem that much more biting. There was nothing holding it back.

Erin walked back over and pulled out the "C" volume of the encyclopedia. She found the little corner of the plastic wrap where it was bunched together and poked her finger through. Pulling back the seal, she rubbed her hand over the dimpled cover. She loved the sound of the binding cracking when she opened it for the first time. The hard, folding pop that would emanate when she ran her index finger down the seam in the middle. She carried the book over to the corner of the room where Harley was sleeping. His long legs splayed out in such a way to almost make a little armrest for her. Harley's belly raised and lowered rhythmically. He could breathe uninterrupted even when Erin put the full weight of her back against him. A 120-pound frame will do that. She settled down in between his outstretched paws and began flipping through the pages, stopping where it had a listing for the Christmas Star. Also known as the Star of Bethlehem.

Erin looked at the pictures of wise men looking up in the sky. Her eyes darted over the words detailing what they said they saw that night. How it served as a beacon to lead them to where Jesus was born. She looked back outside into the night sky and could see nothing that resembled the drawings in the book. Nothing whatsoever.

The sound of the floorboards squeaking behind her pulled Erin from her intense reading. Eli was standing directly behind her.

"Hey, girl," he said with the warm tone she had become accustomed to. Her face lit up immediately.

Erin got up and hugged him around his midsection. "When did you get in?" she asked, keeping her voice at a whisper.

"Late. We had some car issues."

"I'm happy you're here."

"Me, too. Can't sleep?" he said. He had a wry smile in his voice. As if he was pegging her for being overzealous about the coming days' events.

"Yeah. But it's not . . . not because of this stuff. I didn't feel so good all the sudden."

Eli put his hand on her head. "What's going on?"

"I don't know. Just felt like I was gonna puke."

"You feel okay now?"

"Little bit."

"Well, why don't you go back to bed then. It's pretty early. Even for Christmas."

"Okay."

Erin walked over to where she had rested the encyclopedia on the carpet, catching Eli's eye.

"What were you looking at?" Eli inquired, his voice in mid-yawn.

"Oh, just curious about stuff."

Eli took the book and smiled at it. Erin watched his face.

"You don't believe in this kind of stuff anymore, do you?" she asked.

"Well, if I didn't, I don't think now's a good time for a philosophical discussion. Let's wait a few days," Eli said, hoping to redirect the conversation back to sleeping.

"It's important to me. I need to know what's going on here."

Eli saw in her face that it was vexing to her. He nodded and sat down on the floor against the wall. The window to the left of him.

"Okay. A quick one. What's your question?"

Erin pointed the drawing in the book. Eli had his own doubts about what Christmas was all about but wasn't about to play the role of the bitter atheist. Especially on Christmas morning. Wait until New Year's, at least. Erin was looking up at him with a look that stated, *Everyone else has steered me wrong, so whatever you say I will believe.* He typically avoided such pressure, but the mood was enchanting enough that he welcomed the dialogue.

"The Star of Bethlehem. Sure, what's your question?"

"I don't see it."

"You mean tonight?" Eli looked out up at the window. "No, I don't suppose you would."

"I mean, that one there looks pretty big, but nowhere near big enough."

"Yeah, I think the idea is that the star only appeared on the first Christmas Day. A thousand years ago."

"A thousand years ago?"

"Well, I guess you could say one thousand eight hundred and eighty-three years ago."

"And it only stayed bright like that for one night?"

"So the story goes."

"And then it just went away?" Erin asked, almost accusatory.

"Well, it was a signal. I guess like a road flare. God telling the three guys where to find the manger."

"It should come out every year. That would make more sense."

"Well, it might just appear when amazing things happen. People see stars."

"Do you believe that story?"

"Well, I believe Jesus was a real person, if that's what you mean. But, you know, I read that astronomers now can actually chart what the night sky looked like. Even way back then. And the best they can figure was that an object that bright in the sky more likely happened in the fall. Not in December. Some speculate that it wasn't a sign from God at all, that it was just a comet or a supernova or something."

"What's that?"

"It's um, it's all the same stuff, pretty much. Volatile matter."

Erin frowned. Eli had taken the conversation in a direction that wasn't getting to the core of Erin's grievance.

"So today isn't Jesus's birthday then?"

"Well, it's the day Christians have chosen to celebrate."

"Why today? If you're saying that he was really born in the fall, why not October 10th or whatever?"

"I didn't say he was born in the fall. I said when people apply today's known science to the story of the Christmas Star, they find nothing that correlates with a massive light in the sky in December. The best they can come up with is sometime in the fall."

"I don't know what I'm supposed to think now."

"Well, keep thinking, that's the best I can tell you."

"Tell me what you think."

"About?"

"About Christmas. I'm really confused."

Because Eli had been out of the house for most of the year, he hadn't been exposed to this new version of his little sister. When he moved out, he left behind a generally happy, playful little kid. Now she was grilling him on the minutia and inconsistencies of the most sacred holiday in his parents' chosen religion. He now wished he had given her the Santa Claus version of things. But he didn't believe. And he knew she'd have been able to read that in his face.

"Okay. I think Jesus as written had a good message. I think he shaped much of the world. As for him being the son of God and being immaculately conceived, I can't say. Miracles. Walking on water, that sort of thing. I just don't know. But even if those are just stories, his message of sharing and peace and helping others is a very good thing. So that's what I'll choose to take from all of it."

"So if there was no Jesus, there wouldn't be peace and sharing."

"No, I think humans would have come up that eventually. Through evolution."

"Oh."

"And don't forget, there were plenty of Christ's followers who did terrible things. Holy wars and such."

"Oh," she said, looking more confused. "So as humans go on, they're becoming more peaceful and kind because of evolution."

"Yes. As time goes on, the consensus is toward a more communal outlook on society. The more knowledge we accumulate, the less we need religion."

"Oh," she said.

Erin tried her best to digest his words. Her upper lip curled in curiously antagonist way. She finally relaxed, seeming to accept some of that and then asked, "What is immaculately conceived?"

Eli paused and glanced at the clock, which now read 4:15.

"Ask your mother," he said.

January

thirteen

The New Year had stayed the same.
It made Ian realize what a manmade
concept time was.

The clocks turned over to 12:01 a.m. and somewhere in the house Helen was making a right-hand turn on the little rectangle in her head. But it felt remarkably similar to 1984. It was still cold. He was still the only smart one in his family. Only now it was one more calendar year he would have to regrettably claim celibacy. He had already made up his mind at what age he'd claim he'd lost his virginity. Sixteen. That was a good year. Not absurdly early, not pathetically late. He decided it didn't matter if he actually closed sexual escrow between now and the end of the year; anyone he'd meet at college would know that sixteen was his year. Although he wouldn't go around broadcasting it or have t-shirts made up proclaiming the dates and locations like some concert t-shirt.

Ian was in the basement of his house. There were two giant utility sinks that he was using to defrost the chicken water. Typically, such backbreaking manual labor would have been reserved for his eleven-year-old sister, but Eli told him about their Christmas morning chat a few weeks ago. And Ian was encouraged by her skepticism. Seeing Erin as a potential atheist piqued his interest and as a result, he sought to spend more time with her. A testament to Ian's commitment was that he didn't just relegate this time together to sipping hot chocolate and watching *You Can't Do That On Television*. If he was going to attempt a full conversion of sorts, he needed to show his dedication. Much in the same way Christian missionaries will endure the harshest of climates and disease to pass along God's message, Ian was willing to endure the most demeaning of chores to pass along his own antithetical message. That God was no more real than Godzilla or Smurfette or any number of fanciful creatures designed to push an agenda. Godzilla's was most certainly antinuclear power with a healthy dose of anti–US imperialism. Smurfette was more difficult to place, but Ian assumed she had to be some subtle offshoot of the militant feminist movement. Either of their philosophies being more pleasing to the taste than Jehovah's.

Ian watched as Erin clomped down the stairs in her snowmobile suit and moon boots. He couldn't help but comment.

"You're still wearing that stupid thing?"

"It's warm."

Ian nodded and turned the watering cans over. A cylindrical mass of ice slipped out of the steel container and landed hard inside the sink with a heavy crack. It slipped to the left side of the sink, illustrating just how uneven the support structure was beneath it. Ian proceeded to fill the tank with water.

The basement was divided into three major areas. It couldn't quite qualify as unfinished, but one also wouldn't want to spend any more time down there than necessary. There was a storage room down a long corridor. The room on the end had large windows that opened out, almost in the same fashion as the front of a corner store. Perfect for the display of seasonal items. It would often weird Erin out to come down in the middle of summer to see a Styrofoam Santa looking back at her. But she also knew that Helen didn't venture in there after the Christmas lights were taken down promptly on January first. So, anything that Erin wanted hidden from the rest of the family, or Helen in particular, could be safely stored in the window room. There were plenty of cubbyholes underneath the windows that would be secure until at least next Halloween.

The other storage rooms held old toys that the children had long outgrown but Helen insisted on keeping. "One day you'll all have children," she'd say. "And they don't make this Fisher-Price parking garage set any more." That was true actually—they didn't. Most of Helen's other idle threats involving the virtues of saving just produced excess clutter.

To the left of the utility sinks was a door leading out and another larger room. The kids would often play soccer or hockey on the hideous green tile, until they eventually all got ripped up. The dirt floor seeped up from beneath, and Erin started to believe the stories that the basement once held liberated slaves from the South.

She would test her bravery by walking down the long corridor of storage rooms. To the right of the corridor, the basement opened up into the traditional furnace and hot water heater locations. These would always click on just as she was making her descent into the depths of the basement, forcing her into retreat. Today was no different. She stood at the end of the hallway, looking down. There was always a dark corner in this basement, no matter how many lights were turned on. Too many twists.

Ian had filled both dispensers of water and set them down on the tile. He looked over to see her starting down the hallway. For a moment, he thought it would be a fine time to scare her. But then he noticed that there was something cute about the way she stood. Her hips cocked to her left side, her hat hanging down in her right hand. Her awkward little body pushing out a little round butt through her snowsuit. *Now, if Beth had that kind of curve, maybe I could have gotten somewhere,* Ian caught himself thinking.

Ian shook his head as if he'd just been splashed with water. His face crinkled with disgust at himself that such a thought would even make it into his brain. He moved his eyes to the chipped tile and once again began to analyze how such a thing might happen. He had sexual frustration, but how on earth that translates to an incestuous thought, he had no idea. *No, it wasn't a sexual thought. It was merely a statement of geometry.* He was making a geometrical observation and the human eye has been trained since childhood to seek out rudimentary shapes. That's what was happening. Round is more appealing that flat. Erin had a round little butt and Beth's was flat—thusly, Ian's eyes were conditioned to look toward the round one. *It had nothing whatsoever to do with attraction, for the love of Darwin.*

Ian brought forth the deepest and most older brother voice he could summon.

"Hey," he scolded at her.

Erin jumped and then laughed at her jump.

"You ready?"

The walk from the basement steps to the chicken coop was close to a hundred yards. It felt like ten feet in the summer when it's 75 degrees with a light breeze. On a January morning hauling a twenty-pound can of chicken water, it might as well have been a mile. Water sloshed out of the little slots at the bottom of the feeder with every step. The can would bang against one's leg, sending more icy water against the snow pants. If you sought to hold it upright so it wouldn't swing, you required the strength of Lou Ferrigno in his prime. Within seconds the weight became unbearable and the process of dropping it to the ground only caused more water to splash out, this time down one's chest. It was miserable work for someone of any age. That Ian offered to help Erin with it endeared him to her beyond words.

For months, Erin had been given the task of watering the chickens. Her parents would say it built character and taught the lessons of a valuable day's work. That was debatable. One thing that it did teach Erin was that she had no interest in farming when she left the house. The freshness of the eggs and romanticism of growing one's own food were lost on her because she had known no other. Such values are impossible to instill in children because they have no reference point. Spend a year in the city and she'd long for the fresh air that one finds only in the deciduous forests of upstate New York when it's ten below.

The air was still that morning. If there was a saving grace, it was that there was no wind. Encounter wind at ten below and one can feel the moisture being sucked off their eyeballs. Nostrils stick together when sniffling and the snow is so dry it squeaks like a freshly polished floor. The moon shone through the trees stripped of their leaves, casting a menacing shadow across the snow. Gray and thin. Prior to their connection, Erin had to make this journey alone. She loved that she now had company.

When they reached the chicken coop, Ian dropped the can to the ground, wiping his wet hands against his pants.

"Ugh, to hell with that bullshit."

Erin giggled.

"I know. It sucks, huh?"

"Yeah, I'd rather buy my eggs at the store."

"I know, right?"

Erin loved that he seemed to be on the same page that she was. Although it didn't really require much for anyone to qualify their chore as "bullshit."

"It's so nice of you to help me, Ian."

"Yeah."

Ian thought about adding a "Don't worry about it," but then didn't want to her to completely get the idea that he was digging this in any way.

"So, Ian?"

"What's up?"

"Why are you doing this?"

Ian unlatched the door to the chicken coop. It was coarse wood, looking like a few railroad ties had been glued together. Felt as heavy as some, as well. He stepped in the coop and hauled the water in with him. The chickens cooed and clucked at the intruder. Although little else. Chickens aren't much interested in life at this hour either.

"Whataya talking about?" Ian asked. He was uncomfortable with this line of questioning. For some reason which he couldn't quite place, he didn't want Erin to know the only reason he was helping her was that he hoped to fuel her hatred of religion. If he could turn Erin against their father, it would help his cause at being more comfortable at family dinners and perhaps even get the family to think more rationally about other life issues.

"Well, I know this is no fun. And you've never offered to help me before. Did I do something?"

"Do something?"

"Yeah, what changed?"

"Nothing changed, I just felt . . . okay, that changed. I just realized that you and I don't have a lot of time together with me going to school and all, and I just thought you could use the help."

Erin nodded. That seemed to sink in. Ian had mastered the technique of how to properly counterfeit emotion. Years of manipulating his father into thinking he actually respected his point of view had provided him with ample rehearsal time.

"I love you, Ian," Erin said through aching eyes. She had been wanting to say that to his face for the longest time. She knew it would make him uncomfortable but didn't want him to run off without him knowing. If her tear ducts worked normally, now would have been a good time to cry. But nothing came. Just that persistent ache around her optic nerve.

"What's that?" Ian asked. Although asked in a way one does when their hearing is fine but their ability to emotionally receive the statement is severely handicapped.

"I said, I love you. I truly do."

"Yeah, that's cool."

Erin waited for a response and didn't get one. Ian was hoping the conversation would end.

"Do you love me?"

"Sure."

"Sure? That's kind of a funny way to put it."

"What do you want me to say, Erin? We aren't dating here. Jesus."

Erin looked sheepishly at him. All she wanted was an "I love you" in return. She'd have to settled with "Sure."

"Okay, back at you."

"Can you at least look at me?"

Ian put the can down. Looking his baby sister in the eye and delivering a soulful "I love you" weirded him out to no end. He assumed he did love her but didn't enjoy being put on the spot and asked to push it out verbally. He felt the same sense of anxiety welling up in him as when he was forced to perform first grade math at the Country Token. Backed into an emotional corner but still unwilling to surrender his naturally guarded state.

"Erin, I can't give you what you need."

"Do you even know?"

"Yeah, it's pretty clear. You're like a little puppy dog that needs constant praise. I'm not into this free exchange of emotions like you and Mom. You need a friend your own age."

"I don't really have any."

"That's not my problem."

"So you like me when I argue with Mom and Dad about going to church but nothing else."

"All right. This is the kind of conversation that married people have. We are not married. Just stop. Do you want help with this shit or not?"

"Yes, please."

"Then shut up."

Erin put her hands to her sides. Ian saw the hurt in her eyes but wasn't about to give her an inch. An apology? Out of the question. So he did the best he could.

"Please," he said without a hint of irony.

Erin saw that she wasn't going to get any further and stomped over to a stack of hay bales. She grabbed the twine with both hands and hauled one down, dragging it inch by inch across the concrete floor of the chicken coop. Ian seemed satisfied with the silence he'd created and went about lugging the water can into its rightful spot. Erin grabbed a rake off the wall and began the process of collecting the day's droppings into one pile. The sound of bamboo strips scraping against frozen concrete filled the audio for the next minute. Ian knew the silence was driving her crazy. Their time at the pond together, their time at dinner, Erin would always be chatting. He realized it was because she didn't have any friends at school and all this schoolgirl chatter had been bottled up in her all day. A melancholy fate in which he was the release. Erin held out as long as she could but didn't want to let the time pass with another human and not converse.

Finally, she baited with, "Why do you hate Dad?"

Ian had pulled a handful of hay out of the bale and had begun to replace it where Erin had raked.

"Hate's a pretty strong word. You sure you're comfortable with that?"

"That's the way you make it seem sometimes."

"Then maybe I do. I've never stopped to analyze it."

"But why don't you like him?"

Ian sprinkled another handful of hay around the pen and grabbed a basket to start collecting eggs. Erin could tell by his body language that this was a topic he felt relaxed with. His whole face stiffened up when she asked him to say, "I love you, Erin." But when it came time to freely criticize his father, this was a world in which Ian had plenty to say and felt very relaxed saying it.

"He's a dinosaur. His ideas don't work anymore. I don't respect his job. I don't respect that he cowers in fear under the rules of some made-up bearded man in the sky. And I don't respect that he lets you run around with a gun."

Erin grabbed the dustpan and began raking the little black and white droppings into it. She was angry with her father lately but also felt bad hearing him taken down to size.

"I think he's a good dad."

"That's because you're a kid. And what about that talk you had with Eli? The Christmas star being bullshit. I thought we were on the same side."

"I don't think I've made up my mind yet. I mean, parts of it seem silly, but then other things I don't get."

"Like what?"

"Like where'd we come from?"

"We evolved. From apes."

"Okay, but before that."

"There were dinosaurs. "

"So before that, then."

"There was nothing. Just a bunch of chemicals and weather."

"So, before that."

Ian looked at Erin. "Okay, you haven't learned this in school yet, so I'll help you out."

He stood up and grabbed her rake. Then he collected of mass of hay and chicken feces together on the floor, pushing them into a little pile.

"See, first there was this big ball of stuff. All the little bits of matter that would ever be. And it exploded."

Ian began swirling the feces around in a circle, spreading it out over the floor. Little bits of white and black chicken poop making up the known galaxies and dark matter.

"So, every molecule the universe would ever need came from that explosion. The parts needed to form Earth and all the things on it. That's why people say we're all just star dust. Same idea."

"So, God made the Big Bang?"

"No, of course not."

"Then where did that come from?"

"Don't be an idiot, okay?"

"But where did that come from, then?"

"No one's figured that out yet."

"So maybe God did make the Big Bang?"

"No. Definitely not."

"But how come? If no one's figured out what happened before that, how do you know?"

"Because that would be magic. A big mystical guy with a white beard and a long cloak in his little white house in the clouds. It's stupid."

"But it seems like a ball of stuff appearing in space out of nowhere and then blowing up and making everything is magic too. Why did it explode?"

"I can see this is too complicated for you."

"I'm just asking questions, Ian."

"Well, I told you, the scientists haven't figured that out yet. But I'm sure they will soon."

"All right. But all that still doesn't explain why you hate Dad so much."

"That's just as complicated," Ian said. It was true that he didn't really have a good answer. But he had to give her something. He raked his little demonstration back into the dustpan and stood up.

"I guess because I'm smarter than he is," he concluded.

fourteen

Erin used to dread lunch hour. It was the one period during the day when it was obvious to everyone that she had no real friends.

Sitting alone in the cafeteria was tortuous because the assumption was all the noise and laughter that floated around was directed at her. A self-martyring position to be sure, but one that was not entirely inaccurate. That was until she realized that she was allowed to go to the library at lunch. The library was free of social clichés, as verbal communication was discouraged.

Computers hadn't quite made their way into the public school system by this point and if they had, they certainly wouldn't have reached Elizabethtown Elementary School. No, all this library had to offer was books and silence. Erin was free to find a corner cubicle and fold open her lunch sack and eat her peanut butter and honey sandwich in peace. Her brown bag had been reused so many times that it no longer crinkled. It was like that one cotton shirt that is washed to the point it transforms into silk. Her mother had put too much honey on it and it had begun to seep through the peanut butter layer and initiate the dissolving of the bread. It didn't bother her that much.

It served its purpose to make her no longer hungry and it really made her appreciate a warm meal at the end of the day. She didn't qualify as a bookworm because that implied a dedication to homework or scholarly pursuits in general. And Erin preferred comic books. She like the primary colors and few words of Richie Rich. So what if all the stories were the same. They were calming.

The ladies who ran the library were happy to have the company. Even though there was only a brief hello, it made them happy to picture Erin absorbing all that collective knowledge. It didn't matter that she wasn't really there for the books. If the janitor's closet had a place to sit, she would just as readily gone there. Erin had made it halfway through her ziplocked bag of generic brand corn chips when she heard a light thump against the windowsill. The sound a bird makes when it loses its depth perception. She looked around the wall of her cubicle to see Jamie Peterson outside, waving at her. Jamie had the remains of a cigarette between her lips and was clutching her arms together. She pointed frantically at the window at the bottom of the cubicle. It had a winch mechanism that would open at the base. Erin knelt down and opened it enough to have Jamie wiggle in.

"Ugh. Thank shit you were here. I snuck out for a smoke and got locked out." Jamie was always coming up with awkwardly formed profanity such as "thank shit." It amused Erin.

"Sure," she said, smiling at her.

Jamie wiped her face with her sleeve and gave it glance. Upon noticing that her discharge was more than a sleeve should be asked to overcome, she began looking through Erin's backpack. "You got a Kleenex or something in here?"

It didn't bother her. "Yeah, top pocket."

Jamie promptly found one and proceeded to blow her nose into it as if calling for geese. Erin watched and wondered if this was what boys found attractive. When she watched Jamie check the Kleenex to see what came out, she wondered further.

"So, remember that scene. Like a month ago?"

Erin looked away as if she were guilty of something but then knew there was no denying what she had seen. "Yeah. Kinda."

"You didn't tell anyone, did you?"

"No, course not. What would I say?"

"That's cool, 'cause I can't get kicked off the bus. My dad would kill me."

Erin nodded. "Yeah."

There was a brief silence while Erin tried to formulate which part Jamie's dad would likely be upset about. Getting kicked off the bus and having to drive her to school or giving up oral sex so easily on a simple dare. She'd never met her dad, so it was hard to say.

"That was some funny shit, though. You kinda freaked out."

Erin smiled. "That was funny."

Jamie wiped her nose again with Kleenex and shoved it into her jeans pocket. "So, you have any questions, Erin?"

Erin paused, not quite sure she wanted the conversation to proceed any further. "Whatya mean?"

"I mean you seemed sorta confused by what you were looking at." Jamie spoke with the self-assured swagger that comes with being in on something the other person isn't.

The dilemma was that Erin was pretty sure she didn't want in on it. She froze. She wanted desperately to make a friend in Jamie but feared a response in the negative would render her too juvenile for Jamie's taste. A response in the affirmative and she feared Jamie could easily sniff out her statement as being a lie. So she balked.

"What was I looking at?"

"I was sucking him off," Jamie said candidly. Which was the only way Jamie knew how to say anything.

Erin nodded as if it were suddenly all clear. Then she realized it wasn't.

"Why?"

"Guys like it. You'll see. It drives them crazy and they'll love you forever."

"So, you just put it . . . ?" Erin made a motion to her mouth with an expression to follow.

"Yeah. Well, there's like a whole technique to it, but yeah. I can show you sometime if you're interested, but not here."

"And guys like you for that?"

"'Course they do."

The word "respect" had yet to enter Jamie's list of possible nomenclatures for what else the boys on the school bus thought of her.

"Huh," was all Erin could say. This was all new to her.

"Don't you want guys to like you?" The concept that some girl might not possibly care what a boy thought of her was news to Jamie. Sparkling human insight was being felt all around.

Erin hadn't thought about it. She had to admit that she was at the point now where she wanted anyone to like her. She wasn't enjoying being the pensive loner anymore. She liked Jamie's abrasive style and that she could teach her things about boys and life. Erin suddenly felt herself awash with unbridled enthusiasm. She tried to think when the last time was that she had brought a friend home to her house. She may have had a birthday party once or twice in kindergarten. And she was pretty sure her mother had playdates set up for her when she was a toddler. It would be on the heavy side of pathetic if that wasn't the case. Erin felt for the first time that she had to make a move. Jamie would be an ideal person for her to bring home. She might even help her track down the weasel. Although she would wait to see how the friendship developed before bringing that topic out of the bag.

"Do you want to be friends?" Erin asked with sincerity so heartbreaking that it would certainly have made her parents weep to hear the desperation in her voice. Well, Lyle anyway.

Jamie looked at her curiously. She was enjoying the exchange in the way older kids do when they can control every aspect of the conversation. Erin asking so directly to take their casual relationship and move it into the "friends" category struck Jamie as pathetically desperate. And that most certainly was not the kind of girl that Jamie fashioned herself to be. She had graduated to all things involving boys, and few things would set her back more than playing house with a fifth grader.

"What is that supposed to mean?" she asked defensively.

"I don't know. Do you want to come over and play sometime?"

"Play? You mean like with dolls?"

"I dunno. We could skate at the pond or read comic books maybe? I like to draw too."

"Uhh, no. No thanks," Jamie snorted through her congestion. Once you've crossed over into performing oral sex in front of a captive audience, most traditional forms of female middle school behavior are instantly rendered obsolete. And Jamie wasn't even sure if Erin's suggestions would have classified as traditional. But they were most certainly lame.

"Oh, okay," Erin said quickly. As if she knew she had come on too strong and just wanted the whole conversation over with. She was crushed and wanted nothing more than to crawl under the desk and cover herself with some blankets. She would have cried if her stupid body knew how.

"Well, don't cry about it. But if you ever want me to teach you more about that other thing, let me know. No big deal. I gotta go." Jaime grabbed another Kleenex and promptly filled that one, as well.

Jamie got up and left. In keeping with her rough-around-the-edges persona, she didn't fail to leave her used tissue on the desk where Erin was seated. She stared at it with resentment while she watched Jamie sneak her way out of the library. She felt the same way as she did every Sunday morning when she would stare at her church shoes. The tissue was a symbol of the utter rejection she was saddled with. Even more so since it came on the heels of a rare opening up of her emotions. It served as a reminder as to why she spent her whole life hiding in a virtual plastic bag.

Erin then debated Jamie's offer. If she said yes to her offer of sex education, then it was possible she could arrange for Jamie to come over. Erin could show her just how charming and fun she could be away from the entrapments of school milieu. And Jamie could show her just how her exploits had made her a wise and classy young lady, Erin thought as she continued to stare at her used Kleenex.

fifteen

The Virgin Mary was missing her left ear.
There was a crusty patch of snow still caked
on below her nose, which made her dour
expression all the more remorseful.

Concrete had a way of accentuating expressions of sorrow yet wasn't
the best medium for capturing joy. This particular display was weathered to a point where only the most devoted of Christians could pull
spirituality from her. Erin still wasn't sure where she stood on that
issue. Instead, she was trying to picture where the sculpture came
from. Her class had just watched a film reel on the history of the
assembly line. Henry Ford and his innovative techniques. Erin began to
wonder whether everything she came across was manufactured in the
same way. This analysis would last only a week, but that was enough
time for her to picture women in hairnets and safety goggles piecing
together sections of the Blessed Mother. Hundreds and hundreds of
them shaking down a conveyor belt in some industrialized part of
town in some state she'd never been to. A primary station of some
swarthy, strong, yet equally out of shape men would hoist the main
torso out of a kiln. She would be blast-cooled with liquid nitrogen
while later sections of black women in military birth control glasses

would attached the limbs. Still another station would process the Baby Jesus. Complete with a coiled iron bar sticking out of his backside. These would naturally be supplied by a low-cost subcontractor. They would then all be affixed to their rightful spot in her arms as they rumbled past, sliding into a pre-drilled hole then sealed with plumber's adhesive. They would then fall off into packing crates full of shredded paper and onto huge eighteen-wheelers to a final resting place near you.

Erin stood by herself in one such cemetery on a crisp Saturday afternoon, studying the five-foot sculpture that stood to the right of the mausoleum. Her feet skewed apart, her hands hanging at her side, unsure of where to lay. She wore her light blue snowmobile suit and puffy black moon boots. Erin loved the minimal effort that such an outfit required to put on, and her mother didn't hassle her about wearing too little. Erin would often choose the cemetery as a place to run around, since it was almost always deserted. The grounds were always kept clean and she had never been given the impression, either through family or popular culture, that cemeteries were to be seen as places of dread. To her, it was just another park. In January the trees hung bare and the wind whistled through the broken windows in the crypt to produce an ambient hum.

Her father told her matter-of-factly that the mausoleum was where bodies were stored in the winter when the ground was too hard to dig. She had responded with an "Oh," and that was the end of it. No further questions required. This pleased Lyle. Erin had put her search for the weasel on hold for a week while she adjusted to post vacation school. Plus, no more chickens had died since the one incident and she hadn't seen any tracks leading either to or from. Her father had fixed all the holes in the coop, but she didn't think that served as enough explanation. Perhaps he'd found an easier meal elsewhere. Or perhaps he'd frozen to death on one of the nights where the temperature had dropped to minus eleven. Or maybe the retarded kid next door had eaten him. *Did they do that?* She suspected not.

Erin picked up a small stick that was resting at the base of the sculpture. The bark caught in her wool mittens and she tried unsuccessfully to pull the little fibers way from the rough bark. When she grabbed it with her other mitten, a similar fate ensued, serving only to extend her predicament. This had to end. Little clumps of snow were starting to cling to both the twig and her mittens, driving her mad. She sought out a nearby grave with which to strip the bark clean. A smooth surface on the stick would rid her of all the day's ailments. The rough marble slab was a good height for her, well-aged and perfect for whittling. She rubbed the stick back and forth, shredding the bark and giving it a nice sheen. Dark brown flecks were now imbedded into the little grooves and imperfections in the headstone.

Erin was admiring her cleverness when she stopped to glance at the words chiseled into the marker. What caught her eye that morning was that the birth year and death year were the same. It was the headstone of an infant. Erin had never made the connection before that children sometimes died. The only person she had known to pass away was her grandmother. Her father's mother. She was very old and that's what old people did. This was something new to her.

January 20, 1957 to June 11, 1957
To our most special baby girl.
We miss you daily.

She read the inscription. Some young couple had loved this child intensely for five months and then had to bury her. There was no name carved nor parents' names to assign these mournful words. The first six months of a child's life can be agonizing for all parties involved. They had birthed her and changed her diapers and woke up crying with her in the middle of the night. They held her against their chests and heard her first throaty, chubby giggles only to have her taken away before that sound evolved into a voice. They had spent the months debating what her name should be, thinking her personality would give rise to something appropriate. But that never came. They had probably screamed at her to stop crying and then one day would have done anything to get those cries to return. They may have even spanked her bottom when she thrashed around on the changing table. Such actions would have faded into memory had the child lived on. Because she didn't, this was all they had. The stone gave no indication of why she died.

Erin looked at the patch of ground where she stood and the whole place suddenly was enveloped with a new meaning. The realization that this peaceful place held in it the remains of children younger than her frightened her like nothing had before. She caught sight of the decaying statue of Mary behind her. Holding the cracked and chipped Savior-to-be in her arms. Perhaps that's how small this child was when she died. Frail and helpless. Erin felt a wave of terror pulse through her skin. The weight of some responsibility. The realization that she was mortal and she had better do something meaningful really quick or she, too, could be buried nameless and without parents in a sparsely kept plot.

Erin racked her brain for a purpose. She thought of the weasel and how had it torn apart her chickens and she wanted to kill it. She thought of her parents and how she wanted them to be happy and in love again. She thought of her brother Ian and how they were growing so distant and she wanted to prove to him that she was fun and interesting. She thought of Jamie Peterson and how she wanted to be a pretty girl that boys would permit performing oral sex on them. At least, she thought she might. Perhaps that last one wasn't the best way to gain purpose.

Erin suddenly wished she had a friend to share her thoughts with. She was growing weary of "daddy-daughter time." She felt her father was trying too hard. Hanging on to something that was no longer there. This is certainly the type of odd discovery that he would have loved to rattle off some life lesson on. But Erin was fairly certain he would completely miss the point of where she was coming from. Plus, she was sick of hearing about his mother. *She died. Get over it.* She felt a tinge of regret when the thoughts raced through her brain, but it was true. How could she apologize for it? *I barely knew her and she wasn't all that nice to me when she was around.* Erin remembered how her father stared at her during her funeral. She knew he was checking for tears, and when they didn't emerge, he took it very personally. *I faked liking her. I couldn't fake tears*, she thought. *I was all faked out by the time she finally died.*

Erin looked around. It was the first opening critical stance she had taken about the whole incident, and she felt a rash of guilt because of it. Standing in a place so full of concrete religious figures made her feel the various apostles and saints could read her thoughts. But what did it matter? They weren't Santa Claus. Mary and Jesus didn't take orders for Christmas and that was really the only viable threat at this stage. And anyway, she didn't think anyone was listening anymore. She had stopped praying for material things long ago, thinking that perhaps

God dealt only in the kind of items that weren't readily available at the local strip mall. *Turns out he doesn't deal in either*, she thought. She had prayed for a best friend and she prayed for a baby brother and she prayed for her father to quit being so sad. But none of these wishes transpired. Erin remembered asking her father why God wasn't answering her prayers. On anything. Lyle gave the tepid response, "It wasn't in God's plans." It was here that Erin began to realize what a convenient answer that was. She was pretty confident God wasn't sharing his plans with her father, and if he was, he really seemed to be able to rationalize away anything with that response. Erin began to grow bitter at all the religious symbols that occupied the cemetery. She thought about all the times she had wished and prayed and sat through church and none of her prayers were answered. All the times she had suffered through walking up in the cold and wearing those terrible clothes and it suddenly hit her what nonsense it all was.

Erin stared at the grave of this little girl and wondered how her parents rationalized her death. Did they tell each other it was all part of God's plan? *To make them stronger? To make a cuter baby next time?* Erin grew angry at the possibilities of whatever inane babble grieving parents might go through to justify the death of an infant in God's eyes. The only one she could think of was that God hated them for making fun of lepers when they were kids. Lepers being the only biblical deformity that she could think of at the time.

She pulled her mitten across her hand so that her fingers pulled tight across the end. She started to wipe off the chips of bark that had embedded themselves in the cracks of the weathered marble. Another wave of shame crept across her as she sheepishly bent down to pick up the big pieces and remove them from the matted grass that lay beneath the headstone. The few patches of grass that were exposed around the infant's grave were more like tundra. The rest was hardpacked snow that had a layer of crust on it. It was ugly. And this little girl deserved better.

Erin took her stick and began to break apart the snow. She brushed the section away as best she could. She began to feel determined to care for the plot. The nameless infant in row E adjacent to the crypt would have the most cared for space in the cemetery. She wouldn't make up any excuses for why this child lived for such a short time and then died. It wasn't in anyone's plans and it was just one of those rotten things that happens in life. Erin began to think the whole concept of religion, its sole purpose, was to make people feel better about tragic circumstances. The coldness of real life is just too painful to take at face value, so a long time ago, humans thought up religion as a way to alleviate some of that pain. She would remove all the religious items from around her grave and make sure the child was told what really happened.

The cemetery that no one went to.

February

sixteen

Saturday visiting hour at the penitentiary was
Lyle's favorite hour of the week. Because he
worked the night shift, he wasn't privy to the
societal microscope.

That is, loved ones attempting to push a condensed form of emotion
through slotted Plexiglas. He would watch as mothers and wives and
the occasional daughter would walk past him and give a look of utter
resentment. As if he were the one who manipulated the men in their
lives into exercising poor judgment. Being February, the women would
come bundled in huge parkas and ski jackets and always give the
same line that they needed to keep them on. This was all nonsense
and was just an excuse to try and smuggle something to their beloved
to make the time go faster. Or better. The former typically entailed
pornography. The latter, M&M's.

Lyle sat on a raised platform that was surrounded by chain-link
fencing and looked out over six stations. Each segregated by a blend
of chicken wire and particleboard. The communications board in front
of him looked more like the kind of high-tech equipment that the
Q-tip-haired lunch lady would do the announcements from in high
school. Decidedly low-tech. It made Lyle recall the times he would

volunteer in the front office as a way to get out of Home Ec. *How little my life has really changed*, he thought.

During the holidays, visitors would bring with them bags full of forced sentiment in an effort to make up for lost time. After the post–New Year lull, it was strictly business. "Honey, can you sign this document from our lawyer?" "Sweetheart, here's a picture of little Sally in the second grade." "Hey jackass, I'm itching again. Go to the clinic."

Lyle loved the dynamic. He didn't watch television or read celebrity magazines, but this dank, poorly lit room had more than enough nuanced drama to go around. It was perfect for satiating the voyeuristic impulses that a healthy percentage of people possess. Lyle was just fortunate enough to have a living, breathing outlet. With a pension.

He was assessing his good fortune when a woman with straight brown hair approached him. Her hair hung out of a wool hat. She had thick eyebrows and lips that were just slightly above wire thin. Lyle accepted her personal items and passed her the clipboard to sign in. There was no eye contact made. When she removed her gloves, Lyle noticed the age. He recognized the smell instantly and was reminded of apple conditioner when mixed with the oak of a home fire woodstove. The smell carried with it enough of a reversion that it worked him up. He looked up to see where it was coming from, but she had already moved on.

As she walked over to her assigned seat in station number six, Lyle glanced up again. He rolled his chair forward in the booth and watched her inch forward and put her elbows on the table in front of her. She waited with a forlorn sense of purpose. Like this was something that was more of moral obligation than a burning desire. She wasn't there to provide comfort for someone. Lyle had watched enough of these exchanges to know when someone was just making an appearance. It then hit him. He turned the clipboard around to see that the woman's first name was Anna. He had skipped over the last name and then looked back at her. It was his Anna. The girl whom he had dated in high school off and on for a few years. And here she was, sitting here waiting for her criminal husband to come up to the glass and greet her. With a smile? With a tear? In an instant, all the hurt and anger and bitterness he felt when she last hung up the phone on him came roaring back. He felt sick. Sick that something that was so long ago could still cause juvenile emotions to well up in him like a schoolboy.

When Helen had appeared in his life, Lyle had forced Anna out of his daily thought routine. This was successful for the most part, but every so often an image would creep in. He would have a full night's worth of dreams that she would solely occupy. Bizarre, nonsensical stuff that at the time seemed so vivid but on reflection was strictly ludicrous. The two of them locked out of his parents' house, longing for a bedroom in which to dry-hump, but he just can't find his keys. The date wears on and she loses interest. One of those maddening repetitive dreams that one knows will never satiate the urge. Lyle would wake up ornery and frustrated. Partially because he never got to commence with the aforementioned dry-humping but mostly because Anna was resurrected from the basement of his subconscious. This could go on for days after Anna entered one of his dreams. He'd eventually push it aside and go back to his normal routine, but her aura remained somewhere in him. Like a dormant genome waiting for a full moon with which to torment the host body.

As Lyle watched her speak, moving her hands in a confident way, passing her man a few sweet smiles, he envied him. Somehow down the road, this man, this deadbeat criminal, had more going for him than Lyle did. He began to wonder how soon after Lyle she met him. How many men in between before she settled with him. Was there a child involved? He hated the fact that he even wanted to know. He desperately wanted one of the other guards to take his place, but by the time he explained why, she'd be gone. He would be stuck checking her out. He hoped she wouldn't recognize him. He had aged terribly and now had thinning hair, a dated moustache, and a prison guard's uniform. But the eyes don't change. *I'll just keep my head down*, he thought. *It'll be over before it's started.*

When she was finished with her talk, she approached the glass. Lyle felt a wave of nervousness that he wasn't prepared for. Should he say something clever or biting? Rub it in her face that she ended up with the person behind the glass. Or maybe he could just fixate on the clipboard, she wouldn't notice, and he could move on. He wondered why he had never seen her before this evening.

She arrived. Her hands grabbed the pen. He stared at her left hand. He didn't want to look at her face, but he had to. He had to know if she really was as beautiful as he remembered. His eyes moved from her pen rolling across the sign-out column to her face. Her naturally long eye lashes, deep brown eyes, her crescent moon eyebrows. But she did look up. And they made contact.

"Lyle Cook. Jesus Christ," she said with the voice of an exhausted woman.

Lyle just nodded. There was no point in pretending as if he didn't know who she was. For years after they last spoke, there wasn't a day that passed that he hadn't thought about what he'd say to her if he ever saw her again. It was one of those drawn-out conversations on the telephone that is mostly periods of dead air. Never one to enjoy burning up phone minutes, Lyle said something that he was confident would be the last word, and sure enough it was. Now that the long anticipated reunion was here, nothing came to mind. It was perfectly akin to fine pasta sauce that begins subtle and exquisite yet is spoiled with too many ingredients. The more you add, the more all the flavors cancel each other out and you're just left with a rudimentary paste that has the flavor complexity of boiled celery. That is what Lyle's emotions felt like the instant Anna was finally standing before him. All the tell-offs, all the insults, all the hurt and embarrassment and the wanting and the hating, just condensed in one wholly forgettable sheepish nod. He took the clipboard back and jotted the time down as if she were any other visitor.

Lyle felt himself reverting. He wanted so badly to bring out the mature man with four children and a wife of twenty-three years, but that wasn't coming out. He could tell that she had stayed the same. *Refined. Educated. Athletic. All the things I am not.*

"Fuck, this is awkward," she said. *Then again, perhaps she had lost some refinement.*

Lyle took a breath. He looked up from his position. Ashamed to be in his prison guard uniform. His polyester pants. His uncomfortable shoes. His shrunken physique. Bony in some parts, like cookie dough in others. He was a mess. She was everything. *But wait. Think. What would Erin do? Channel your most precious and proud creation and assess the situation the way you think she might.* He hated that after all this time, Anna still held some power over him. That even though her choice for a life partner, whomever she deemed more worthy than he, was locked up. Lyle could make his life miserable if he so chose.

"I don't feel awkward," Lyle responded. His mood calm. His emphasis on the last word ever so slightly. As if to suggest he was feeling something but he wouldn't allow her to make him feel uncomfortable. He passed her back her keys and identification.

Anna laughed with a snort. "That's cause you're on that side of the glass."

"We all make decisions in life."

Anna gave him a defensive look that suggested she wasn't in the mood for a lecture.

"Okay, take care of yourself," she said turning around and putting her gloves on. Lyle did not respond, although he thought of what an empty response that is for one person to make to another. As if it's in one's instincts *to* inflict harm on oneself, and by giving that statement, the person—typically a stranger—was passing along some form of noncommittal concern. Lyle hated false sentiment. So he simply nodded again.

Anna left without saying a word. He watched her turn and his eyes couldn't help but follow her legs down. She was short, not even five-four, but her legs remained perfect in his eyes. His mind instantly flowed to a time in her bedroom when he first watched her change her clothes. Pulling her jeans up around her knees, she'd bend over slightly to get them around her thighs. Her hamstring was able to capture a perfect blend of definition and femininity. Lyle closed his eyes in disgust with himself. He had once forgotten Michele's birthday but could remember virtually every intimate exchange he ever had with Anna.

Lyle had always wondered why he could so easily remember certain moments of his life while years could go by and he couldn't tell anything significant about any of them. A man of faith, he explained it away by hoping it was all a part of God's plan. You remember certain things because you will one day come to lean on that knowledge. It may seem trite at the time, but there's a reason for it. He prayed that was the case. Otherwise, it was simply that she had fantastic legs.

The moment that he had prepared for his whole adult life had come and gone quicker than most bowel movements. And that was precisely how he felt. It was that uninspired and uneventful, and his life was the same. Nothing was resolved and nothing had changed. He had finally accepted that Anna was just a part of who he was. She had come into his life during a period when he was desperate to define himself, and like it or not, she would forever be imprinted on his core. Like a poem or song or sermon that touches the listener in a very deep way. One remembers when they first heard it and how it changed them. People can do that, as well. Even if you occasionally wished them dead. He wished he could know if he had affected her in a similar way, but it would be impossible to know.

He quickly looked to God to see if they would ever cross paths again. He decided the most spiritual way to go about this would be to flip his pen up in the air. If he caught it after a perfect flip, he would never see her again. *Got that, God? That's the deal, right?* Lyle flipped his pen and he caught it. Right as rain. Anna was now out of his life. By the time his mind cleared, he had noticed that she had long left the building. And Lyle was already halfway through checking in the next visitor.

⌐

Lyle made his way to his car to find Anna leaning up against it, waiting for him. Apparently, God didn't take his flipping the pen assessment seriously. *I'll be giving less in the collection plate tomorrow, thanks.* Lyle pulled his hat over his head and pretended that she was waiting for someone else. Although the only person she could be waiting for wasn't going to be walking out these doors for another decade or so. And it seemed a fantastic coincidence that she would mistakenly be leaning up against his car.

"So, Jesus, what have you been up to?" She came walking to him with that confident stride. The kind that a woman gives when they know they have the upper hand. Lyle remained with his guard up. Working at the prison taught him to second-guess every conversation he had, since either the inmates were sizing him up for a weakness or the other guards were looking to dump an extra shift on him. Lyle stopped by his car and looked her in the eye for the second time. She still had it. *Dammit!* he thought. *Why couldn't she have been tossed in a vat of acid or something to take that look off?*

"This is pretty much it," he said with a shrug of his shoulders. His body language was restrained but his tone implied, *If you don't like it, you can get the hell off my car.* They had reached the ever-awkward "hug or hand shake?" moment in their brief reunion. Lyle had no interest in hugging her as she stepped forward. He knew that to feel her head against his chest would be too much to bear, so he promptly extended his hand as if he were sitting down for an interview.

Anna took it reluctantly and nodded with a skeptical smirk. Lyle still didn't know what angle she was trying to play, so he made an effort to lead the conversation.

"So, the gate didn't open for you, or . . . ?"

"I wanted to talk to you, Lyle. It's been decades. Isn't that weird?"

"You waited out here for three hours to talk to me. How did you know when my shift would end?"

"I didn't."

"How did you know this was my car?"

"I assumed."

"What gave it away?"

"It's practical."

"In what way?"

Now Lyle was thoroughly confused. It had warmed up the last couple days in upstate New York, but that still meant it was a balmy 34° outside. Lyle studied her face, waiting for her to respond. All she did was smile at him. And he hated it. Like she was taking pity on this sick animal at the pound. *She wants something from you*, he decided. *End this now.*

"Well, it's cold out. And I'm tired."

"Maybe we can go somewhere. I'll buy you a cup of coffee."

Lyle raised his thermos as if to say, *I have my own and I'd rather choke on it*. But instead said, "And what would we talk about?"

"I don't know. Aren't you interested to know what I've been up to? I wanna know what you've been doing."

Lyle stepped forward, openly defensive for the first time.

"I can't get your husband out early and I'm not smuggling anything in for you."

Anna laughed. "My husband." She made another step forward toward Lyle. She was wholly aware of the impact her eyes had on him. She had taken care of herself while Lyle had not. She was as fine a woman as she had been when she was seventeen, and Lyle didn't look a day under sixty, even though he still had ten years to go. He loathed her for it.

"Is that not who he is?"

"Oh, that's who he is. I just forget sometimes."

"Then I'd guess you're lonely."

"I'm fine, Lyle. Just wanted to catch up."

"I can't imagine how that would benefit either of us."

Anna stepped forward. He read it as a come-on. He couldn't understand why she was taking this approach but knew whatever her angle, it wasn't genial.

"Would you stop being such a prick? God, you haven't changed."

"Whoever gave you the impression that people change? I have nothing to offer you, Anna. I'm not rich. I'm not handsome. And as far as conversation goes, my life's as boring as they come."

"That's not true. I can see in your eyes that you're happy. There's a happy soul in there somewhere."

Lyle stepped past her and smirked as he opened his car door.

"Oh, I've known lots of happy people at one time or another," Lyle said. "And then I got to know them better."

He closed the door of his car. He was very content with his closing line. As he felt around the steering column for the ignition, he gazed ahead with a satisfied grin. *Spot on*, he thought. *Delivered with confidence, but with just a hint of intrigue.* He felt like he was the seedy detective in an old pulp paperback that would then drive off into the dead of night. He could still feel her near the trunk of his car. She hadn't left. He knew she was counting on him to roll the window down and offer her a ride, or at the absolute minimum, pass her a longing look. To indicate he was still smitten with her. *Neither's gonna happen, sweetheart.* Unfortunately, the other thing that didn't happen was his engine turning over. It hissed and wheezed and grinded against the engine block, but little else.

Lyle closed his eyes with a sigh. No matter how great you think your last line is, if your car doesn't start, you might as well have pissed your pants. Humility never tastes as bitter as when it plays second course to haughtiness. Lyle pulled the key out of the ignition. *Dammit! I had ended it perfectly! I was home free!* His eyes moved over slightly to see Anna still in the same spot. She started walking toward him with the same self-assured walk. It was as if the upper hand just wasn't meant to be his when she was around. They could be sixteen or fifty-six. She would win, be it from simple survival of the fittest or just really crappy luck.

Anna arrived at his door and tapped on the window with her keys. He desperately did not want to turn his head to the left, but every second he waited would have made him seem that much more like the desperate, lonely, out-of-his-league teenager he was thirty-some years ago. He pulled off his watch cap, leaving his hair tousled but not in a sly, hipster way. Rolling down the window, he looked up at her and smiled. "Yeah, I'll take a black coffee and a cheese Danish."

Anna nodded, "It was never clever. Even the first time you did it."

Lyle nodded back without looking at her.

"Sounds about right." His tone was self-accusatory, as if he'd been caught speeding and there was no way out of it.

Anna looked at him with sympathetic eyes.

"Need a jump?"

Lyle suddenly felt a rush of adrenaline shoot to his groin that he hadn't felt in decades. *Yes, please,* he thought. *You have no idea.*

seventeen

Helen pushed the business end of a pin
through the coarse canvas template. The material buckled and then gave way to the needle,
dragging with it a swirling band of color.

She was seated in a spring-coiled rocking chair. The kind that death
row inmates might cobble together if they were so inclined. The springs
were thick, like they had been stripped from the suspension of a
Kenworth, complete with years of oxidation. It was a dreadful piece of
furniture. But it moved silently and the brown afghan cover afforded
it an odd sense of inebriated charm. She had spent the better part of
her Saturday evening cooking a tuna casserole in silence. Then eating
it with Erin in silence. This all culminated with Helen finally cleaning
up. In—yes—silence. There still lingered the unspoken tension with
Erin over her cavalier use of the family firearm. When Erin retreated
to her bedroom to read her magazines, Helen was relieved. It gave her
a chance to make some much-desired headway on her most recent
sewing endeavor.

Helen did needlepoint only from predesigned kits. The kind
that came with a little pattern of a train, complete with the precise
amount of thread one would need. The proud artist in her cried out

to break free from the restraint of the little dotted lines that formed the mass-produced shape. This was in contrast to the defeated artist in her that had used up all her creativity trying to make a go of the comic strip thing twenty years ago. Her conquered ego was triumphant in the end, as negative energy typically is, and she resigned herself to merely tracing the shapes like a toddler's connect-the-dots book. This current craftsmanship featured a country house with a picket fence and sun shining in the background, all tied together with obligatory sentiment. This form of artwork carried with it the same graphical precision as the original Space Invaders possessed. Blocks beget blocks.

"Grandfather" continued to tick away with the precision of a metronome, and her rocking had slowly fallen into step with it. She had a cup of tea next to her that had long since been reduced to room temperature. She had forgotten to take the tea bag out so there it sat, saturated and dense, with the romanticism and potency of used chewing tobacco. Needless to add, she no longer desired it. This was the fate of many a tea bag lately. As she was nearing the completion of a particular needlepoint, she focused on little else. When she paused to analyze the absurd focus that her menial task occupied in her life, she stopped. Abrupt and in mid-form with the needle pushed through. So sudden was her mental block that she failed to even recognize the needle had wedged itself in between the nail on her left thumb. A tiny bulb began to form underneath. Finally, the pain shot through her bone, sharp and direct. She pulled it away and brought her thumb to her mouth.

"Damn," she said out loud.

It was the first human voice she had heard all day. How pathetic that it was hers. Perhaps more so was that both participants in the

monosyllabic exchange were the same person. Helen Cook. Alone in a
house full of people on a Saturday night. It was here that Helen decided
she needed a job. Her hands returned to their rhythmic motion, the
chair began to rock, but Helen's eyes lost their gaze. She had made up
her mind. She would find a job. She would enter the workforce and
make a friend to spend Saturday nights with.

If she hadn't already used up her one allotted life assessment moment
for the evening, her next realization would have filled in nicely. She had
not worked since she and Lyle were engaged. Her last job was in the
file room of a law firm. She never saw the light of day and would spend
hours opening corrugated cardboard boxes and emptying the contents
into filing cabinets. That was the extent of her time "employed" outside
of the home. What possible skill could she offer this new workforce
that was half her age? She was just turning the corner on a squiggly
border when Lyle came through the door.

He closed the door behind him deliberately, pushing the door closed
as if he were fighting some urge that was begging him to go back
outside. He kicked the heel of his shoe against the thick doormat,
sending brown flakes of slush skittering across the carpet. He removed
his scarf and placed it over the coatrack. Then his hat. Then his coat.
He didn't remember one instance of his drive home from work. He
didn't even remember getting out of the car. He remembered Anna's
dark eyes. The smell of her hair. *She still used the same apple-scented
shampoo after all this time?* Her voice was still scratchy and sexy, the
way a '40s lounge singer's might. Raspy but still feminine. Lyle hating
thinking about her. His thoughts competing with one another. That his
first love still possessed that nameless allure that caused him so much
pain. That his wife of twenty years was waiting patiently for him to

return home from a long day's work. This wasn't like him. He could fight it. Helen would see his longing and embrace him the way she did when they were dating. She would sense the drift in his heart and speak to him in a voice so tender that it would make Anna's seem like Mercedes McCambridge's after a pack of cigarettes. Helen lifted her head from her needlepoint. *Here it comes*, he thought. *Save me, dear wife, from this vile temptress.*

"Is it too much to ask you to kick those boots off outside? I vacuumed today," Helen said in a tone most unpleasant.

Lyle stared at her with the kind of stoic wonder that comes from being let down by all five senses simultaneously. A strange form of awe. He didn't think it was possible for her to come across less alluring. *This was a test*, he concluded. *The Lord is testing me. Like Job.* He still had one boot on. He envisioned hurling it across the room and it connecting cleanly with her face. Closing her mouth and getting more soot-laced snow across her carpet in one swift motion. If God *were* testing him, giving Helen a satisfying kick in the mouth just might go over. After all, he'd still be maintaining his fidelity while scoring a satisfying blow to Helen's emasculating persona. *Did Job seek out petty, superficial victories during his test from the Almighty?* Lyle wasn't sure. He'd have to look it up.

"There's a plate for you in the fridge. Couple minutes in the microwave should be fine," Helen continued as she fixed her gaze back to her needlework. And her thoughts drifted back to what possible career she could puruse with no skills in her mid-fifties.

Lyle bent down to remove his other shoe and saw himself in two places at once. For the first time since he could remember, his life and everything in it could go in different directions. He thought of Helen saving him a plate of food. Opening a pungent can of tuna fish into a worn-out piece of Pyrex cookware and dowsing it with Wise potato chips. Throw in some cream of mushroom soup and you had yourself the ready-to-eat meal that was awaiting him beneath a thrice-used piece of tinfoil.

Then there was the fantasy he'd left behind in the parking lot. It was highly likely that he was imaging all the signals he'd interpreted from Anna, but it made him feel more like a man nonetheless. All that remained in his head were flashes of some pent-up rendezvous with Anna. A look over her shoulder with the wind tossing her hair just so to signal, *Okay, let's do it. Just this once. For old times' sake.* A drive to a seedy motel room so intoxicatingly naughty that he'd likely ejaculate in his pants with only the feel of his underwear to get him off. *That'd be okay*, he wagered. *I could go longer when the real thing comes along.* Sex so clunky and awkward that only the two involved would recognize it as lovemaking. The post-orgasm gaze that would ensue. A whole life apart to make up for.

And then there was this. A reality so absurdly lackluster in its tone he half thought he was on stage with Ralph Edwards. He even cocked his head to one side to see if there was, in fact, a curtain behind Helen. There was nothing there. Just Helen in her night-robe that clung to her in the most unflattering of ways. Just his yellow and brown kitchen that was the best his income could afford. And just the five-hour-old dinner that was approaching a black-hole-like concentration with every second he wasted. A food source so dense no taste particles could escape it. This was the path he'd chosen in life. And it was congealing one molecule at a time.

He walked past Helen with the stride of a beaten man. He was a sucker. A sap. The kind of goody two-shoes nobody who would surely die having fulfilled not a single fantasy in his head. He picked up the plate of food and held it over the floor. It had the weight of an anvil. Soaking wet. He searched for some meaning in this plate of food. Some sign that he'd done the right thing by doing nothing. When no such sign materialized, he noticed he was standing behind Helen. Just over her shoulder. The perfect angle to let the food land right in her lap. He then glanced at what she was working on. Her hands moved with the precision of an organic loom, almost lulling him into a submissive trace. Her predesigned artwork that no doubt resided in at least several hundred other homes of similar taste and income bracket. He moved his eyes around her head to see what it was specifically that she was working on. It read:

Home Is Where The Love Is

A wry smile tightened across his eyes. After all that time and all her nasty ways, this had to be what she really thought of her life. This had to be the sign he was searching for when he kept himself guarded from all of Anna's questioning. Despite all their problems and all their routines and the fact that there were merely married in IRS standards only, this is what mattered. At least he thought it did. This had to be the omen he was looking for.

Damn, he thought. *It's gonna have to do.*

His mind began racing again to the way that Anna looked in her jeans. They fit her perfectly in all the proper places. A confident walk, shoulders back, with well-worn denim that clung to her thigh just so. He began staring off into space, replaying Anna's walk away from him over and over. That perfectly lit four-second sequence. He considered finding the downstairs bathroom to quietly rub one out after Helen went to bed. Just him and that perfect walk to guide him to a much-needed release.

Helen apparently had been talking to Lyle during this whole time, but he wasn't aware of it until the drone of her voice was replaced by silence. Unsure of what to do, he filled the gap with the most logical thing.

"You looked amazing in those jeans," he said, his eyes still fixed at the same spot on the wall.

Helen set her needlepoint down on the kitchen table and cocked her head up at him. Her profile looking more birdlike than ever with her reading glasses pulling her eyes ever so delicately from her sockets. Lyle, on the other hand, found his eyes sagging. He couldn't get the image out of head and looked down to greet Helen's face with the same enthusiasm he felt the last time a catheter was slipped down his urethra.

"What did you say?" she asked.

Lyle could feel the skin on his face pulling down, producing jowls that would rival those of Harley. Multiple rings were forming under his eyelids. Like the mighty sequoia, they revealed his age.

He couldn't think of a response. His best material had been used for Anna. His best delivery he wanted to save for the downstairs bathroom after Helen had retired for the evening. Lyle fixed his gaze into her eyes while his brain raced for a response that doubled as an explanation.

"What?" was the best he could muster.

"What did you just say?" she repeated pointedly. "I looked amazing in what jeans?"

Helen straightened her chair. Lyle looked down at Harley curled up under the table. He felt a swell of envy for the beast. He pictured himself crawling underneath the table and going to sleep. Lying his head on the Great Dane's belly and not worrying about anything. Least of all how to maneuver his way out of his careless slip of the tongue. His mind raced again.

"Oh, sorry, my mind was drifting. It's from a country song. Heard on the radio on the way home."

Helen returned his stare back at him. Checking for any telltale signs that she was his primary victim in some vast conspiracy. The writer in her played out all the possible reasons why Lyle would be lying to her. The cartoonist in her could see tiny word bubbles forming above his head. Filled with all the symbols that appears above the numbers in a keyboard, signaling profanity. The storyteller in her pictured Lyle as the ringleader in some underground prison escort service in which he was bribing the wives of inmates. In exchange for sexual favors, Lyle would give them additional access and smuggle in contraband. *Access for access*, she thought. After more than a minute of crafting an elaborate scenario of Lyle's infidelity, the realist in her concluded that Lyle was too boring, too unattractive, and too exiguous to attempt anything close to an affair.

"Okay," she said, grabbing his hand with dubious charity. Passing him a smile with her eyes. And once again, sweetness followed.

eighteen

Heather Moss had always seen her faith as a gift. The way an elite athlete or artist might view their abilities.

Gifted people are able to see the world on a different plane. Mathematic prodigies can visualize complex patterns in numbers and assess multiple outcomes, while most others can stare at a set of numbers indefinitely and never derive anything meaningful from them. Similarly, most people can read a religious text and see it as simple blueprint or a place of direction and comfort. Stick to the outline and you'll be fine. Still others would look at the Bible as merely a collection of letters formed into archaic words that formed sloppy sentences. The culmination of which carried with them the weight of a strand of hair and nothing of worth could be derived from any of it.

Heather, in turn, saw the Bible as the diary of the universe. A thousand or so pages in which lessons to all of life's answers were played out in one way or another. It is said that there are really only ten basic stories in all of literature, and every work of fiction—be it novel, film or otherwise—is a derivative from one of these ten basic outlines. Just ten. And the first place they all appeared in one concise, easy—or not so easy—to read format was The Good Book.

In the month that had passed since her outburst at Sunday school, Heather had been searching for the source of her anxiety attack that was somehow initiated or related to Erin's questioning. The Mosses had thus far been unable to get pregnant so Heather suspected the two were somehow related. It was painful for Heather to see all those beautiful children each Sunday at the church and not be able to make one of her own. So she went to the Torah for answers. She told her husband, Thomas, that under the right circumstances, she could hold the Bible in her hands and literally hear the answers to the questions she asked of God. The right circumstances varied from day to day. This depended on what sort of external stimuli Heather required to charge her up Bible auditory senses to full efficacy. On this evening, the right circumstances entailed being penetrated in a multitude of creative ways with Thomas giving it as much as his arthritic spine would allow. Heather's hair thrashing wildly, Thomas gripping her hips, while Heather gripped her King James leather bound edition of the New and Old Testaments.

Heather viewed intercourse with her spouse and her commitment to God as a symbiotic relationship. After all, they had committed to each other in a house of God, by a man of God, and under the threat of God's wrath if they didn't hold up their end of the bargain. Thusly, Heather holding her Bible in both hands while Thomas worked his supple magic was, in their eyes, a much more holistic pairing to their lovemaking than say alcohol, lingerie, or scented candles. It had all the elements that a committed couple seeks in intimacy. The raw, prehistoric style of intercourse that has served our species well for a millennium and the spiritual guidance that formed the basis of western civilization.

Thomas grabbed her hair and pulled her neck back just enough to force to her to arch her back in that most sexual of ways. Heather thrust her backside further into the air and held the Bible to her forehead. She loved the way the bumps and grooves in the leather binding felt against her fingertips. It worked beautifully with the athletic sport floozing that accompanied it. Heather briefly dropped it and quickly snatched it back up to keep the pages from opening. Being that this particular copy of the Bible was inscribed on the front cover by her grandmother, the sight of her Nanna's slender cursive would be enough to dry the passion with the proverbial quickness. And she had to know what was going on with her. The answer would come. And if it didn't, well, she would eventually.

And she did. Much before Thomas. Heather stopped receiving him with the same enthusiasm and opened her eyes. Her body still moving back and forth to his rhythm. She stared at the book for a lengthy beat and then pressed it to her forehead once again.

"Erin," she finally said. Out loud.

Thomas ceased all movement. Her tone was that of a terrified woman. Like she had just seen this girl Erin, whomever she was, leap in front of oncoming traffic. "What's the matter? Did I hurt you?" he said with his deep calming voice. He pulled out and guided her away from him.

Heather turned to her side and lay on her back, leaving Thomas wagging in the wind with a hefty case of frustrated gonads. He could tell from her tone that he'd be rubbing one out solo once she fell asleep.

"No," she said, bringing her knees to her chest and her Bible along with it. "I'm just done."

Thomas spooned up beside her and pulled the covers over both of them. Heather was staring into the distance with her eyes wide open. And Thomas could feel it. When you're connected with someone on every level, you can sense in their skin if their eyes are open or not. You don't need to be facing them. Thomas pulled his hand up around her torso and pulled her pelvis against his.

They began slowly breathing apart. Heather's breath quick and deliberate. Her heart like a humming bird. Thomas continued his steady inhale. Eventually their exhales coincided and they breathed as one. When they reached a comforting level, Thomas broke the silence.

"Who is Erin?" he asked after a stoic beat. He assumed it was a girl, but then again, she could have meant "Aaron." He knew that it wasn't a romantic rival. There were no men, certainly none within a hundred-mile radius, who could compete with him sexually.

"A little girl in my Sunday school. She's . . . ten. Or eleven, I think. I don't know." Heather gave the answer right up. As if she had been anticipating the question the whole time.

Thomas thought for a moment, taking a breath to analyze all possible scenarios of why she might blurt out this child's name during sex with him. Coming up with exactly none, he simply nodded and said "All right."

"She's the girl that freaked me out last month. No, not last month. Before Christmas. I told you about this, right?"

"A little bit."

Heather had been hanging onto this for a while, and her fail-safe system of analysis had produced the name "Erin." Past couplings of sex and the Bible had accurately predicted Karol Józef Wojtyla would be anointed Pope John Paul II in 1978. It also effectively produced the Oakland Raiders as the 1981 Super Bowl Champions. Granted, it failed at any precise meteorological forecasting, but for those events in life that really matter, it worked. So she continued.

"She was really testing me that morning. I don't know why. Asking me all sorts of questions about Jesus and where he is now and . . . I don't know. I just got this flood of emotion that she needed protecting. Even more so than if she were my own child. And just now, I asked Him why we weren't having children. And that's what He said: 'Erin.'"

Thomas looked away. For a brief instant, he felt as if his arms were wrapped around the body of a madwoman. It was the vocalizing of this form of delusion that had people burned at the stake. He was fully aware of her habit of occasionally holding the Bible during sex and in a weird way, it turned him on. Like a naughty Catholic schoolgirl kind of thing. But he never for one instant believed that the whole routine was so that Heather could serve as a conduit for God's messages. The Pope and the Raiders were pretty easy calls. Not a whole lot of insight there that you couldn't get from reading a newspaper. Thomas went to church and he believed in Jesus, but when he heard Heather talk in terms such as "He told me," or "His word," it made his penis deflate like a wind sock entering a low-pressure system.

"So you're saying this girl is making you sterile? Well then, we should sue." A flippant response was Thomas's only defense against borderline insanity. He hoped it stifled any further inquiries.

Instead, she nudged him with her elbow.

"I'm saying maybe the reason He hasn't blessed us with a child yet is because I need to protect this girl. Or guide her to some other path.

Something. She has an aura about her. She might not be getting the love she needs at home. Or she could be a musical or intellectual savant. None of the adults around her know it. But I've been asked to lead the way. Does that make sense?"

Thomas could only scratch his forehead. Heather knew, and Thomas intended, that it was to be read as one of those "not in the slightest" kind of scratches.

Heather smiled and grabbed his hand. "Okay, love," she said. "It's not for you to understand."

She kissed his hand in a way that a woman does when she appreciates the ear but little else her man has offered is of much comfort. One can often catch them pulling this same guarded gratitude with the family dog or cat. Heather knew there wasn't much hope in enlisting any further support from Thomas on this latest calling. She knew in her heart that she wasn't crazy and that there was something undeniable about her incident with Erin.

As she felt Thomas's hand relax as he drifted off to sleep, Heather moved her Bible to the nightstand. She knew Thomas thought she was out to sea on this one. Heather really needed another sign from above to cement the goal that she'd given herself. She stared at her Bible, hoping that the pages would flutter or the embossed lettering would glow. Any metaphysical response, no matter how trite, she would categorize as a sign from the Almighty. *Come on!* she thought, but none of those things happened. She was wishing for a follow-up sign so badly that she stared making things up. *If the heater clicks on in the next five seconds, my visions are real.* That didn't happen. *If it starts to rain or snow, my visions are real.* Neither occurred. Heather looked across the room and thought,

If I can throw this book and make it land on the dresser, then my visions are real!

In one swift motion, she hurdled the book across the room. It slammed against the mirror on the dresser, sending a sharp crack through it. The book landed on the wardrobe with an equally loud thud. Thomas shot out of his covers.

"What the hell was that?" he said, sitting straight up.

Heather focused on the book with a contented sigh. *It landed right where I thought it would. And only because of divine intervention. My visions are real. End of story.*

"Nothing," she said.

nineteen

On the rare occasion that the family got together
for dinner, the majority of the participants were
counting the seconds until it was over.

Everyone except for Erin, that is. She would be the last to
understand the subtle nuances that separate human beings. Cause
them to loathe one another on sight. It was her first inclination as to just how meaningless blood relations are. Values and
philosophy are what connect sentient beings, not which womb
they came from. She began to suspect that her parents would
rather have adopted children who shared their values than birth
children who didn't.

Helen had made pasta with meat sauce. The sauce was from a
can. The pasta from a box. The meat was ground up from a cow. It
was safe and savory so everyone would be sure to at least enjoy the
meal. Even if they couldn't stomach the company. Helen and Lyle
would sit on opposite ends of the table like feudal lords. Ian and
Erin on one side and Eli on the other. It was the first day of Lent.
Helen would always mark a religious holiday with a family meal in
hopes of reminding the older boys. Erin just liked having everyone

together. It wasn't until they had each finished their assigned bowl of salad that Ian decided to make a name for himself.

He pushed his wooden bowl aside. "So what's the occasion tonight, Mom?"

Lyle looked up. He knew what was about to ensue. He would confess he was surprised it took this long.

"Today is the first day of Lent, Ian. You would know that if you came to church."

Ian nodded and looked at Eli, who gave a look that suggested, *I'm just here for the free food. Don't involve me.*

"Lent, huh. And what's behind Lent?"

Ian was Helen's favorite, but he still knew how to test her where it hurt. Helen forked a healthy portion of salad and speared it into her mouth with aggression. "Why don't you ask your sister? She still goes."

"All right. Erin, can you tell me what Lent is?"

Erin nodded. "Yes." She finished chewing what was in her mouth and then continued, "Lent is the forty days between Ash Wednesday and Easter. The days representing Jesus's walk in the desert. Answering questions from God or something."

Ian nodded. "And who told you that?"

"My Sunday school teacher, Mrs. Moss."

"You like her?"

Erin paused and looked at Ian, trying to piece together what his angle was. She pushed at her food with her fork. "She's okay," she said in a way that indicated she thought otherwise.

"And you believe that bullshit she's feeding you?"

Lyle threw down his fork. "You can take that kind of language outside, fella."

"Come on, Dad. It is bullshit."

Lyle shook his head. "What, Ian? Why are you so angry?"

"'Cause you're filling Erin's mind with these lies. There is no God and there is no Jesus. It's just stuff you right wingers make up to scare kids into behaving the way you want them to."

Helen took a sip of her wine and shook her head. "I'm no right winger, Ian. Don't you lump me in with your father."

"There is no God?" asked Erin. Lyle and Helen turned to her, their minds racing.

"There, you see? Are you proud of yourself, Ian?"

"If she starts to questioning this nonsense, then yeah, I am."

"I already questioned it."

"When was this?"

"I dunno. Around Christmas time. Mrs. Moss got mad at me."

"I'll bet she did. Good for you."

Lyle was organizing his silverware in front of him. He knew that becoming angry would only serve to fuel Ian's caricature of him.

"What did you say, Erin?"

"I just asked her where Jesus is. And she couldn't tell me, so she got mad."

Ian made a "good for you" face toward her.

"It just didn't make sense to me. We do all this stuff and behave this way 'cause of this book that these people wrote. But we can't see Him or talk to Him or ask Him questions."

"Some people can, Erin."

"Yeah, right. Those are called crazy people."

"Father Houghton is not crazy, Ian. Please have some respect."

"Sorry to break it to you, Dad. People who hear voices in their heads are crazy. People who talk to imaginary friends are crazy. What do you want me to say?"

"I agree with you, Ian," said Erin.

The table went to silence. The clinking of silverware was all that was heard as Helen and Lyle looked at each other. Finally, Lyle spoke. "I respect both of your opinions. And your right to question. Your mother and I just happen to feel differently." Ian let out a smarmy snicker that Lyle glanced over at but pushed through anyway. "But Erin, we would still ask that you continue to come to church with us."

"How come? I don't believe any of it."

"It would mean a lot to us. When you're sixteen, then you can decide whether or not you wish to accompany us in the future."

"Fine, but I've already decided."

Ian laughed. Hard.

"What is your problem, young man?"

"You. You're my problem. How many innocent people did you lock up today?"

Eli finally jumped in. "Come on, Ian. What are you doing?"

Lyle put his fork down. "You're excused, Ian."

"No, I wanna know. How many innocent black people did you execute this week?"

Lyle folded his napkin perfectly and looked at Ian. He studied which direction to take the conversation. Whether it was best to just let the whole thing go. But he couldn't. The dinner was already shot, so why not just keep going? He looked at him hard and said without a hint of irony, "I don't work at Planned Parenthood, Ian."

Ian stopped. "What's that supposed to mean?"

"It means that I know how you think. How those teachers have poisoned your mind. How they've taught you to hate authority and refer to people in the military as baby killers. But just ask yourself, who has killed more babies?"

"You're such a hick. You know nothing."

"You're opposed to killing people who've done terrible things but you're in favor of killing people who haven't harmed anyone. Who haven't even had the chance to live yet."

"Ah, see? That's the point. They aren't people. They're things. Little mass of blood and guts but nothing more. Like a zit."

"A zit," Lyle said, despondent and shaking his head. He looked at Helen. "Proud of that comparison?"

Erin was sitting in silence, watching the back and forth. She didn't like where the conversation was going and wasn't sure what to believe.

"It's a woman's choice." Ian came back as if reading a bumper sticker. Helen nodded at Ian. "That's right, Ian. Thank you."

"And what if that fetus happens to be a girl? Same deal?" Lyle asked while taking a fake sip of his water.

Helen put down her fork and left the table.

"I hate you. I can't wait to get the hell out of here. Good luck, Erin."

Ian got up and left. Lyle pushed at his food with a piece of bread. Eli and Erin remained at the table, each hoping for their own excuse to leave.

"Who loves these family dinners?" Lyle said in a sad attempt to break the tension. He smiled at Erin, hoping for a return that would not be granted.

"Can I be done?" Erin asked. Her plate barely touched. Lyle nodded and watched her get up. Eli waited for Erin to leave the kitchen and then looked over at his father. There was a hint of sympathy in his eyes. Lyle looked at Eli and poured the rest of his beer into his glass. Eli took the glass and followed with a healthy sip.

"Do you ever wonder how we all turned out so different from you, Dad?"

Lyle shook his head. "Not once."

"Why?"

"Free will. But you don't subscribe to that, do you?" Lyle asked.

"I don't?"

"You can't."

"Why can't I?"

"Because you told me once that humans are just animals," Lyle said.

"We are just animals. Maybe smarter. Sometimes smarter," Eli countered with a bit of hesitation, debating who really was smarter.

"Right. So, if we're just a collection of matter, then we have no decision making. It's all preprogrammed. We both think the way we think due to the chemicals in our brain."

Eli thought for a moment. "So there's no scenario where you might consider ending a pregnancy?"

"I can't think of one. That's for God to decide."

Eli sighed, not wanting to go down that road again.

"What about you?" Lyle asked.

"What about me, what?"

"Is there any scenario where you might consider that collection of blood and guts a miracle and not to be interfered with?"

"I can't think of one."

"And I know why."

"I have a feeling you're going to tell me," Eli said with a smile.

"If there is no God, there are no miracles. Everything is just science. Or a coincidence."

Eli nodded. He let the silence sit in for a moment and then laughed. "Don't you wish you had a beer now?"

Lyle nodded. "Kinda."

Snow cutting through high beams always reminded him of outer space. Like when a spacecraft goes into hyperdrive, or at least hyperdrive as illustrated by those effects guys in the movies. Eli always looked forward to when the car on the opposite side of the street passed him and he could click the high beams back on and just like that—back into space warp or whatever the moniker of the day was. The drive from his parents' house back to his basement apartment in the woods never got old. The road curved and dipped with the kind of magical fluidity that a car's suspension was designed for. Nothing too jarring but just enough to keep the driver awake. The canopy of trees hung low as if in a tunnel, creating a state of perpetual shade. In the fall, when the trees were every shade of yellow and red and orange, a stiff wind would come through and shake the trees just right to disperse a steady flow of leaves. Raining down as if in slow motion.

Eli recalled when he first got his license, taking Erin for a drive on this road under those very same circumstances. She was seven at the time. They were driving so slowly, the engine was precariously close to stalling out. They would see errand dustups of leaves swirling around and Eli would ask his sister to describe that image as best she could. Erin decided it was as though a whole batch of them were trapped in some translucent clothes dryer. Although "translucent" was Eli's contribution. When it came Eli's turn, he said that whirling band of colors was what their mother's casserole looked like when he threw it back up the next morning. And she let out a heart-stopping giggle. So genuine and pure. Her laugh shot through him.

The memory was enough to cause him to take his foot off the gas. And as his car slowed, Eli was reminded of his most recent heart-to-heart with Erin. Her questioning of everything having to do with Christmas. The rancor in which she spoke. A touch of venom emanating about why she was even being burdened with having these questions. Eli stared ahead. And eventually his car rolled to a stop, the tires crunching over the gravel and sheets of ice.

He pulled his hand off the steering wheel. His leather gloves creaking as they opened and then closed again, finding their way to rest in his lap. *Was that really the last time anyone had heard Erin's laugh?* The emotion that was running through him made him think the answer would be a resounding *yes*. He wasn't so much a part of her life anymore so it was possible he was overreacting. Still, something was amiss.

Eli was far enough apart in age from Erin that he never saw her as direct competition for his parents' affections. She was young enough and he old enough that when they would go places together, she could be the adorable younger sister. This in contrast to the annoying younger sister, as Ian saw her. They had grown apart when Eli moved out of the house, but the bond they shared from their earlier days together was something that didn't need to be spoken. It just was. He could return from months away and they could carry on as if he were living in the room next to hers the whole time. There was no grace period that had to be endured before they got back to the way things were.

Certain friends are like this throughout life. It doesn't matter how long you're apart and you don't need constant reminding of what the other means to you. When Eli began to realize that this was the kind of friend he had in Erin, his heart ached. He wished he had stayed talking to her longer that Christmas morning. She was reaching out to him for some form of guidance, yet the detached older brother who just doesn't want to be bothered came out instead. Granted, he tempered this with some half-assed middle ground, but that wasn't where his mind lay. He just wanted to go to bed. He felt the aching tinge in his eye socket as he thought of her.

A portion of his soul wanted to go racing back to the house this instant and run up to her bedroom and assure her that what she was going through was normal and that she had every reason to hold on to her faith. *Don't become jaded like the rest of us.* Still another found the idea of quelling his loneliness by establishing some heartfelt correspondence with his younger sister more than a little pathetic. Eli was lonely, but Erin wasn't the place to start making up for lost time. When the emotion of his predicament finally hit him, he hung his head. The fist he was making with his glove relaxed. The tension that had been building behind his eyes finally let go. And he wept.

twenty

The small-town oddities for sale at the
Country Token filled emotional gaps, not
practical ones.

The kind of miscellaneous clutter that is used to occupy bookcases and nightstands and windowsills. A sixteen-inch porcelain angel. A sewing thimble candlesnuffer. A trilobite. Just as horseshoe crabs have been in oceans since the dinosaurs, so too have trilobites been in gift shops. The Country Token was no exception. They were there, right next to the locally harvested geodes. Erin had a purple such rock in her hands. It wasn't something she would ever buy but it had a nice solid feel to it. Plus, it sparkled.

She had spent that Saturday morning chopping firewood while being pelted by sleet. Her father had an aversion to arbitrarily giving children money, but if they were willing to swing an axe for it, he'd cough it right up. In hindsight, after watching his eleven-year-old daughter swing a slippery axe above her head in 36-degree precipitation, he'd wished he'd just given her the money. But she wanted it bad and they did need more firewood. The timing just worked out.

So there Erin stood in the Country Token with a wrinkled five-dollar bill and some newly acquired sniffles. Strands of wet hair matted against the side of her face from a raincoat that needed updating. The little cinch cord having lost its plastic clasp years ago when it belonged to someone else. Someone that it actually fit. Ken Metcalfe had been watching her off and on from above his reading glasses for the past half hour. Not because he'd pegged her as a shoplifter but because he, too, could tell that the money she held in her hand was the whole world. And she was determined to spend it there. Instantly charmed, Ken knew he'd be cutting her a pretty good deal before she left. Within reason, of course.

Erin moved down the aisle, glazing over Christmas ornaments and window decorations. Mostly secular in origin. Reindeer. Santa Claus. The pagan inspired tree. Her eyes finally caught a glimpse of dozens of porcelain figurines. All of them of the Baby Jesus. Some sculpted. Some blown-molded. Some carved. But all at half price, since The Season had passed. Erin stopped to take them in. Her eyes quickly scanned all the myriad interpretations, mediums, and price points in which this, arguably the most important event in human history, had been mass produced. She tried to picture the types of homes that would feel comfortable with something so tacky. And then wondered if perhaps it was what she needed to feel closer to God. Maybe that's what she was missing in her relationship with Him. More merchandise. For going to church regularly, her family didn't possess a lot of Christian memorabilia. She reached out her hand to a petite wooden figurine. The features weren't so realistic as to be frightening. The naturalist approach might feel nice in her hand. Plus, wood and manger seemed to go together quite nicely. Her fingers came within inches of the piece when a voice came from behind her.

"That's not the one I would have picked."

Erin turned to see Ken standing behind her. A wool button-up sweater. Gray. A cup of coffee in his hand. Black. His reading glasses in the breast pocket.

"What's wrong with it?" Erin asked, feeling that his advice was almost an affront to her taste.

"The craftsmanship is fine, if that's what you mean."

"It wasn't what I meant."

"No, I didn't think so. I was teasing you."

Erin didn't take to teasing. She got plenty of that at home and wasn't about to accept it from the business school dropout running the corner swap meet. Not that she assembled her criticism in those terms, but one could rightly make the assumption. Besides, her wrinkled face with mouth slightly agape was more than enough contextual clues for Ken to make the read on his own.

"I'm sorry. That's just my way. Your brother didn't care for my way either."

"Which one?"

"There's more than one?"

"Yes."

"Well the one that you gives you rides to school sometimes."

"Rarely."

"Well, him. You've passed me occasionally when I'm out walking."

"His name's Ian."

"What's your name?"

"Erin. What's yours?"

"My name is Ken."

Ken extended his hand to Erin. She looked at his hand as if he had just offered her a live suction eel to digest. But when her eyes reached his face, she realized there wasn't a hint of malice anywhere. This man was genuine. Her gut didn't ache. She accepted his hand but then was confused once more.

"What's your full name?"

"Ken Metcalfe."

"Mr. Metcalfe."

Ken nodded. He recognized instantly that Erin had never been introduced to an adult by their first name before. He wasn't about to pass judgment on her parents and found her formality endearing.

"You don't want to call me Ken?"

"No."

"How come?"

"'Cause I'm a kid."

Ken set his coffee cup down on the shelf and folded his arms as if he were about to embark on some meaning of life speech before her.

"Well, you know, a lot of times kids can be smarter than adults."

Erin looked up at him and grew sour. She began to feel as if she had pegged him wrong. He wasn't ill intentioned, just ill of wisdom. A common misconception that runs rampant through academic communities is that children possess some omniscient view of the world. They attribute it to purity of heart that has yet to be corrupted by the failings of capitalism. Being a kid, Erin knew better. She knew that children were just as capable of having malice in their hearts as grownups. Perhaps more so, since they haven't yet acquired the decades of life experience it takes to assemble a moral compass.

"Only someone who doesn't have kids would say that."

Erin turned and walked down the aisle, her interest in the manger scene subsiding after yet another adult put intellect on a higher plane than wisdom. Ken pursed his lips and reconsidered the direction of the conversation.

"I apologize. It wasn't my intention to be condescending. You're right—I don't talk to many children. Certainly none with your acute sense of purpose."

Erin turned. "I don't know what that means."

"What I meant before was that I was impressed you were looking at the nativity. So many kids these days aren't that interested in anything involving religion."

"Oh, I'm interested. Just more at the absurdity of the whole thing."

Ken stopped and leaned against the wall.

"Now why would you say that?"

"'Cause I think it is."

"Do you go to Sunday school?"

"Mm-hmm." She nodded without looking at him.

"And none of that has really sunk in or touched you?"

"Not really. It upsets a lot of people, though, you know?"

"In what way?"

"I'm not easily fooled."

Ken realized that he might be better off not engaging this child in a theological discussion. He knew where he stood, but ultimately he feared that if he pressed things any further, he might lose the sale.

Still, it was a slow day and he could use a little banter.

"So, your assumption is that those who believe in the Bible are easily fooled?"

"Yep."

"Who else besides you is not easily fooled?"

"My brother."

Ken nodded. It was all falling into place.

"Well, I'm certainly not going to tell you what to think."

"Thank you."

"You're welcome."

Erin turned away to walk back down the aisle. She grabbed the same nativity figurine off the shelf and trotted up to the counter. Ken followed, unsure of how to proceed. He could sense that this young lady was getting some specious guidance and didn't want to participate in influencing her decision one way or another. He just sensed that despite her age, she would be up for such an exchange. Intellectually, he determined, yes, she was a suitable sparring partner. But not today. Ken flipped up the little section that divided the customer from the proprietor and stepped behind the register.

"Well, as a fellow college graduate like your brother will one day be . . ."

Erin looked him in the eye and passed him the five-dollar bill.

"Whomever that nativity scene is for, I think they'll really like it."

"I doubt it," Erin said with a cold sadness.

"How come?" Ken gave her back her change.

"She's dead."

Erin turned and walked out of the store. Ken stood behind the counter, holding her receipt and feeling the same overwhelming sadness about Erin that seemed to be creeping through a number of people in Elizabethtown that winter.

twenty-one

Ian chipped away at a quarter-inch of ice to
reveal a block of creamed spinach. He had been
looking for it for over a month, and it finally
turned up at the bottom of the ice cream section.

Ice cream didn't move too quickly in the winter months, so every so
often they needed to reshuffle the inventory. When Ian took the job
stocking frozen foods, it was the middle of July in upstate New York.
Which meant a great place to get out of the humidity and mosquitoes.
When it became apparent that he would need to keep the job going
in order to pay for his car, the whole conceit quickly abandoned its
novelty. The irony was that in the summer, he would bring a turtleneck
and hat and gloves to work. Now it was much warmer in the freezer
than it was in his car on the way to the supermarket.

The spinach was the result of a produce fight he had gotten in with
Doug some months back. Doug thought the idea of the two of them
working together would be fun. So he showed up one day, threw some
frozen vegetables around, and then realized he could do this at home
and his mom would clean it up. Doug retired from his job in frozen
foods after ninety minutes of work and left Ian to wonder where that
last block of frozen spinach had gone. Now that he'd found it, he'd

resolved the one moderately curious issue about his place of business. He stared at the cube of vegetable mash one last time and then tossed it into the trash.

It had been two months since his uncomfortable exchange with Beth at her father's Christmas party. When he would drive past her at the bus stop, he'd wonder if she ever told anyone about the incident. Unlikely, since she didn't seem to be making any friends around school. And since the story didn't exactly paint Ian as the class stud, he even resisted sharing it with Doug. *Maybe one night*, he thought. *When we're thirty and catching up over some beers and high school comes up, I'll break this story out. Let it ferment a few decades.*

Ian pulled back the cardboard edges of a box of TV dinners as little flecks of snow shot up with every perforation. *Someone put very little thought into making these and someone else will put just as little thought into eating them* ran through his head as he stacked identical Salisbury steak meals on top of each other. This wasn't true for the very first one ever made, he decided. That had probably required a great deal of thought and planning and—dare he suggest—chemistry. After that, however, it was just monkey skills. He related this to his own life and how once a particular skill is acquired, there is little more reason to keep at it. He was as good at stacking frozen foods as he was ever going to be. There was no more consistency or timing or agility required than he possessed at that very instant. When Ian realized that he was, in essence, what his father had become, only forty years younger, he froze in his tracks. He was working a job purely for money, only without the added incentive of a family to guide him through the monotony. Working a job solely to pay for car insurance seemed like such a fundamentally backward endeavor. He needed his car to get to his job to pay for his car. Because really, what else did he need his car for? He had no girl, he had no real friends, and other than school, he never really went anywhere.

It wasn't until Ian heard the metallic clicks of Doug Vaughn's jacket that he broken his self-induced trance. This familiar audio was coupled with the recently filed laugh of Beth. The two of them together. Shopping for who the hell knows what in the middle of February in a place where they both knew Ian worked. Ian looked up to see Beth's arm hooked around Doug's in such a forced execution of affection it made his parents' yearly hand-holding seem romantic. It was a truly unnatural pairing. The kind of coupling that Darwinism certainly should have prevented. Like a warthog mating with a naked mole rat. Neither species worthy of evolutionary sustention, but one still suspiciously out of league with the other. Ian got the sense that they had been walking around the aisles of the supermarket for a solid half-hour until they ran into him. Doug delivering the much-prepared first line.

"Hey man, you're still here?"

Ian gave the two of them the brow furrowing of lifetime followed by an equally ambiguous, "Yeah. Still here."

Beth, seemingly the ringleader of this whole charade, couldn't wait to chime in with her preordained line, "Haven't seen you since the Christmas party. Why'd you run off like that?"

Ian thought for a moment. *Why did he run off like that? Or more important, what version of the story did Beth so obviously relay to Doug?* He watched as the two of them shared a calculated chortle. Their choreographed "cover the mouth and turn" routine reeked of inadequate rehearsal time. *Oh, I get it now,* Ian thought. The whole scenario was obvious. Ian was known, at least within this newly formed clique of two, to be as flaccid as boiled celery. His tongue leaped into defense mode, perhaps prematurely.

"You tell me, Beth. You were there."

"Oh, I was there. But something else sure wasn't."

Doug and Beth shared another preordained laugh. Ian knew how he looked. He was pushing a cart full of low quality foods while wearing a black tie, red vest, and winter gloves. In addition to his obvious social deficiencies, he also couldn't perform under pressure.

"I see you two are getting along famously. What's your story?" Ian asked, looking directly at Doug for the first time.

"Just trying to help out where you couldn't, man."

Ian was almost without words. Did people really talk this way? Did these two shit sticks really go out of their way to seek him out on a Thursday night for no other reason than to humiliate him? He sort of got Beth's rationale. She was embarrassed in front of her parents. But what possible angle could Doug be pursuing?

"So, you two came all the way down here to . . . do what? Show me that you're eating my leftovers, Doug? Congratulations."

Beth stepped forward and released her arm from Doug's.

"Leftovers? Hey, you prick, you couldn't even get started."

Ian looked Beth up and down.

"Well, your face and your body made it difficult."

Doug finally made the connection that Ian's comments were just as much directed at him. He stepped forward and gave Ian a two-handed shove in the chest. Ian stepped back awkwardly and fell *backward* over the box of spinach, landing hard on the tile. Beth let out a cackle that felt as much forced as it did vengeful. Ian slowly rolled over. His hip hurt. His shoulder hurt. But mostly it was the combined humiliation of being on a linoleum floor in a public place wearing his grocery store outfit while being laughed at by this pair of charlatans. They had turned to walk away when a brick of frozen spinach came hurling through the air and hit Doug in the back of the head. It connected with an empty thud, breaking the skin beneath his shaggy hair and sending ice fragments darting over Beth's face.

"Owww! Fucker!" he shouted, turning back to face Ian. Beth looked over at him and gave him a shove that read, *Go be a man and fight!* That is until she, too, was hit with a brick of frozen spinach.

Ian stood armed with a small cardboard box full of his weapon of choice and proceeded to hurl a few more their way as Doug charged. A messy, slaphappy spectacle masquerading as a fight ensued on the floor between two rows of refrigerated cuisine. Beth ran over and gabbed Ian's hair, clawing and kicking him in a desperate attempt to salvage her pride.

Ian's manager tuned the corner and shouted down at them, "Hey!"

Beth and Doug got in one final shot and then sprinted down the hallway and out of the store. As the world turned to slow motion, Ian saw the two lovebirds scurrying away from their verbal and physical assault. His manager trudging down the hallway with her misplaced concern. And Ian's thoughts raged. He stewed at how much he loathed his current condition. How much he hated school and life in general. How much he despised all the social constructs and his family life that were all slowly conspiring to bring him to where he was at that instance. And to make the moment more insufferable, he really wasn't hurt that bad and his shift wasn't over for another two hours.

March

twenty-two

Ian had always enjoyed his social studies class. He felt that because he read the newspaper and engaged in class discussion, he understood the way the world operated far better than his contemporaries.

My dad reads the Bible. I read The New York Times *editorial page. I am worldly. I am enlightened,* he would remind himself. This self-congratulatory tone was not enough, however, to shield Ian from most of the senior class knowing about his vegetable dustup on aisle eleven. What went down. Who lost. And what embarrassing anecdote proceeded the whole thing in the first place. Ian had found himself drifting into a state of constant malaise. He had become so adept in the art of ignoring people that it almost served as his major. Constantly reading, shoe tying, adjusting items in a book bag or locker. Anything to avoid eye contact. Ian transitioned so seamlessly into a state of perpetual floor-examining that when his teacher started class with a provocative question, it strained his neck to look up.

"The United States is no better or worse than the Soviet Union," Mr. Nightingale said.

The class had been subject to much of the Cold War tensions of the time, and to hear such words coming from their teacher quieted the class.

"I thought that might get your attention. Well it turns out it's true. How many of you have heard of the concept of moral relativism?"

No one raised their hand. Either due to no one knowing or no one wanting to participate.

"It's the idea that posits all morality is subjective. In the case of the U.S. and the Soviets, who are we to say we are right and they are wrong?" Mr. Nightingale watched as the class shuffled in their seats. He relished the position of being a high school teacher. Students at this age were perfect for being indoctrinated. A media-numbed captive audience who knew nothing of history and therefore would never present a thoughtful challenge.

"Now, I am an atheist. So I don't believe in God, a creator, any of that stuff. But I also recognize that belief comes with a price. And that price is, since there is nothing above man to tell us what to do, all human morality is simply opinion. I liked Brezhnev, you like Reagan. So what?"

"But the communists kill people," said Tammy Brackett in the back of the room.

"We kill people too. Ever hear of Vietnam? Korea?"

"Yeah, but didn't we go there to help them?"

"How does killing all those people help them?"

"Killing bad people helps the good people."

"But who's to say who is bad? See, that's the point. I think murder is wrong. And I certainly hope you all do, as well. But there's nothing that proves it's wrong. Like, I can prove how far my desk is to the window. I can measure it in multiple ways. But you can't prove to me that the communist collectivization was wrong. Many people benefited from it and more equality was achieved. And I'm certain you all support equality."

The class had now been spun into a circle and no one dared say they were for "inequality." Not without suffering the punishment of being an outcast. Mr. Nightingale looked to his favorite student in the front row.

"Ian, any comments? You're never at a loss for words."

Ian had started scribbling in his note pad. He liked the idea that he was his own God. That he could create his version of morality. Where everything he did was justified. Ian looked up slowly. "Um, no, I guess not. I was just thinking what a refreshing concept it is to say that no one is better than anyone else. It would be nice to live in a world free from being judged all the time."

"I agree," said Mr. Nightingale. The class was silent for a bit and then Tammy chimed in with one final question.

"So, if there is no right or wrong, then I can say America was on the side of good in Vietnam?" asked Tammy.

"Well, you can say it. But you'd be wrong," said Mr. Nightingale, completely missing the irony.

twenty-three

It's challenging to pinpoint the exact moment
that a human brain switches from being
guided by the decent to that of the indecent.

A common quest of psychologists is to decipher, categorize, and then ultimately rationalize antisocial behavior. *This is a direct result of that. Or this could have been avoided if only that were done.* Oddly, there were bad people long before religions and psychologists and tenured professors. Long before humans were exposed to harmful external stimuli and subversive popular culture, they did bad things to each other. In light of all intellectual pursuits to quantify and understand depraved behavior, it is perhaps just as likely that in some cortexes, immoral behavior is just hardwired. It will lay dormant and come out when it's ready, regardless of how well that child is nurtured or fed or educated. Illicit behaviors come in all intellects, incomes, and ethnicities.

It was a Saturday morning that found Erin, her legs folded in front of her, seated on the couch. A brown and yellow afghan covered her legs while scattered remnants of Fruity Pebbles were soaking up an overzealous pouring of milk in a well-worn yellow

Tupperware bowl. She felt cozy curled up with a hooded sweatshirt and a familiar episode of Foghorn Leghorn flickering on their fifteen-inch Zenith. Lyle and Helen had left for the morning to look at new kitchen tile. It had been decided that with their tax refund that year, they would finally replace the brown kitchen carpet. Erin loved Saturday mornings alone. The hours in which she could truly feel content were becoming scarce, and curling up with some cereal and cartoons really hit the spot. The rain pattering on the windowsill only added to her comfort.

Ian entered the room and sat down on the brick around the woodstove.

"Hey," he said.

Erin looked over at him and smiled. "Hi," she said with genuine happiness.

It had been some time since Ian had been the one to initiate conversation with her. Typically, it was Erin who would seek out verbal communication, but on this morning Ian was feeling particularly lonely. Seeing Doug in the supermarket with Beth hit him more than he anticipated.

"What are you up to this morning?"

"Nothing, just wakin' up slow. Kinda nice not having Mom and Dad around."

"Tell me about it," Ian said with a breath of anxiety.

Erin and Ian had bonded lately on their mutual distrust of all things Bible related. But once that bitterness had been talked around, the relationship didn't leave a whole lot to chew on and they ended up right back where they started. She eleven and he seventeen. He searching for a release for his sexual frustration and she longing for the kind of acceptance and closeness in a relationship that she wasn't finding anywhere.

"Are you still going out with that one girl?"

"Going out with what one girl? Who's that again?"

"The neighbor girl. The one you gave a ride to."

"What makes you think we're going out?"

"I dunno. You went to her Christmas party."

"Well, yeah, I did. It didn't really work out. I don't think we're gonna be hangin' out too much anymore."

"Okay," Erin said, bringing the bowl to her mouth to drink some of the orange milk. It made sense to her. She was desperately curious as to why they weren't hanging out anymore but worried that Ian wouldn't deem her worthy of sharing. *I'll impress him with some older person talk. Teenage boy speak,* she thought. That would be the most effective way of illustrating her maturity. Erin continued to play with her cereal while her mind raced to think of something. She could tell Ian was about ready to head back to his room and spun through all the adult subject matter she could think of. She knew there was not going to be a new president anytime soon and that might cause him to rant uncontrollably. They had been doing complex fractions at school, but that didn't strike her as having much follow-up material. She could always bring up the new tile that the kitchen was soon to have. *It certainly will make the room look better*, she thought. And right when Ian placed his hands on his thighs in a manner that suggested he was ready to get up, Erin asked him the most mature, sure-to-have-follow-up question she could.

"Was it because she didn't blow you?"

Ian removed his hands from his thighs and gave Erin a most curious glance.

"Say that again?"

Erin got a sheepish look on her face as if she had used the wrong verbiage or mispronounced something essential. She figured there weren't that many syllables to screw up as she understood the terminology, so she tried again.

"Did you stop going out because she didn't blow you? Maybe? Or something?"

"What do you know about that?" Ian asked. His tone on the fence between amused and defensive.

"Oh, I know stuff. I know that it's something boys like."

Ian nodded, *That was true.* Although he immediately felt the urge to impress his younger sister. He didn't want her knowing that he had yet to receive the forbidden foreplay. He chose to keep the mood light and not play into his own insecurities. Even if it was distinctly out of character.

"Yep. That's true. No arguments here."

Erin looked at Ian and then down at her feet. Bare, with her toes curled up in a fist beneath her flannel pajamas. She was dying to know. She had to know if that had happened to Ian. And if he loved the girl that did it to him.

"So," Erin said.

Ian developed a nervous look.

"Yeah?" he asked

"Has that ever been . . ." She stopped, unsure of where this conversation might lead but couldn't help it. "Has that ever happened to you?"

Ian laughed. "Course it has," his shoulders shrugged. "Couple times."

"Oh," Erin said. She sounded disappointed.

"What do you care? Why are you asking me this?"

"I dunno."

"Well, it's creepin' me out, so stop it."

Erin shifted positions again on the couch and folded her legs over the other way. She was perfectly convinced that this was the moment where Ian would get up and walk away. But he didn't. He remained exactly in the same position. Erin began to realize that this is a behavior that young men deliver when they want the conversation to press on but don't want to be the initiator.

"Do you want to see what I made in the basement?" she asked.

"Sure."

Erin took the final step off the creaking, unfinished stairs and onto the cool basement floor. Taking a few steps into the center of mudroom, she felt the humidity increase. The only light came from the sunken basement windows. She walked down the hallway and entered the storage room with the storefront-like windows. The furnace working away on the opposite side of the hallway. She stepped into the room and opened one of the cabinets beneath the window.

"See? This is where I'm going to keep him," Erin stated proudly.

"Who's he?" Ian asked.

"The weasel. When I catch him."

"Catch him or kill him?"

"Either one, I guess."

Ian nodded and followed with, "That's cool." He gave a surveying glance around the place. It was quiet and dark. And a place not often visited by parents. He thought about where he was in his life. About how he arrived at this spot. He pictured a winding staircase like something out of *Alice in Wonderland* and each step had a particular event on it. On their own, the steps mean nothing, but line them up and place them accordingly, and he would arrive at his current mental state.

"So, you love me, huh?"

"Yes. How come?"

Ian closed the door to the storage room. And turned around to face Erin, taking the little metal hook and slipping it through the hoop. Locking the door.

"There is a way you could show me without having to tell me all the time."

Erin looked at the closed door. Up at the lock. Then at her brother. Her heart raced as she felt an intense anxiety never before felt. She felt a wave of guilt at her own actions. That her weirdness, her inability to express emotion and her loneliness had all conspired to place her in that room at that moment.

"What's that?"

"Well, remember that thing you heard that boys like?"

"Yes?"

"You could try that on me, maybe."

Erin stopped. She wasn't sure what to think. She so longed for her brother's approval and affection. She also knew their relationship would never be the same regardless of her response. She thought of her dad. Their daddy-daughter time. A conversation from a year ago came oscillating back. She could hear his voice in her head. *There will be days when life hits you with a speed bump. Just don't turn it into a fork in the road.* This was one of those days. Regardless of how she reacted, the days of playing pond hockey were most certainly over. The days of watching Saturday morning cartoons with a soggy bowl of cereal were over. No more board games. No more fishing in the stream. She couldn't look up.

Ian, meanwhile, had cleared his mind and stopped rationalizing his behavior. He thought of his social studies teacher and how much he was grateful for his talk on moral relativism. *Who are we to say the communists are bad? One society's morals have no bearing on another's. Morality only exists if God exists. God does not exist. Therefore, there is no objective right or wrong.*

Erin stared at the floor. She started to see shapes and colors form along the fibers in the worn utility carpet. She heard Ian undo his belt.

"Okay," she said. And chose the fork in the road.

twenty-four

Nothing else of note occurred during the
month of March that year.

april

twenty-five

The wood had bent where the knot once was. The fibers curved around its neighbor in the chicken coop wall to produce a quaint peephole from which to view outside.

Still, with the rank odor of stale droppings and the temperature in the low teens, the conditions would have to truly be wretched for quaintness to ensue. As it happened, the wind had been howling all morning, so any relief from the burning and stinging of a windchill in the negative numbers was welcome.

Erin was seated on a hay bale. Her little legs extended straight out with the heels of her boots just barely touching the stained concrete. Her feet flopped to opposite sides the way they always did. The way a little girl's do. Although she wasn't feeling much like a little girl. Her vagina ached. There was a throbbing pressure that coiled through her uterus up into her abdomen. She rubbed the inside of her leg with her mittened hand and then returned it to its original resting place. The stock of her rifle. She felt more comfortable stroking the barrel of her weapon than she did addressing the various physical ailments she had been feeling.

She had ventured out that morning with renewed purpose to kill the beast once and for all. Last month's incident had left her feeling more isolated than even she thought possible. And it had happened since. She knew what she was doing was vile on more levels than there were levels for, but it seemed to be the only way she and Ian could communicate. There were brief exchanges by him when he'd return home from school. They went something to the effect of, "Do you want to go show me your hiding place in the basement?"

To which Erin would say, "Okay."

Incest would follow and then Ian would return to his room. Perhaps most disturbing of all was the normalcy of the whole sordid affair. The blasé routine with which it was played out. This is what was to be expected out of Erin, as far as her relationship with Ian was concerned. When the family would meet for dinner, it was almost strictly in silence. Lyle and Helen would speak about their days but the contribution from Ian or Erin had dropped to nothing. They never argued. They never asked questions. At the very least, this was something that Erin would have entertained. Yet even that had dried up.

During school Erin would sit in class, staring straight ahead. Afraid that if she breathed in the wrong way, someone would know. She began to think everyone was clairvoyant and would rat her out to her parents. On Saturdays Erin would lie in bed, wishing that she had a friend who would stop by. Someone from school to ask her to go play or to come over and watch cartoons. But it never happened. It wasn't until April rolled around that she decided the weasel needed to be dealt with. She had admittedly forgotten about her former bloodlust for the rodent yet had recently spotted it out the kitchen window. And she needed a distraction. The weirdness that embodied every molecule of her family life the past several months had made it essential that she developed a pastime. Pond hockey with Ian was now out of the question since incestuous oral sex had been brought into their already awkward relationship. Hunting local marmots seemed to be the next logical progression.

There were fewer than a dozen chickens left in the coop by this point. Lyle had helped build a separate enclosure inside the main barn to tighten them up a bit. They still produced eggs and they still required plenty of care and feeding. Perhaps not surprising, Ian had ceased helping Erin with her morning chores after their "routine" had become routine. Much in the same way the husband ceases to buy flowers after marriage. Erin had started to learn a lot about men and how they operate.

She scraped the barrel of the gun across the concrete, leaving a tiny black question mark shape. She stared at it briefly and then saw a flicker outside the peephole. Another flash broke the field of white behind it, indicating to her that there was movement behind the walls. Erin brought her rifle up off the ground and held it next to her side. She began to think how cool it would be to shoot something through the knot in the wood. She wouldn't even have to go outside. She quickly hopped down off the hay bale and pushed it onto its side, sliding it against the wall so the top rested perfectly below the hole in the board. Just enough to allow her to rest her weapon in a prone position and aim the barrel out the space. The only dilemma being that she couldn't quite see out to tell what she was aiming at. Details. But there was something scurrying around just outside the door and it was playing right into her plan.

Flapping gently in the breeze was a Styrofoam container. A tan clamshell with the remnants of a specialty sandwich containing two all-beef hamburger patties, coupled with some form of altered Russian dressing, cheese, and assorted vegetables. Erin had found it at the cemetery the afternoon before when she went to clean the Lonely Girl's grave. It was left just as it lay now, only on a bed of frozen moss by her burial place. Like she had done so many times before, the cemetery seemed to lull her into a state of hyper-analysis. She wondered whether it had been left there by a mourning family or simply by the maintenance crew. And whether its owner had hoped to return. She suspected it was just a coincidence that the litterbug chose her grave as an ideal disposal site. She had accepted that whomever the parents of Lonely Girl were, they had long since left town. And they wouldn't be so disrespectful as to leave a half-eaten fast food burger on her final resting place. Erin wasted little time deciding what to do with it.

Erin brought the stock against her shoulder and watched the flicker of shadows cascade across the piece of fluttering polystyrene. She knew her weasel had returned. She started to view its imminent death as a form of catharsis for all her internal rage. Perhaps killing this scavenger would fill her with the confidence she needed in order to tell Ian to go away. To get affection from girls closer to his age who didn't come from the same womb. Erin squinted her eye and took a breath that tasted like metal coming off the cold edge of the barrel. She would put a bullet in this animal and then confront her brother and explain to him that what he was doing was wrong. She would bury it in the dirt outside the chicken coop as a symbolic gesture. She would tell Ian to go away and seek help.

The hay bale smelled fresh. It crinkled beneath her jacket as she positioned the .22 to her left. She heard the distinct sound of snow compacting outside, followed by the soft snap of torn Styrofoam. She squeezed the trigger and the sharp pop of the rifle pushed the stock back against her shoulder. Her bullet grazed the side of the knothole, splintering the wood and sending a thin crack through the rest of the board. Erin pulled back, startled by her poor judgment in thinking there was plenty of space for a clean shot. There was silence.

Followed by the unmistakable wailing moans of Edward.

Erin backed off the rifle instantly, letting it rest on the hay bale. She put her little mitten to her mouth and sat down on the cold floor, bringing her knees to her chest. She could hear him crying in terrified breaths. His lungs heaving up and down to catch up with the adrenaline. He threw his body against the side of the barn, causing the boards to ripple as a singular unit. Erin scampered back a few inches and put her hands over her ears. His noise was unbearable, sounding like a more like Holstein calf halfway through castration. Erin pictured him writhing around in the snow, spilling red with every flail of his torso. She pictured his neck pulled apart, with all the little tendons loose like strained pasta. Basically, she pictured what her horror magazines had taught her to picture. And she had to see it for herself.

Erin stood up and held her arms straight at her sides. She looked at the rifle on the hay bale and made a brief motion for it. *What if I need to finish him off? That would be the Christian thing to do*, she thought. She then remembered that she was going through a hatred of Christianity phase and left the gun where it was. Edward's moans had subsided somewhat, but his pounding against the side of barn had slowed to an even pace. Every four seconds. Bang. Wait. Bang. Erin wiped her chest clean of hay and stepped forward across the floor. The rubber in her boots creating little pockets of suction with each step. When she reached the door, she knew that the next ten seconds would define her life forever. She closed her eyes to soak it in.

When the door opened, she saw Edward. Sitting with his back against the chicken coop, throwing his torso against the side of the barn. Erin made a frown and put her hand to her mouth. Each step she expected to finally pull around him to reveal the true extent of his injuries. But as her little boots squeaked into the dry snow, she saw no blood. There were no exposed organs, no gushing arteries pumping hot sticky plasma into the frosty air. Just poor, sweet Edward. Sobbing into his chest, clutching his ear and rocking with all the might of a grown man into the barn.

Erin saw her overturned fast food clamshell lying in the show by his feet. He was clutching the remaining portion of the sandwich in his stubby hand. It shook with every heavy sob he took. Erin let out a remorseful sigh as she soaked in the fact that he was not dead—and so far as she could tell, wasn't injured. She took another step toward him and reached out with her hand.

"Hi, Edward," she said with as pleasant a greeting as you might find at a school bake sale. Erin had witnessed the effect a syrupy tone had on people from her mother at church. It had a way of disarming those expecting the worst. She hoped it would prove similarly successful here.

It was not to be. Edward screamed at the sight of her and pushed himself in the opposite direction. His eyes lurched out at her from their sockets, bursting forth their angst with strained blood vessels.

"I just want to see if you're okay," Erin said. It was delivered with the same cheerfulness as if she were asking, *How is your punch? More ice?*

Edward looked at her with his thick black eyelashes matted against his lids. His nose dripping with translucent goo that collected in a pool on his brightly colored ski jacket.

"NO, IT HURTS!" he sobbed.

There had been little progress since their first encounter several months ago, in terms of Erin's ability to interact with handicapped people. In fact, her overall social skills had developed little. But being faced with this poor soul who was suffering as a result of her careless-ness instilled a newfound sense of maturity. Borderline manslaughter has a way of doing that.

"Can I just see real quick?" Erin pleaded. She was quickly losing her hosting voice. Between Edward's screams and the initial gunfire, it was a safe bet that someone would be around shortly. Erin suddenly felt a wave of defensiveness pass through her. She anticipated the lecture she would receive from her mother and Edward's parents. The disappointment that would befall her father and the inevitable rescinding of the gun privileges and privileges in general. She made another motion toward his head with her mitten.

"NO, MINE!" Edward screamed.

Erin was running out of time.

"Christ, let me see!" she screamed and wrestled his hand away long enough to see that he hadn't been shot. She wasn't even sure where the initial bullet had run off to. Stuck through Edward's earlobe with laser-guided precision was a toothpick-shaped splinter. Jagged and worn with little flecks of blood spattered here and there, but otherwise it looked pretty natural. Like Edward had been christened an honorary member of the Dani tribe out of Indonesia.

Erin took her mitten off and grabbed his hand. She had watched her father do it to her grandmother at the retirement home and it seemed to comfort her. Since she and Edward seemed to have shared more than a dozen personality traits, Erin logically assumed it would work on him. For the moment it seemed to and she felt a wash of relief glide through her as Edward calmed himself. His breathing relaxed and he had begun to sniffle through his tears.

Erin sighed and pursed her lips together. Relieved that, if one wanted to get technical about the whole thing, she hadn't shot anyone. And grateful that she would surely live to hunt that wretched marmot another day.

"Look at me, okay?" She was now reciting lines she seen on television. That is how people in control talked when they needed to do something rash.

"I'm going to try pull this out of your ear. Can you stay still for me?"

"NO! NO! NO!" Edward pleaded. Even in his fractured mental capacity, he knew this lass was not qualified to attempt such a procedure.

Erin reached for his ear and Edward thrust himself back against the barn again. She quickly realized that removing the object wasn't going to happen too quietly.

Erin now faced the dilemma of how to return Edward to his home in such a way that it seemed as if the piece of lumber jutting through the side of his face was all in childhood fun. Erin wasn't much into dolls or decorating, but she was aware that normal girls around her age were busy chatting, dressing up pets, braiding each other's hair. This was in sharp contrast to Erin's newly acquired pastime.

"Okay, come with me."

Erin knew what she had to do. And it didn't entail anything involving the preservation of dignity. But these were the sacrifices that one had to make when greater threats were at hand. She held Edward's hand as she guided him back into the chicken coop and seated him on the very hay bale that she had used to shoot him. She stood her rifle up on its side and began looking around the shed.

It seemed logical enough as the story played out in her head. *I ran into Edward in the backyard.* She snapped out the clip from the rifle. *I happened to have this toy rifle with me and invited him to play the injun.* She picked up a few scant chicken feathers and began sticking them in various places around his snowcap, creating a headgear of sorts. *I'd seen this nature show one time where injuns have wood in their ears. My mistake.* Erin was happily playing through the exchange she'd have with Edward's parents. The more it played through in her head, the more she began to see it actually working. The absolute worst-case scenario would be that they'd question whether she herself was not lacking in some facilities. *And they'd be right to*, she thought.

She looked back to see that Edward had snuck the rest of the burger, now pressed so tight between his fingers that it was escaping through them as if in a grinder. He giggled in that way that only he did as he shoved the rest of the mess in his mouth and laughed. "HEY HEY! YEAH! ASSHOLE WHO WOULDN'T FUCK ME!" he chortled.

Erin stopped tucking chicken feathers into his hat long enough to ponder with utmost sincerity. "What was that?" she asked.

If there were a saving grace to all the lesser qualities of their home, it was the view out the kitchen window. Resting comfortably on the second floor, it gave the sink user, typically Helen, a gorgeous view of the horse pasture out back. Lining the property were two massive pine trees and a creek that ran through the property. On this Saturday afternoon, Helen felt content in herself as she watched the beginnings of a snow flurry cascade down across the field. The snow had managed to sublimate the last few weeks, so she welcomed the sight of fresh powder to cover the imperfections in her landscape. Snow had a way of cleansing things. If only superficially. She looked up at the ceiling, hoping it would be torn off its moorings and allow a light flurry into the house. Cleansing all of the odd tensions that had invaded of late.

Helen had fallen off her quest to find a job and had been derailed further by the awkward dynamics seeping through the silent meals. She could usually count on Lyle to poke and prod at her at least once a week for some physical exchange, but that, too, had subsided. The thought of another woman never entered her mind. After all, who would? Helen would, of course, but their marriage had reached the point where she felt that the weekly sexual procedure was merely the wifely thing to do. It didn't cost her anything and was a very efficient way of preserving a low level of stress. But when his masculine interest diminished, she found herself missing it. It reminded her of her high school rationale. *Even if you don't find someone attractive, you still want them to find you attractive.* At least that was the family proverb that had gotten her through most of life.

It was about this time, Helen internally debating why she wasn't getting the sex that she didn't want from the husband she didn't love, that a peculiar visual disturbed her introspection. Entering the corner of her window frame from the left side was Erin, guiding Edward through the windswept field as if a bloodied Korean War casualty. His hand held tight in one of her mittens, the .22 rifle in the other.

Edward clutching his ear, his clumsy steps exaggerating an already sloppy wardrobe through the crusty snow. Helen dropped the wooden spatula that she was cleaning into the sink and bolted to the porch. It fittingly landed with an inconsequential thud. Like so many things these days.

Stepping out into the frost and down the steps without her coat, she crunched her way toward the two figures. As she got closer, she wondered if this was how the marines of the Chosen Reservoir looked. Bloodied and disheveled, weary desperation, confused and frostbitten. When she arrived within arm's length, she realized her analogy was far too dramatic. They both looked a little stressed but nothing a little Swiss Miss couldn't alleviate. She snatched the gun from Erin's hand with a screeching "What happened?"

"Nothing!" screamed Erin back at her. "Really nothing!"

Edward removed his hand from his ear to show the fragment protruding through his earlobe. Erin looked away guiltily.

"Except that," Erin said sheepishly. Hoping her previous emphasis on "nothing" would override any accidental flesh wound.

"Oh my God. Get inside, both of you!" screamed Helen.

Erin continued to hold Edward's hand as Helen grabbed hers. She attempted to pull them back to the house as briskly as possible, she still in her slacks and blouse and they dressed for the weather. She fit in rather nicely, herself another misfit to join their already awkward chain. Helen almost seemed to relish the renewed purpose of her day—an exciting little mission with which to implement some much-needed parenting. And if it served as a reason to finally get rid of that vile weapon, then so be it. She'd march them back to the fire, provide comfort, nourishment, and some quick medical care. But not before making them kick their boots off. She did just vacuum the floor, after all.

When they stumbled into the kitchen, Edward became even more anxious. A new surrounding coupled with strange people yelling and pulling on extremities has a way of doing that.

"Mommy, it hurts!" he bawled. His sporadic movements increased. He started flapping his arms against his side. The heavy, wispy rasps of his meaty hands against his snow pants echoed over the polished floor. Helen sat Erin down at the kitchen table.

"Stay," she barked at her. "Can you sit?" she asked Edward with the calm of a Buddhist librarian. Erin was simultaneously impressed and annoyed that her mother could so rapidly change her tone. Almost in mid-sentence. Edward the victim and Erin the perpetrator. It had already been adjudicated.

"Don't hold it like that. It's still loaded," Erin suggested to her mother. Helen was grasping the rifle in a precarious fashion. Like a chimpanzee would, having taken it from a vanquished human foe. Erin thought about telling her to hold it over her head in victory but decided against it. A round might end up in her ear. And for real this time. Helen looked at the rifle and then walked it over to the kitchen closet. The place where all the boots, umbrellas, and dozens of coats were tossed. She pulled some of the coats back and shoved it in the corner.

"I'll deal with that and you later."

Erin gave a despondent full-body "Fine," kicking her feet out and slapping her arms to her legs.

Helen returned to the pantry and tore open a box of instant hot chocolate. She filled a cup with water and then put it in the microwave.

The room sat still. Only the sounds of Edward's occasional sniffle and the humming of a first-generation Amana range.

"Can I have some?" Erin asked as her mother began to stir in the powder. Helen just glared at her. As if withholding the cocoa would serve as apt punishment. Erin had managed to sit Edward down next to her, and she assumed the next logical step was to distract him with some hot chocolate while the splinter was removed.

"Do you even want to hear what happened?" Erin pleaded.

"Does it matter?" Helen said.

"Yes."

"Okay. When you take him back home."

"When I take him back?"

"That's right."

"Well, I didn't shoot him. And it was an accident. I was trying to aim through a hole in the wall, and it hit the wood and I didn't even know he was out there!"

Helen approached Edward with the tweezers.

"No Mommy! No Mommy!" he cried. Erin felt such sympathy for him as he spilled his hot chocolate in the process. His hands now coated with it and his snow pants slick with a chocolate residue.

"Jesus, kid!" Helen yelled, causing him to jump.

"Mom, you can't talk to him like that. Calm," said Erin. Her earlier impression of her mother's mental agility had faded. Patience was apparently as fleeting as sweetness in this home.

Helen just nodded while she set the tweezers down on the table. She then grabbed a shot glass from the cabinet and a bottle of bourbon from back inside the weird little cubbies that were on top of the fridge. Erin watched curiously as she lined up all the items. She grabbed a bag of marshmallows and ripped it open. She then walked over to Erin and whispered in her ear.

"Okay, here's what we're gonna do. You distract him with some of these and while he's looking down, I'll just dive in and snatch it out."

"Okay . . ." Erin said. Erin wasn't familiar with this side of her mother. She was hoping she would never see it again but was trying to absorb the moment for posterity. *She's gotta be bored*, Erin thought. Noting that her mother possessed none of the skills necessary to execute what she just described.

Erin stood up and grabbed the bag of marshmallows. She didn't need to speak as she walked them over in front of him. Edward took a brief glance and reached his hand in the bag. In one fluid motion, Helen dipped the tweezers in the bourbon, took a shot for herself, slammed the glass back on the table, and darted the tweezers in the general direction of Edward's ear. The splinter slid out of Edward's ear with the ease of a serrated arrowhead pulled from a deer carcass. Edward yelped in pain, dropping the mug and sending the bag of marshmallows all over her newly cleaned floor. The hot chocolate acting as a nice adhesive.

"Hey, I got it!" Helen said, proudly displaying the splinter to both of them. She seemed as surprised as anyone. Edward held his ear, a grimace of pain coupled with a wave of relief. Helen picked up the mug and walked over to the sink.

"Here, I'll get you some more."

Erin followed her, cautiously stepping around the mass of processed sugar.

"Let him finish them and then walk him back home."

"What do I tell them?"

Helen looked over at Edward. He smiled at them through his dry tears and chocolate-lined lips and mouthfull of tiny marshmallows.

"You're good at keeping secrets, aren't you?" Helen asked. The words made Erin's knees go weak. She probably would have thrown up if she had partaken in the cocoa. She felt as if she were back in school and the paper and glue of some crafty project were being passed out. Only this one was grim. All the paper was green and gray. Like the basement. Her mind flashed through all the things that her mother didn't know about her. It was a long flash. She wondered why she would ask that. *Does she know? Is she testing me? There's no way. It's just a coincidence.*

"Yeah, I guess," Erin said.

"Tell them he fell down in the chicken coop," she said. And finished the rest of her shot.

twenty-six

The plastic booths at fast-food restaurants
are designed to be uncomfortable. The idea
is to discourage loitering.

If patrons don't have a comfortable place to sit, they won't stay long. Heather Moss wondered if the same rationale was applied during the manufacturing of church pews. If those in charge had outfitted the chapel with hammocks instead of ornate wooden boxes stuffed with newspaper clippings, maybe the general populous would stay longer. Or maybe it was making them feel guilty for every infinitesimal act of human nature that was to be blamed for diminishing attendance. Heather was still weighing that out.

She flicked the giant button on the cushion with her fingernail while she and Thomas waited for the services to start. They had arrived at church early that Easter Sunday as Heather prepared to deliver one of the readings. There was that, and her ongoing anxiety about teaching Sunday school with Erin Cook present. She had other episodes of varying nature in which God gave her the name "Erin" as an unhelpful answer to her equally vague question. Well, it was either God or some random synapses in her brain. Thomas was growing weary of

Heather's "visions" but the adoring husband in him kept chalking it up to her "creativity." Noncommittal and vague compliments were always a safe way to go.

Heather wanted Thomas to feel what she was feeling, and so far any attempt to convey her emotions at home at been met with the same reaction. She had delicately suggested that they arrive at church early to see if a more spiritual setting would provoke a deeper reaction in Thomas. "Deeper" being Heather's synonym for "any." Thomas just as delicately suggested that perhaps a hand job in the church pew was the stimulation he needed to reach a higher power. It was statements such as this that had kept Thomas celibate the last several weeks. Under duress, of course.

Heather grabbed Thomas's hand and stopped him in the midst of folding a paper airplane out of the morning's pamphlet. She closed her eyes.

"Do you feel anything?"

"Yes," Thomas answered. His back flush against that of the pew. His head staring straight out at the altar.

"Well? What?" Heather pleaded in a whisper.

"Feeling . . . horny. Man need . . . sex," Thomas said, as if he were gliding his fingers over a braille manuscript.

Heather sighed while Thomas let out a muffled laugh. It rang deep and melodious through the empty church. She pulled her hand away and went back to practicing her assigned reading. Doing a last-minute scan to see if any unpronounceable biblical names were on the horizon.

As the hour worn on, other faithful followers filed in. Similar to the insurance industry, the older you are, the higher the premiums. The elder patrons, typically those with the most unwavering faith—otherwise known as those *closest to the end*—took residence in the forward pews. The younger families toward the back. It was here that Heather waited for the Cooks to arrive. And when they finally did, at three minutes before ten, her emotions rang out again at the sight of her.

Erin was wearing her traditional outfit but moved as if the weight of the world had been thrust upon her. Yet her face was stoic. Her equally traditional pout had been relegated to a somber glance. Void of emotion. Any sign that she was a little girl had been eradicated by something. The rest of the family were not much better off. Heather watched as the Cooks filed into a pew in the back as if sneaking into a dirty movie. A mix of guilt and not wanting to be seen. The parents had managed to convince the older brothers to attend, but it looked like they had brought reading material of their own. Some well-worn paperback that she couldn't make out.

Heather motioned for Thomas to look her in direction.

"Oh no, Thomas. Look at her."

Thomas turned. Not in an uncaring way, but clearly not making the emotional connection that was vexing Heather.

"Oh, poor baby. What's happened?" Heather pleaded. She held her hand to her breast. Massaging it, hoping it would aid with some clarification.

Thomas raised his hand. "Is that question meant for me?"

"Stop it. Don't you see?"

"No. And I'm not looking either. This is weird, Heather," Thomas said.

When the organ started, Heather brought her focus back to the upcoming reading that she had been assigned. Father Houghton gave his usual introduction of hope mixed with guilt. Hymns were sung. Other readings were read.

When it came time for Heather's reading, she stood up and ran her hands along her skirt to smooth it out. As soon as she took her first step, the crisp click of her shoe hitting the polished tile floor, she felt the audio sucked out of the room. The gravity of her reading suddenly hit her. It was Easter Sunday. Theoretically a more important holiday in the Christian way of doing things than Christmas. This was the time when Jesus performed the miracle of all miracles by rising from the dead. If there was ever an opportunity for her to connect with Erin, it was this time. Even though she had walked down this very aisle on her wedding day, the walk of Easter Sunday in 1985 felt like a marathon. She could feel the tendons around her rib cage compressing with every breath.

When she reached the podium, she flipped through her pages. Finding the proper passage, she looked up to face the congregation. Hoping to settle on a fixed spot in the back of the room, she instead nestled in on Erin. As if sensing her eyes upon her, Erin slowly raised her head and gave Heather the same fixed stare. But there were no feelings of dread. No scary music stings that would accompany such a look in a horror film. Just a sad girl who wasn't in the mood to be challenged.

And Heather began.

"A reading from Corinthians.

'For I delivered unto you first of all that which I also received, how that Christ died for our sins according to the scriptures; And that he was buried, and that he rose again the third day according to the scriptures: And that he was seen of Cephas, then of the twelve: After that he was seen above five hundred brethren at once; of whom the greater part remain unto this present, but some are fallen asleep. After that, he was seen of James; then of all the apostles. And last of all he was seen of me also, as one born out of due time.' The Word of the Lord."

The parishioners responded with a murmured "Thanks be to God," and the choir director started a hymn, yet Heather remained at the podium. She put her hands up.

"Sorry. Can I just say something?" Heather said.

The music stopped and the people who were typically not paying attention picked up their heads.

"I know we don't normally do commentary after readings, but I just wanted to sort of dissect what this is saying. I know the language, even though it's an English translation, probably doesn't make a whole lot of sense. It's hard to follow. Trust me, it was hard to say!" The congregation chuckled meekly, appreciating a change in pace.

"What does that mean? As one born out of due time? Maybe it means a preemie? In this case, it's Paul's words. Was Paul's birth an immaculate birth? I don't think so, but what I think it means is his birth wasn't normal either but despite that he grew to be an apostle of Jesus. That's pretty important. I do think Christ will come again, as we say every week in the Creed. But I'm not sure if it will be a big spectacular glowing light from the sky with clouds parting. It may be humble. None of us know why we're still here and what our purpose is, so we shouldn't take life for granted, least of all this Easter Sunday. Anyway, that's all."

The congregation stared at her. Not accustomed to such interruptions; they weren't sure how to respond.

Heather caught herself and stepped down off the podium. As she walked back to her seat, the click of her high heels was met with a competing audio. That of faint clapping. The mixing was so precise that she needed to change her stride to fully grasp it. But there it was. A clapping so methodical it could only be interpreted as jest. As she stepped past the aisle, she looked to see where it was coming from.

Finally reaching her pew, Thomas gave her a pleasant smile.

"Good job," he whispered to her and gave her a pat on the leg for support.

Heather turned around once again. The clapping had stopped. The service was moving on. But all of the Cooks were looking at Erin. Keeping her head looking straight, she glanced over at Heather, passing her a sad, knowing smile. One that would continue to haunt Heather for the rest of her days.

twenty-seven

It wasn't a motel, but Lyle felt the same sort of seedy underpinning that he was embarking on the greatest, if not simultaneously the most drawn-out, deception of his marriage.

The others had primarily consisted of the emotional kind. Several years into their nuptials, he once pretended Helen was another woman during sex. He had reached that physiological barrier that many PhDs speak of to justify their own infidelity. The one that says, biologically speaking, humans are compatible with one another for only three years. Lyle had come up limp one night and the only thing he could do to keep himself erect was to pretend he was having a dirty little affair with the checkout girl at the grocery store. He then spent the better part of the year racked with guilt over it. Still, it was better than the misery he'd endure from Helen if he failed to be aroused. Helen's guilt could hold out longer than his.

His car was parked in the lot at the River Street Diner. He'd received a small handwritten letter at the prison from Anna. It read:

Dear Lyle,

As my first love, I cannot shake the feeling that we have a bond. Even though we've started our own lives and have been out of each other's thoughts for a generation, I felt a sense of home seeing you again. An excited warmth that you can only feel from the one person you first exchanged an "I love you" with. And I'm so sorry for any ill feelings between us. If you feel bad, the way I feel, please tell me. I will be at the State Diner on Wednesday at 5am. I hope to see you there, Lyle. I never intended for you to feel this way about me.

Anna

It had been folded over and over the way a high school letter gets tormented being passed through class. Lyle had read the letter dozens of times since he'd received it at work. He left it in his locker and would study it each afternoon when he'd arrive. At his dinner break. And every morning on his way out. Tonight, he brought it with him. He sat in his car and would gaze from the texture of the paper, to Anna's gliding penmanship, to his own face looking back at him in the rearview mirror. He tried to remember what he looked like the last time he was sitting in a car awaiting a date with Anna. And then tried to promptly delete the word "date" from his choice of words for the rest of the evening. *This is not a date. Get that shit out of your head right now. This is a meeting. A business meeting to catch up on old emotions that might possibly lead to sex.* Lyle leaned his head back and looked at the foamy carpet on his car ceiling. *Christ, you're a douche.*

Lyle began to wish that she wouldn't show up. He still wasn't off his usual schedule so far as the whole "getting home on time thing" was concerned. He took his gloves off and rubbed his rough hands together, feeling their coarseness. It made him feel his age. *And that was the point,* he decided. To remind him where he was in life. But then waiting in the car with his stomach in knots, with blood pumping into his groin with every passing memory of Anna, he also felt seventeen. *What a pathetic mix. No wonder I'm a mess.* His mind was racing with every awkward moment, every foolish thing he'd ever said in her presence, and every instant he wished he'd behaved differently. There seemed to be more of these than others, he quickly realized. And it brought a childlike grin to his face. Yet another facial reaction he hadn't elicited since he didn't know when.

He turned to watch Anna pull up in her car. He had always pictured she'd be driving a Saab or a Volvo or some European automobile that instantly gave people a hint of her class and success. He hadn't quite gotten over the reality of her driving a Toyota Tercel hatchback. It looked like she had gotten it used too. Lyle found himself wishing that their conversation would reveal her failures and heartbreaks. He hoped she would reveal her life to be that of one defeat after another. That would make him happy. There was plenty of schadenfreude to go around these days. Plentiful despite all the conflicting lust he felt just seeing Anna step out of her car. A long coat flowing gracefully in the wind pulling across her waist just so. *She had a waist.* As opposed to the other woman in his life. His childlike pettiness was equally prevalent.

Anna did not look around. It wasn't in her nature to survey her surroundings. To see if she had gotten there first. Confident people didn't do that. They took things as they came and could deal with it. Lyle was the polar opposite. He had to arrive early. He had to watch her walk in and collect his thoughts. Prepare a commanding opening line that would impress her.

He pulled the cheap metal handle of his door and pushed hard against the weight of it as a cold blast of air swirled around the car. Putting her letter in his jacket pocket, he pushed the door closed.

The breakfast crowd at the State Diner consisted primarily of cops and nurses in between changes in their respective shifts. Lyle spotted Anna sitting in a booth, putting the finishing touches on some order. Most likely coffee. He took his hat off sheepishly and held it against his chest as Anna looked up, making eye contact with him. He stood there for a good twenty seconds, waiting for a smile of acknowledgment. Something to warm him like her letter did and put him into a comfort zone. When it didn't happen, when Anna merely met his eyes and returned to her menu, he shriveled back to his natural posture. The one resembling a prehistoric carnivore. Against his better instincts, Lyle stepped forward past the eyes of what were clearly regulars at this hour. When he reached Anna's booth, he lifted his head and pulled the note out of his jacket pocket.

"I got your letter," he said. He had been planning a different opening line. Something a touch snappier than the *Super Friends* dialogue he offered.

"I'm happy you came," she said, finally smiling. Her gaze still distant. "Did it sound familiar to you?"

Lyle sat down and slid across the red leather booth. "No. Should it have?"

Anna nodded as she shook a packet of sugar into her recently arrived coffee. "Yeah, remember? One time when we hadn't talked for a while, I wrote you something similar. I figured it was safe to break that out again."

Lyle knew precisely what she was talking about. "I don't remember," he said. He was lying to her already. He hated himself for not being able to just talk to her. He always felt the need to gauge where she was going and then delivering what the "cool guy" might do. The problem was that Lyle was never further removed from being the "cool guy" than he was at this moment.

"It's weird seeing you again. I wasn't sure whether you'd come after the other night," she said, finally looking him in the eye. It made his heart ache to see her face. To see her in a brighter light showed how beautifully she had aged. He wished she hadn't. Not because he had fared far worse but because he got flustered in front of a beautiful face. He decided that's why people were always so honest with him. No one ever got flustered in front of him. Lyle finally sighed deep in his chest and decided to stop with the internalizing. *Just enjoy the conversation with someone not Helen.*

"Weird in how terrible I've aged?" he said, smiling beneath his moustache. If there was one thing Lyle could do well, it was engaging in self-deprecating humor. Low-hanging fruit.

Anna smiled. "No, why do you say that?"

"Come on. I know what's going on up here," he said, motioning at his face. "And here." He rubbed his belly that hung out over his belt buckle. "And here too," Lyle said as he pulled his wallet out and tossed it on the table.

Anna let out a girl-like giggle. "I was so embarrassed seeing you at the prison. God, I can't imagine what you must think of me."

"I could say the same thing," Lyle said, reassuring that there was no judgment. "This isn't where I thought I'd end up."

"Whatever happened to that cooking thing? Did you ever make a go of that?"

Lyle had forgotten. When in high school he would speak so often about reinventing American cuisine. He used it many times to impress Anna on dates on the research he'd done and the things he would do to become one the great chefs of his generation. He thought about how quickly dreams fade away when reality intrudes.

"Oh, I'm doing it. We've got the best Salisbury steak in the New York State penal system. Ask your husband."

Anna nodded. "You should have stuck with it."

"Well, life gets in the way sometimes. Did your life work out exactly the way you wanted?"

"No, it didn't."

"Did you ever say anything you regretted or you didn't see through?"

"Yes, I'm sorry, Lyle."

"About what?"

"Well, I touched on something," Anna said, looking down and pretending to be shy.

"Do you think I'd be sitting here talking to you if my life were perfect?"

"No. It's weird. When you talk to someone you see every day, there's somehow always plenty to talk about it. But when you're sitting in front of someone who you haven't seen in twenty years, there's nothing to say. Why is that?"

"It's because with your friends, you know what's going on in their lives. You can ask them about things you know about. That's not the case here," Lyle said with a shrug.

"We aren't friends?" Anna asked defensively.

"No. I don't see how that word describes us."

"Then what are we doing here?"

"I think you hit on it. We're both bored. Lonely. Maybe sad," Lyle said. And she nodded. A period of silence followed. Plates and saucers dinged softly together. The dusty vents pushed out heat, making the blinds vibrate slightly. Lyle looked past her to observe the other patrons. He noticed they were the only ones seated together. It made him aware that they were also the only ones talking. Their conversation ripe for eavesdropping. He became self-conscious and his posture shrunk down even further. Anna had been stirring an individual serving of nondairy creamer into her coffee for much longer than necessary. She tapped her spoon on the side of her weathered mug and looked up.

"So, I wanted to confess something to you."

Lyle inched closer. He wanted to make sure he looked her in the eye for whatever was coming next. *This is it*, he thought. *She's going to say seeing me again rekindled that old flame. She's going to ask if I'd be open to an affair.* Lyle couldn't believe his fortune. *Don't seem desperate*, he pleaded with himself. *Be curious at first—noncommittal.* In that moment, he was the most handsome, confident man in the world.

"You obviously know what my husband did," she continued.

"I do," Lyle stated, channeling his inner Tom Selleck.

Anna looked around the diner to make sure their waitress wasn't approaching. She took a delicate sip to collect herself.

"The truth is, I did it."

Lyle broke his gaze. "You did what?" he asked, sitting back in his seat.

"I was driving that night, not him."

"You . . . you were driving?" Lyle's mind flashed to the details of her case. He had immediately pulled her husband's record following their first encounter. An involuntary manslaughter conviction.

"We switched places before the police arrived. I have the job, the career. Him going away for three to five years would be far less devastating to our lives than me."

Lyle remained stoic in his seat. He tried to remember the specifics of the accident. A thirty-year-old woman crushed against a dumpster by a pickup truck with a snowplow while walking her dog. Anna's husband had claimed he didn't see her. She was walking where she shouldn't have been. It was messy in all the ways an accident can be messy.

"You killed that poor woman?"

"Yes."

"Jesus, why are you telling me this?"

"Just to see if I can trust you."

"You shouldn't be telling me these things, Anna. I work for Corrections. I'm basically a law enforcement officer."

"Can I trust you?"

"To do what?"

"Keep our secret."

Lyle looked around. He was racking his brain to figure out what game she was playing. He knew that she knew he was still smitten with her. He looked at her lips. An innocent pout was forming. He shook his head, trying to shake off what he had just heard.

"I mean, um," Lyle stammered. He stared at Anna, who was confident as ever and seemed inches away from smiling.

"Was it on purpose?" Lyle asked. His tone accusatory.

Anna just shrugged, the way a little girl does who is caught in a lie but knows she can just bat her eyelashes and make it go away. Lyle put his hands to his face. He couldn't get the images of his head. Anna and her husband finding this girl walking her dog. Seeking her out.

Dragging her remains against the pavement.

But can you keep a secret, Lyle? My evil deed in exchange for an early morning frolic? I'd call that a fair trade for an idle existence.

"Oh my God," Lyle said beneath his fingers.

"So?" Anna asked.

Lyle slowly removed his hands and put them on the table. He saw that they were shaking. He clenched his fists in an attempt to hide his nerves. He looked down at his hand and noticed his taunt knuckles only made it more obvious. Anna reached over and put her hand on his fist. Gently peeling it open. Resting her fingers in his open palm. Her hands were perfect. The nails were perfect. Feminine and elegant. Even the temperature of her hands was perfect. Lyle stared at them. Not grabbing her hand but not pulling it away either.

"So, what?" he asked without looking up.

"Can I trust you?"

Lyle raised his head and caught her eyes. He and Anna were sixteen again. Sitting in a parked car, soaking wet from a run into the stream behind the ball fields. She looked perfect. He felt alive. Which in this relationship equated to putty in her hands.

Lyle nodded regretfully. "Yes," he said.

Anna squeezed his hand. "Good. Thank you." She let his hand go. "'Cause I was just kidding."

Lyle cocked his head. "Come again?"

"I was just checking to see if I could trust you. With a secret. Andy was driving that night. Not me. Total freak accident."

"What's wrong with you?"

"Just playing. Testing. Remember?"

"No, what on God's earth is wrong with you?"

"Come on, Lyle. Remember that game we used to play? Who bites first?"

"No."

"I win again. Anyway, I'm glad I can trust you because I have something much less risky for you."

"You were testing me?" Lyle's head was spinning. He couldn't put two and two together if asked. He saw the walls behind her melt into some cheap knockoff of a Salvador Dali painting.

Anna reached into her purse and grabbed a bottle of bourbon. She put it on the table. Seven hundred and fifty milliliters of a beautiful amber elixir. Defined corners of a rectangular bottle, catching the light just so.

"I was wondering if you could give this to Andy for me. It's his favorite. Our anniversary is coming up. I used to have a nurse sneak stuff in for me, but now she's at the hospital so you're the only person I know there."

The color slowly drained from his face. He was no longer the most handsome man in the world. He was pretty sure he wasn't even the most handsome man in the diner. Lyle stared at the bottle. He looked at the short-order cook behind the grill. He looked outside at his beat-up car and the 35-degree rain that was starting to tap on his windshield. And for the first time since he failed his mother on Christmas Eve, he wanted to cry. The breakfast had gone exactly as he had initially predicted. But he went along anyway because the idiot in him hung on to the minuscule chance this gorgeous, classy woman wanted to sleep with him. That was never going to happen and she was using her feminine charm to manipulate him further.

Anna smiled at him with her eyes. "It's so good to be able to talk to you again, Lyle. And have a friend on the inside. Means a lot."

Lyle smiled back. His smile a façade for a new fantasy. One that didn't involve hotel rooms or clumsy, naked fluid exchanges. He pictured himself smashing the bottle on the tabletop and leaping across the beige linoleum, grabbing her perfectly styled hair with his chapped blue-collar hands. His eyes tightened as he could hear the sounds of the dishes hitting the floor mixed with her muffled screams. The other patrons turning in horror as he slammed her gaping mouth onto the corner of the table. Her teeth would shatter, cutting her gums and her esophagus as she gasped for air, sucking in bloody bone fragments. The corner of his mouth curled as he pictured himself jabbing the broken shards of her husband's anniversary hooch into Anna's neck over and over until her head was connected only by a meaty piece of chipped spinal column. His whole essence relaxed with the notion that after all these decades, he finally stuck up for his dignity and tore her to literal shreds. It was about this time in his daydream that Anna spoke up and broke him from his trace.

"What do you think?"

"Sure thing," he said. And moved the bottle into the seat next to him.

may

twenty-eight

There weren't assigned seats in Ian's third period government class, yet for the bulk of the school year he chose a seat at the front on the left-hand side.

This gave him a good position to engage Mr. Nightingale in a variety of topics. Since they agreed on virtually every issue, it was more of a monologue that fluctuated in octave, but Ian loved having a comforting mouthpiece to spout off with. Come May, however, Ian had resigned himself to the back of the classroom. No longer the freewheeling spirit he once was, he carried with him the internal stigma of knowing he had vanquished any hope of being considered among the school's elite. No matter how fluid one's understanding of the essential role that government can play in one's life, engaging in statutory incest was certainly among life's great levelers. He had begun to understand how the throngs of people behind bars would develop a sense of shared comradery. He used this backward logic to picture himself as a sort of victim, like all those black men in jail. *After all, if there is no free will, then we're all ultimately victims or beneficiaries of nature,* he reminded himself.

When Mr. Nightingale called on him, Ian merely shrugged it away with a "Sure," or "I dunno." Gone were the venomous rants toward Alexander Haig and Margaret Thatcher, the latter being the one woman whom men could openly mock. It felt good to hate something in common.

Ian had resigned himself to doing the bare minimum at school for the remainder of the semester. Within a few weeks' time he would be hours away from home at freshman orientation and able to redefine himself. There would be no backlog of gossip and social categories that had allowed others to prescribe who he was. He could create a new version of himself, free from the stigma of being a prison guard's son who'd never been laid and worked in the frozen food section. Ian had been staring out the window when Mr. Nightingale began passing out the senior papers. Ian glanced down at his, which had written in beautiful script:

C- See Me

There was a time not that long ago that seeing such a grade in his favorite class would have caused Ian tremendous angst. The comforting part of becoming a true nihilist is that because nothing matters, nothing bothers you. Ian glanced down at the paper and then pushed it aside as his once bonded instructor walked back to the front of the room. When the bell rang, Ian shuffled his way to Mr. Nightingale's desk.

"You wanted to see me?" Ian asked with the same enthusiasm that one receives a traffic ticket.

"Yes, who wrote your paper?" Mr. Nightingale shot back once the last student had left.

"Me?"

"That's your handwriting but not your words. What's gotten into you?"

"Nothin'."

"Are you disappointed with a C-minus?"

"Not really."

"See? The old Ian would have been."

Ian shrugged. "I don't know what to tell ya."

Mr. Nightingale pushed on. "The only reason I didn't fail you is that I can't prove plagiarism in this case. And there's a large part of me that wants to send you off to school with confidence. But I wouldn't be helping you at all if I didn't say that this was disappointing."

"Okay."

"Is there something going on? Something at home, maybe, that you want to talk about?"

"No."

Mr. Nightingale sighed and shook his head.

"All right, I'm sorry your time with me needs to end on this note. We had some wonderful discussions and I just hope you can find that fire again at your university."

"Okay."

Mr. Nightingale put his hand up, relenting. "That's it. We'll see you around, I guess."

"See you."

Ian left the classroom the same way he walked to the front of room. Stoically. Barely lifting his feet, his hands shoved deep in his baggy corduroys with a backpack tossed over one shoulder. A previously feisty young man who had stripped himself of all emotion. Mr. Nightingale became crestfallen. The last week of high school is typically among the best times in one's life. The weather is perfect, the trappings of adolescent social constructs are removed, and the freedoms of adulthood are on the horizon. Even better than real adulthood, since someone else is typically footing the bill. And yet, as Ian turned the corner and disappeared out of sight, Mr. Nightingale realized that he had none of those things. Sentiment was not something that came easily, but seeing such a promising young fellow leftist lose his passion caused a sense of loss that surprised him. That his efforts in molding him had been fruitless. A waste of time, sure, but more so a waste of direction. If he had foreseen the turn Ian was going to take, he would have placed his fellowship in another student. All those nights nursing a bottle of Merlot while writing comment after comment in the margins of Ian's papers. *What was the point of all that?* he thought. He came close to a feeling of guilt but then remembered that the beauty of working in academia is there are never any real-world consequences to one's failures.

And there's always another student coming next year.

twenty-nine

Lyle entered the kitchen through back door carrying a brown paper bag. The temperature had risen to a consistent 60 degrees and that was enough to change the storm doors over to the ones bearing screens.

He loved the sound the screen door made when it banged against the frame. A signature sound of summer. He couldn't hear it and not think of his childhood. Bursting out of the back door of his parents' house to go make mischief on his own or with the boys across the street. The hums of insects and thunder providing a consistent soundtrack. He recalled that they had devised some elaborate scheme where they would catch crayfish and sell them to local fishermen. They had managed to accumulate a few dozen of the crustaceans and kept them alive in his parents' utility sink for weeks. Until it became clear they didn't have much of a business plan and the basement reeked of decaying animal matter. But that screen door did open and close about a hundred times that summer. And it was glorious. He had just returned from dropping Ian off at college for the weekend, so he found himself in a particularly sentimental mood. Seeing Helen seated straight up at the kitchen table helped bring him back to reality.

"What's in the bag?" she asked.

"The drop-off went fine," he responded. A direct assault on her greeting. Or lack of.

Helen passed him as fake a smile as she could muster. She didn't like the implication that he was more concerned with Ian's education than she. *If it were up to you, he'd be on his way to plumbing school,* she thought.

"What did you talk about?" Helen asked.

"Not much, actually. He's pretty buttoned up these days. I think a change of scenery will do him good."

Helen nodded. Despite her natural inclination to disagree with Lyle, it was hard to argue that. Lyle set the bag on the table and pulled out a bottle of bourdon. *The* bottle of bourbon. The one that Anna had asked him to smuggle into the prison for her husband and he sheepishly said that he would. The instant he moved it from the table in the diner to his lap, he had thought, *Yeah, that's not happening.* And it didn't. He had wedged it in his trunk next to some emergency blankets and the spare tire. He had forgotten about it until he needed to move some things around to load Ian's bags for freshman orientation.

"Where did you get that?" Helen asked.

"Guys at work gave it to me a while back. Forgot it was in the trunk. Found it taking Ian's bags out."

"Eli bringing him back?"

"Yes."

Helen pulled the bottle close to her and started to pick away at the wrapping at the top. Lyle watched with curiosity and amusement. Her picking wasn't one of urgency.

"Help yourself," he delivered with not so subtle derision.

Lyle stood across the table from her and watched her movement shift from that of a nervous tick to one of purpose. She wanted the wrapper off. Lyle had never known Helen to be a consumer of spirits. They kept a few bottles in the house for company, but since they never had company, there was no need to replace them.

She continued to pick at the wrapper until she finally tore a big enough edge to grab onto. Swirling the foil around the top of the bottle, she let it fall to the table and said without looking up to face him, "I'm not in love with you anymore."

Lyle moved his gaze from her face to the floor, staring at the brownish-orange utility carpet. He slipped out of his jacket and tossed it over the back of the chair. He stared at his feet pointed inward, the way people with no confidence stand. He glanced at himself in the glass and saw his hunched-over posture. He had nothing going for him but always held onto being faithfully married as a source of great dignity. Now he was officially married in paperwork only. He weighed his options of what to say.

"I know," was the option he chose.

"That's it? That's your response?" she continued.

"It's disappointing to actually hear you say it. But it doesn't surprise me."

"Then why didn't you say anything?"

"What do you want me to do? Yell? Beg? That's not what a man does."

"Well, this can't go on. No one is happy here. Not me. Not the kids." Helen walked over to the kitchen cabinet and pulled out a small glass. Checking it for scratches, she turned around, sat down at the table, and wiped it with a napkin. Lyle sat down in the chair across from her.

"What would make you happy?" he asked.

"Not this. Not you."

"I'm sorry."

Helen opened the bottle and poured a good inch into her glass, her voice starting to crack. "I haven't done any of the things I wanted to do with this life. None of them. I haven't been anywhere, I haven't created anything," she said, eyes watering.

"You didn't want children?"

"Oh, stop with that. You're not Father of the Year."

"So, it's my fault you're miserable?"

Helen took a healthy sip of the bourdon. Lyle watched with curiosity as she didn't react. The way someone who is used to drinking such an intense flavor doesn't react.

"That's new. Is this replacing your needlepoint?" he continued.

"You're such a loser. I can't believe I wasted my time, my life, my goddamn life on you." Helen now had tears welling. They finally gave way and started down her cheeks.

Lyle closed his eyes. In the back of his mind, he always suspected she blamed him for whatever she was missing. He had never seen this kind of reaction from her but suspected it was always festering back there somewhere. *And this is the day*, he thought.

"So, if you had married a more successful man then your cartoon would have sold, is that it?"

"Go to hell."

"I just want to understand where I let you down. Maybe so we can advise Erin not to make the same mistake."

"Aren't you innocent? Perfect dopey little man and daddy's little girl. I'm sure you've filled her mind with all my wicked ways," she hissed at him. The corners of her eyes pulled tight with rage.

Lyle had never been scared of his wife. He'd been intimidated by her beauty when he was courting her and emasculated by her dominance as the marriage wore on. But being able to see the individual muscles pulled tight around her orbital bone caused a new anxiety. He sensed she had been waiting months, maybe years, for the chance to blow up at him, and perhaps Ian leaving the house was her cue. She had a little bit of alcohol already working through her and a potentially sharp object in her hand. Lyle stood up from the table and pulled the bottle toward him.

"Helen, I don't want to this to get out of hand. I'm going to chalk this up as you being emotional because another child is on his way out of the house. Finish what's in your glass and then go take a walk or something." Lyle grabbed the cap and put it back on the bottle.

"Don't you tell me what to do!" Helen screamed back at him, lunging for the bottle.

Lyle looked at her with confusion. "Are you out of your mind?"

"Give it to me!"

"We are not doing this, Helen. We are not going down this road."

Helen finally stood up and slapped Lyle hard across the face, knocking his glasses off. The pain he almost enjoyed, but the humiliation of losing his bifocals was unbearable. He recalled how much he hated it as a child. On the playground, it was an announcement to the world of just how vulnerable he was. That with one swipe, they had taken away an important part of school combat, the ability to detect your enemy. And then he'd need to fumble around to regain them. Lest they be stepped on and his parents emasculate him further. This was no different. His eyes filled with rage as he grabbed her wrist with one hand and her recently topped rocks glass with the other. His posture straightened and his shoulders rolled back as he prepared to crush the whole concoction against her face. And in a moment of sober hesitation instead, hurled it against the wall. The drywall buckled as the thick tumbler splintered into a cloud of glass and amber liquid.

Helen, too, was seeing a new version of her spouse. Part of her liked it. *After all this time, you're finally sticking up for yourself,* she thought. *Too little, too late, but at least it's masculine.*

They looked over to see Erin standing in the doorway. Her traditional pose, hips skewed to one side, one hand clutching an elbow, her hair hanging straight.

"I'm still here, just so you know," she said.

Lyle looked down and let go of Helen. He was ashamed that he had let Helen drive him to anger. And ashamed that Erin saw it. He grabbed his spectacles off the table and delicately put them back on his face, pushing them up against his nose.

"Your mother and I were, um . . ." Lyle started to make something up and then just raised his hands.

"We were just saying what needed to be said, Erin," Helen finished. She sat back down—exhausted at her rare expenditure of energy, annoyed that he destroyed her perfectly chilled drink, but grateful that the bottle had somehow survived the outburst.

Lyle shrugged. "That's probably true. I don't like how we said it, but . . ."

Erin walked over to the kitchen closet.

"It's okay. We need more of that around here," she said and grabbed the broom, noticing that the .22 was still there.

thirty

The events of the spring had caused Daddy-Erin
time to be postponed indefinitely. There was
a palpable unease throughout the home that
caused its inhabitants to wander about in silence.

They needed each other for a variety of reasons, so they dared not engage in any further dialogue that might erupt into chaos. Ian was still at his SUNY Plattsburgh freshman orientation that week. Erin would be starting middle school in a few months. Lyle was not sure where his marriage would go at that point. He couldn't afford a divorce. Helen hadn't worked in twenty years, so it was unlikely the state would have any sympathy for him.

His relationship with Erin was becoming disturbingly similar to what he endured with Helen. He'd already accepted *that* relationship was beyond repair. It was imperative that he salvage something with Erin. When he knocked on her door that Sunday morning in June 1985, he was drawn to the sounds of a gargling hack. It pulsated intermittently with the light gasps of an eleven-year-old girl and then returning to a throaty reverberation.

"Erin? May I come in?"

He pushed the door ajar to see Erin vomiting into a plastic

grocery sack. The soggy weight of it hung low from her position on the floor.

"Oh, sweet baby. You're sick?" He stepped quickly to her side and knelt down. Resting his hand on her back.

"Uh-huh."

"Okay, well, let's get you downstairs."

"No, thank you," she choked. She looked up at him and the weight beneath her eyes caused Lyle to catch his breath. Her eyes had sagged. The color had dissipated from her cheeks.

Gray, he thought. *My child is gray.* The veins around her eyelids had burst from a morning of dry heaving. Little strands of pink and purple darting from the roots of her lashes. Her hair matted with sweat against her scalp. Greasy and mangled from Erin's constant clutching and pulling.

"Can I help you sit up?"

"Okay."

Lyle pulled her back against the side of the bed and stroked her hair. She leaned into him and with that gesture of need, he knew that it was something beyond indigestion. His mind raced at the possibilities. There had been a recent batch of "Just Say No" campaigns that flooded all forms of media. Perhaps Nancy Reagan was onto something. Perhaps Erin did not say "No." Perhaps Ian had encouraged Erin to do the opposite of whatever this administration encouraged. If Nancy Reagan says drugs are bad, then obviously they must be good. He could picture the whole conversation in his head. But he wouldn't go there. Not yet.

"Did you eat something different last night?"

"No, same as you."

"Okay, well, let's think." Lyle held her head against his chest. He welcomed the sudden return to their closeness but wished it had come under less forced circumstances.

"Have you been doing something that maybe your heart tells you that you shouldn't? Maybe something that might cause me to, I don't know . . ."

Choose your next words carefully, he thought. *Do not judge. Be supportive. When she says yes to the drugs, don't fly off the handle. Be the adult.*

". . . cause me to be disappointed in you?"

Erin closed her eyes and tightened her grip around his waist, clutching his shirt.

Lyle nodded and pursed his lips. Drugs. *How, Erin? Is your life that boring?* First things first.

"Where did you get them, Erin?"

Her eyes remained closed for a moment and then they slowly opened. "What?"

"Where did you get the drugs?"

Lyle felt the release of her grip around his shirt and at that instant, knew that he had gotten it wrong. She sat up.

"What are you talking about, Dad?"

Lyle saw something in her face and knew this child was terrified. Marijuana, for all its foibles, would not elicit that kind of fear.

"I guess I don't know what I'm talking about. What's going on, Erin? What have you been up to?"

"My stomach hurts, Daddy."

"Okay. Can you tell me where specifically?"

"And down here too."

Erin moved her hand down to her groin and the color drained from Lyle's cheeks. He saw this tiny face, her awkward teeth that he couldn't afford to have fixed, her pudgy little arms, and felt the corners of his mouth pull down. And a sting in his eye socket.

"Oh, baby girl. What happened?"

"I'm sorry, Daddy. I don't know why I did it. I don't know what's wrong with me," she pressed, still unable to push herself into a sob.

Lyle briefly thought that it might come out. That this was the instant that caused her to break. He wrapped his arm around her, pulling her closer, almost trying to squeeze a cry out of her as if she were a bagpipe. The analogy that raced through his head caused his eyes to flash open and his head to shake in a vain effort to wash the description away.

"No, don't talk that way, sweetheart. There's nothing wrong. We're gonna figure this out."

Of all the things that Lyle had thought he was going to have to endure that evening, his eleven-year-old daughter's morning sickness was not on the list. It wasn't even on the dozens of backup lists that a father keeps in the worst-case scenario folder. There were no words for a while as Lyle felt his head begin to rock. An effort to calm his impending seasickness. He, waiting for some shake or squeak of a cry finally emanating from his child. And Erin, waiting and needing some form of fatherly advice that she had as recently as two hours ago deemed irrelevant. It was this failure of communication skills, this inability to give the other what they needed, that oddly kept the two of them together. An awkward meshing of arms and legs, twisted uncomfortably against one another, the tendons of hips and lower backs throbbing with the pain of overextension. Yet the comfort of touch superseded all of this. And it served to mask the clumsiness of their silence. Until Lyle's own macabre curiosity and overprotective anger got the better of him.

"Who . . . was . . . it?" he asked. The space between his words dragged so far apart that it almost didn't come out at all.

Erin lay silent, her ankles curled underneath her with her legs folded against Lyle's waist.

"Who were you, um . . ." Lyle searched. He was torn over the word choice. He didn't even think Erin liked boys, much less had a boyfriend, much less would have known what to do anyway. The conservative voice in him threw blame at the schools for putting the whole thought into her head in the first place.

"Who was the boy that, ah . . ." Another pause. He looked to the ceiling. His mouth was dry. Film collected on the sides of his cheeks. It pulled apart when he tried to speak.

"I mean, is it someone at school?"

Erin shook her head no.

Where else? he thought.

"I mean, a neighbor?" It couldn't be the new boy down the street. Even Lyle had caught him wailing away on his pecker in the backyard, and that was enough to convince him his boy-parts were of no threat.

Lyle searched. *What else was there?*

"Church? One of the boys in Sunday school?"

Erin shook her head no again.

Lyle looked across the room. He was out of guesses. He liked it better when their talks consisted of movie magazines and sports stars. It was much too soon to be having this conversation with Erin. *My light. My perfect little angel who is as sweet and gracious and adoring as a goddamned puppy with a bow around its neck! What the hell is going on?* His face swelled with rage. *It's bad enough I even have to deal with this on my day off from my shitty job and my shitty marriage and now my little tramp of a daughter won't even have the ovaries to get her little whorish head out of the sand and come clean as to which pathetic little maggot stuck his cock in her.*

"Goddamm it, Erin, you tell me, right now! You understand? Who the hell did this? Huh? What lucky boy got you first?"

Erin backed away from him, her hand over her mouth in fear. Shaking. Eyes squinting. But no tears. She pulled her hand away from her mouth, each finger pulsating with fear.

"Ian," she said.

It was now time for Lyle's hand to shake. His eyes welled up and then a long stare. He knew that she wasn't putting him on or searching for sympathy or hoping for an outburst. It was just the way it was. It started off as a frown. An unbelieving frown that was steeped in denial and anger but had the pouty overtones of an infant that hasn't gotten his way. Lyle slowly pulled his knees to his chest. As the first tear left his eye, his entire body succumbed to the pain of knowing that it wasn't youthful indiscretion before him. It was something so sinister and wicked that he could feel his core disintegrating at flashes of whatever unspeakable acts occurred. In his own home. Under his own watch. Presumably while he was too busy doing other things. Pining for some hard-core affair with his high school flame.

He watched as Erin watched him. He could see in her face that she feared as much for her own health as for what Lyle might do. To Ian. To himself. She wasn't sure where this was going to go. At least it was airborne now. The stink of incest now circulating their once quaint woodland home like a sour stew. Bubbling on an open pot with rancid produce and diseased meat. This was their home now. And all the doilies and ruffled dustcovers and needlepoint spouting manufactured sentiment weren't going to alter it. It washed over Lyle's soul like he'd been doused with ammonia.

"Oh god! Oh my god!" he sobbed. His rough, shaking hands found his hair and began pulling on it. Tugging and ripping until greasy strands lay stuck between his joints. He kicked his legs. Throwing his elbow against the metal bed frame. It would leave an open wound later, but for now, his rage muffled the pain. His mind was spinning with confusion. *Now that you've thrown your little fit, perhaps you should think of your daughter, you selfish prick. Helen was right. You are selfish. You are a prick. And you can't even think of what your daughter might be going through. It's all about you. How you failed. How you let her down. Open your goddamn eyes and look at her!*

He did.

His eyes were swollen with the sting of salt that hadn't run through them since . . . well, never. Erin was looking down at the ground. Ashamed. She looked up to see her father, eyelashes matted to his face, reaching for her.

"I'm sorry, Daddy. I'm sorry I let you down. I don't know what's wrong with me."

"Oh, baby girl. Please?" His shaking hand reaching out for her.

She grabbed his hand and returned to his lap, putting her head against his chest.

"No, no. Stop. Just stay here a second."

Lyle began rocking her back and forth. He was forty years old again. He was keeping an infant Erin from crying. Unsuccessfully. Lyle closed his eyes tight, holding Erin. Praying that if he concentrated hard enough, if he really believed in God as much he professed to, God would send the two of them back to that moment. He could start over. He could go to school and get a better job and be more assertive. His mind raced over all the places he went wrong. He kept rocking. Waiting for a flash of light or a subtle rumble or whatever happens when a bend in time is achieved. He thought of his failures as man and as a husband. And he kept rocking. He felt Erin grab him hard around the waist and he put his hand on her head. *Keep rocking.* He sniffled a large clump of snot back into his nose and he tried to focus on where they were. This same house. This same house on that old couch of his mother's. Rocking infant Erin. *Keep focused. God will hear me and take us both back to that moment. He'll remember all those Sundays I was dying to sleep in but went to church anyway. All those times that I defended His existence against all sound logic. I celebrated Your son's birthday more than my own. I threw money in the collection plate. You fucking owe me!*

Then Erin spoke and broke his concentration.

"I'm sorry I can't cry like you, Daddy," she said. "But I mean to. I am. In my heart it hurts that I let you down so much. And that I made you cry."

Lyle broke down again and Erin put her hand to his face. His mind flashed to the two of them swimming for the first time. A cheap local YMCA pool. Erin was eighteen months. He spun her around in the pool and she brought her little hand to the side of his face. It didn't matter that he was ugly and poor. He was Daddy. It was this moment that Lyle began his ritual of preparing for her death. What had unfolded before him was something that he hadn't prepared for. And he wondered if it was worse.

And here they were. His daughter comforting him after she had been raped or violated or whatever had happened at the hands of his son. And Lyle was the one who was breaking down. His moustache matted to his face, soaked from tears that continued to pulsate out of his eyes. His mouth open, wheezing for air as he drooled on Erin's head. He caught himself and began to sheepishly dab at her hair with his fingers, wiping it on his shirt.

How does one compose himself after this? he thought. *What's the next step?* He held his daughter against his chest, his heart wanting to push itself out of his rib cage. He felt a migraine developing. The sting of intense heartbreak. She finally pulled away to look at him.

And sweetness did not follow.

thirty-one

The wind chime had five stainless
steel tubes with a thin piece of balsa
wood in the middle.

If the breeze were cooperating, it would echo the last five notes of "America the Beautiful." Of course, only those with a keen ear and a devout sense of patriotism would have picked up on it. The sun had been soft beneath the clouds that day when Lyle was left alone with Erin for the first time. She was just approaching two. He held her up to the wind chime and watched her face lighten as the most delicate breeze passed by them. Lyle was never one for fixating on moments. But this perfect combination that illuminated all five senses at once is what cemented Erin as his most precious gift. If nothing else in his life, the moment where he held his daughter, soft against his arm, her wispy hair tickling his face, the odor of pine, the light tones of the chime, and the expression of utter joy in her eyes were enough for him to know that Erin was his gift to the world. He would never be handsome, he would never be rich, and he would never contribute any more to society than his muscular blue-collar skills would allow. It made his eyes throb as the tendons beneath them welled up with fluid. Erin's cheeks glowed with a peach radiance, her eyes tightening, her smile open with a sampling of teeth. It was a perfect moment between father and daughter.

A scant nine years later, Lyle stared at yet another wind chime. This one he could not hear, and there was no breeze. For it was from the view out the window of the Broome Country Abortion Clinic. His left hand resting awkwardly on his thigh. His feet pointed inward. His right fist clenching his pant leg. Thumb flicking a row of tan corduroy. Lyle bit his lip under his moustache as the memory of Erin and him and the wind chime came flooding back to him. This one was appropriately silent. There was nothing to be gained by whatever song it was playing that late summer afternoon. Lyle looked down at the stained tile floor and let his mind drift, trying to find a song that might help him through it.

_⁂_

Erin lay back against the wafer-thin mattress and winced as the nurse came and grabbed her leg, putting her ankle into the stirrup. It had that cold steel smell, but it wasn't cold. It was clear someone had recently warmed it for her. Moving them in and out. The comparison to cattle wasn't a perfect analogy. Cow meat is eaten and provides nourishment. This altercation would provide no such benefit. Her surgeon had thick horn-rimmed glasses with even thicker plastic lenses. And a smock. Erin kept waiting for one of the doctors to say something but nothing came. They mumbled to each other in doctor speak, referencing the space between her legs and the size of what instruments to use, but nothing that addressed Erin as a human or even a patient. She wished they had put her under. Inside Erin's uterus, the baby boy was sucking his thumb. All of his limbs had developed and the synapses in his two-month-old brain were starting to fire. His gray matter activity processing the makings of a dream. The sound waves of Saturday morning cartoons had wafted in since the child was conceived without provocation. To an observer of popular culture, it cannot be overstated how much the anthropomorphism of animals in entertainment had helped usher in such movements as animal rights, vegetarianism, and the like. *Charlotte's Web* likely stopped thousands of children from requesting bacon. *"I can't eat Wilbur,"* they would say. Yet there was no cultural icon to protect this boy. No highly consumed piece of literature where the hero is an unborn child with acerbic wit. No cartoons with a talking fetus, no assigning of personality, passion, or a silly voice. This was a wart, a blemish, a rotten tooth to be extracted. He was not to be considered life. Microscopic single celled phytoplankton that might one day be discovered in Martian sea ice would most certainly be cause for celebration. *"Complex organic life discovered!"* they would say. But not this boy. It would be a major inconvenience to label him as a life. Best to assign his quadrants numbers and not think about it too much.

Erin felt the doctor insert the speculum into her cervix. The neck of her womb was opened. The tenaculum followed, clamping shut and grasping the cervix. With this, the man with the horn-rimmed glasses was able to determine how large Erin's uterus was. Not very. Her cervix was then dilated with an increasingly larger and larger set of metallic curved instruments. Erin closed her eyes tight, searching for a happy memory. Static. *I'll think about my friends.* Again, that channel was blocked out. The suction apparatus was then inserted through her dilated cervix, puncturing the sack and allowing the embryonic fluid to escape. Gray placenta, ready for the birth of a child. But not on this day. Erin could feel her heart racing as she attempted to steady her breathing. Pursing her lips so tight that she whistled. The doctor turned his head briefly to pass her a condescending smile.

Inside of Erin, the little boy's heart was chugging away at a hefty one hundred and forty beats per minute. The boy who would not be assigned a name jolted at a disturbance in his slumber. Upon the insertion of the suction apparatus, the child reared to get away from whatever it was that had entered his home. It is here that the pointy little Hoover came into direct contact with the child, first tearing off pieces of the bottom half of his leg. He removed his thumb to scream, not understanding what process was taking place but acting on a core instinct to flee from agony. But a scream underwater is rarely heard. Particularly with such tiny lungs. On the table, Erin opened her eyes as her hand grasped the thin paper covering her bed, her fingers tearing through the paper, finding a hole in the mattress. They clawed their way in, finding refuge in the gray filling.

The boy did attempt to escape, as his heartbeat had now bolted to two hundred beats per minute. With the boy's protective membrane punctured, his body was rapidly shredded, fragments of new bone cracking, skin and organs folded amongst each other. All with the ease of vacuuming under the seat of a car. A few sticky parts but it mostly went down easy. Pieces of him darted down a long tube, his heart, which had performed so gallantly mere seconds ago, was now just another scrap of pulverized jelly. Finally, all that remained was his head itself. With his body decimated, the last few electrons darted around in his brain, wondering where the rest of him had gone. They flickered with life one final time, sending the last images of a dream to his cortex. Consciousness had come miraculously into his brain and was promptly vanquished. His skull, too large to be vacuumed, required the use of polyp forceps. Inserting it into the uterus, the doctor grasped the free-floating cranium with the rings of the instrument and pulled it out. His tiny head was then crushed and whatever silly contents and bone fragment may have remained were vacuumed up, as well.

Erin tried to close her ears at the sounds she was hearing, but it was without success. When she finally heard the doctor ask, "Is number one out yet?" she wanted to take it all back. She removed her fingers from the inside of the mattress and could feel something stuck to her hand. She grasped her fist around it, hiding it from the staff as they cleaned her up. She had nothing to show for a springtime of regret. Just a perforated womb and maybe some infected organs. They would heal eventually. The body usually does. The boy, however, would never leave her mind.

Erin walked slowly from the back room to her father seated in the waiting area. Her pelvis ached. Her insides throbbed and her heart was empty. She saw her dad rise to greet her but couldn't look him in the eye. She shuffled across the floor and felt his arm go around her shoulder. He may have said something to her, but she couldn't hear it. Her ears were replaying over and over the sounds from the operating room. Erin opened her fist. Stuck to her finger was a plastic ring. Children's jewelry. The kind one might get from a gumball machine. She wondered at what point that was stuck in the mattress by a previous occupant. And for what purpose. *No matter.* Every fork in the road needs some souvenir from the gift shop.

And this is appropriately pathetic, she thought.

thirty-two

Helen sat at the long kitchen table by herself.
She hadn't moved from her position of rest
for a solid hour.

She had managed to summon forth the energy required to empty a can of vegetable soup into a pot. Yet as she waited, her mind drifted to her daughter. Her fight for a woman's privacy had seen her eleven-year-old daughter's womb vacuumed out and the contents processed into a fine biologic paste. Helen found herself placed in a vexing situation, one that pulled the moisture out of her soft palate. She licked her teeth, pulling a stringy piece of film that collected at the corner of her mouth. These were the common symptoms of Helen when she was vexed. She couldn't bring herself to be happy that Lyle had seen the progressive light that comes with accepting abortion as a clean alternative to childbirth. Not that there was any alternative. *The thing festering in Erin was to be a mongrel, was it not? The product of wicked incest and such an abomination cannot be allowed to live. It surely would have been born retarded, perhaps of sloped forehead and enlarged tongue. Like that creepy neighborhood kid I saw Erin with. No, such children should be put to sleep. Surely that was the only logical answer. After all, it's just tissue. Nothing more. Like a wart that needs burning. A fingernail that needs clipping.*

The water had since boiled out and the little bits of perfectly cubed potatoes and carrots had begun to fry in the pot. Lyle and Erin had left that afternoon in a moment's notice. It was perhaps a cruel twist of fate that Ian was planning to return home that evening. Cruel in an ironic sense, not that Ian would be given sympathy for whatever awaited him at home.

Although Helen was not sure she believed it. Ian, after all, was her creation. Her pet project of a dozen or so years that culminated in college admission. It just was not possible that his hand could have slipped so far as to molest his younger sister. When the door opened behind her, she hoped to see his smiling face.

Instead she saw Erin, her father's arm around her, shuffling across the floor. The life sucked from her. Helen had to turn away at the sight of them. Her confrontation of the lie would need to wait until later. In the meantime, she opened up Lyle's bottle of bourbon. The contents likely to provide ample courage for whichever line of defense she chose.

That evening the table had been set. Helen decided that the best way to deal with a challenge like Erin's abortion was to ignore it head on. She would cook a standard meal, tuna casserole, serve it at a standard time, five-thirty, and discuss standard things. Lyle stared at her with sad, unbelieving eyes. Sunk from a full day of tears. Waiting for her to say something to her daughter. To offer some form of consoling that would help her through the moment. Yet Helen sat upright, as if she were back in the first pew listening to a sermon, spooning perfectly portioned segments of egg, tuna, and potato chips into her mouth.

When Ian entered, Lyle felt his pulse quicken. He had gone over this scenario multiple times since the other night and found every time he played it out in his head, it resulting in him repeatedly punching Ian until his neck snapped. He felt a sickening rage that he never had for any human being in his life. The fact that it was his own son, whatever their differences, made him nauseous.

Ian took one look at the dinner table, the body positioning of everyone seated, and he knew. He knew that they knew and that something was going to go down. When his father's eyes met his, he feared for his life. He deliberately set his bag down on the ground and stepped into the kitchen. Only Helen rose to greet him.

"Hi Sweetie, won't you join us?"

Ian nodded and sat at the end of the table.

Helen wiped her mouth, thinking, *Okay, now we'll have it. Now we'll see who the liar is. My son is not an incestuous monster. This little beast is lying.*

"What's going on?" Ian said. Still holding out a shred of hope that the mood at the table was just a reflection of everyone's collective loserdom.

Lyle swallowed hard and felt his cheeks flush as his looked at his son.

"Ian, do you know where we just came from?"

"No."

As Lyle started to speak, Erin finally did.

"He knows, Ian," she said. "He just knows. What you've been making me do. So stop, okay?"

Ian looked over at Helen, she waiting for a rebuttal. But it was not to be.

Ian's mouth curled down, his eyes fluttering.

"I'm sorry, Erin."

SNAP! The top of Helen's tumbler broke off, slicing into her hand.

Lyle couldn't look at Ian. Instead, his eyes remained on Erin. Watching his most precious being have to confront her molester on her own.

"Do you know what you've done, Ian?" Lyle forced out slowly.

"I don't. I mean, I'm sick, Daddy," said Ian. "I know I'm sick and I need help and there's something really wrong with me."

Helen's world was collapsing. She had convinced herself it was a lie, and confirmation from the rapist that it was not was too much to bear.

Helen pushed her plate away, stood up from the table, and stoically left the kitchen. Clutching her bleeding hand.

"Jesus Christ, Ian, why did you do it!"

"I'm sick, Daddy. I'm lonely and I'm hurting inside."

"But your sister? You're supposed to take care of her, you monster!"

Erin felt something coming on. Was this it? Was she really going to cry? She almost felt a wave of excitement.

"I know! I don't know what else to say, except I know!"

"Do you know what you've done?"

"Yes, but it won't happen again and I'll go get help."

"You'll go get help? This child just had an abortion! Your eleven-year-old sister just had an abortion because you're lonely! Do you know how sick that is?"

Ian stopped.

"An abortion? No, that doesn't make any sense. I never di—"

In the microsecond that Lyle felt the first warm mist of blood tickle his forehead, he regretted that his last words to Ian weren't more prophetic. He wished he had offered something other than anger. His world paused to take in the jagged fragments of Ian's open skull rattling the dinnerware and decorating the cloth napkins with a pulpy blend of pink and deep purple. And while Lyle's other senses began their slow return to full speed, his soul lamented that Ian's last impressions of him weren't one of calmer perspective.

Across the table, Erin was so convinced that this outburst was going to be her moment to cry that she put her hand to her mouth. She wiped the blood off her cheek and saw that it still pumped, gurgling onto the table from Ian's face. His cheek folded outward and his orthodontia-treated teeth were now part of the tuna casserole. *I spent a lot of money on those* blipped through Lyle's brain. Like a burst of static on the television. It was bolted out of his conscious by the screams of Erin.

And there behind Ian, a ravaged and defeated Helen stood holding the .22 rifle. The same rifle that never did get a chance to kill the weasel. The same rifle that would, as it happens, add to Helen's previously cited statistic that guns were far more likely to be used against a family member. Lyle noted that, as well. And for all of Lyle's soap boxing about gun safety, he forgot to account for the occasional fit of rage that can boil up when depression, failure, desperation, and rage all collide.

As Erin paused to catch her breath in between hysterical screams, Helen lowered the rifle.

"I'll make some brownies," she said.

september

thirty-three

Lyle stepped out of his car in the parking lot
of the Adirondack State Penitentiary.
He pushed the heavy car door closed and
took in the late morning air.

It was cleaner than it had been lately. A late August rain had washed away the dust, and the crispness of autumn was upon them. He opened up his lunch pail and stared into it. He had been late getting out the door and packed his lunch full of condiments and salty carbohydrates. Nothing that could come close to nourishment. He sighed and leaned up against the car. Lyle had never wanted to go to work less than he did on this day. It was Erin's first day of school. First day of middle school. And first back among peers since his wife had murdered his son for molesting his daughter. He had dropped twenty pounds since the start of summer and his prison guard uniform was now hanging off his shoulders.

Lyle had always had contempt for the inmates. He never bought the sympathy card that they had made poor choices. And he had never seen any of them do true penitence, as the aptly named building implied. He saw them get old and muscular and addicted to porn but nothing approaching remorse. He felt similarly about those who would visit them. *It's your own fault for marrying such a lowlife*, he'd often think. And yet now, here he was, on the verge of being the face of the other side of the glass. Helen had found herself in Bedford Hills, which had the claim to fame of the only death row for women in upstate New York State. Lyle had yet to make arrangements to go see her. He wasn't sure what to say. Now that it was just Erin and him living in that big house, his loneliness had been exasperated. He wanted to burn it all down and sanitize the property of all the toxic memories. But he had nowhere to go. No job waiting for him. He needed to keep pushing and make his pension.

Lyle pushed himself up from the car and began his walk toward the guard's entrance. He wondered if Anna would make an appearance today. He had only seen her once since the events of late May and made a valiant effort to be elsewhere when he saw her husband's name on the ledger. Now they were back to ignoring one another, just as they had done decades before. She never sought him out to ask about Ian or Helen or the missing bottle of bourbon. Lyle wasn't about to tell her that it was likely the bourbon that helped dull Helen's conscience enough to shoot her son in the back of the head.

The irony of all it was too much for him to bear. His mind would go through the various events of the past year to think if this had been done differently, none of it would have happened. And then the world as it was would come back into focus and Lyle was left with the scraps of a life that remained. He wished he had appreciated how boring and typical his life had been before it all unraveled. It's human nature to never fully appreciation anything until it's gone, but even his loveless marriage seemed enviable when compared to his current state. He had to hold on to whatever was left in his relationship with Erin and keep living for that. But even though his instincts told him to stay by her and hold her hand for the rest of his life, he knew neither would grow out of the pain with that remedy. The fall would usher in a routine. And from routine they could attempt to build normalcy.

Erin was turning twelve that weekend. A September baby born of a drunken New Year's Eve rendezvous. Lyle was never very skilled at choosing the right gift but this year he had planned a much-needed alternative. They would take a trip. A drive to a bed and breakfast across the state line in Vermont. Lyle only had to make it to the weekend. And hope that Erin could do the same.

⌐⌐

Erin sat on the front porch of her house with her feet pointed inward. She had purposely missed her bus and was hoping that a lightning storm would materialize and atomize her into dust. But there wasn't a cloud in the sky. She was trying to come up with some way to explain to her father how she missed her bus when she saw Beth approaching with Edward. Beth looked bright and confident. She walked with a quiet confidence and a classy late summer dress. A far cry from the acid jeans and plaid shirts that had become familiar.

Erin looked down. She didn't want a pity exchange and just preferred to avoid all human contact. Maybe forever, but certainly today. Beth slowed her walk to a stop and stood across from her.

"Hey," she said, holding Edward's hand.

Erin looked up, squinting against the sun behind her.

"Hi, Edward," Erin said. Beth didn't seem to mind that she addressed him and not her.

"Give you a ride to school? Looks like you missed your bus," Beth said. There was genuine sympathy in her voice.

"I don't think I'm going."

"Don't you want to see your friends?"

"I don't have any friends," Erin said, as if she was stating the current weather conditions. *It's clear, high seventies, and Erin has no friends.*

"I'm sure that's not the case."

"It is. But that part of my life is the same, so that's cool."

Beth sighed. She looked back at her house and then to Erin. Beth was one of the few people to know all the details of what transpired in the Cooks' home that summer. A perverse aspect of human nature is to suddenly feel better about one's own condition when the inner workings of an infinitely worse life are revealed. Likely a major contributor to Beth's newfound aplomb.

"Why don't you come with us? Just to be around some other people. I think it'll be good for you."

"How will it be good for me?"

"I dunno. But this isn't." Beth extended her hand to Erin, who looked up at her and then down to her feet again.

"Do you go to church?" Erin asked.

"No," Beth followed.

"Do you think maybe one day you could take me? I haven't been in a while and I don't want to go alone."

"Yes, I will," Beth said.

Erin nodded and continued to stare at her shoes. Knocking the toes together to hear the satisfying tap. Her eyes started to lose focus again. Little dots forming out of the cracks in the wooden boards. Her solitary existence now being marked by a giant exclamation point. She was alone in her house most of the time now. Eli never moved back in from his basement apartment some miles away. Michele made an appearance at the funeral but then quickly returned to her own life several time zones away. One free of the stigma that meant being a Cook in Essex County. Erin wondered how long she would be alone and then realized it would be her decision to change it. To welcome another person into her family. She blinked.

When she looked up again, she saw Edward's hand extended to her. Erin wondered how much he knew of what happened to her family. She wondered what he had been told—and of that, what he really understood. She looked at Beth and saw genuinely sympathy. It was appreciated, but that wasn't what Erin needed. She returned her gaze to Edward and just saw a human hand. That may or not have had any preconceived notions in his brain. That had no ability to judge or offer unsolicited advice. She saw his eyes darting around, not really looking at her or anything else. She examined his chubby little sausage fingers, thick with calluses and torn fingernails. His hand in constant motion, a mix of insecurity and impatience, she assumed. Now *that*, she should could relate to.

And she took it.

thirty-four

On a gray Saturday afternoon in September, Erin found herself walking down to the Country Token.

The first weeks of school were similar to those of years past in that no one spoke to her. What made these different was that her classmates looked at her. Previously she could count on wandering through her day almost invisible without anyone knowing who she was. This year, she could feel countless eyes examining her. The result of being a living victim to the worst case of domestic violence the town had seen since those kinds of records were kept. It was not the kind of notoriety she desired. Erin liked being invisible better.

She stepped onto the worn front porch and decided that times must be tough for the quaint local proprietors. The steps were in need of painting and the potted plants hadn't been tended to for some time. When she pushed through the door, she noticed the distinct lack of any bell, chime, or ring. Just a door. She concluded these were the elements that made up a country store. Without them it was just a building with stuff in it. Other details remained, however: Ken Metcalfe was seated in his rocking chair,

Louis Armstrong was engaged in a duet with Ella Fitzgerald, and the sounds of an upright bass bounced off the wood around them. Erin pretended to look around the store, hoping to catch Ken's eye. When she finally did, he sensed it immediately. He looked up over his reading glasses with a warm, sympathetic greeting.

"Hi, Erin," he said.

"Hello, sir."

"What's wrong, sweetheart?" he asked, slowly bringing his newspaper to his lap.

"How much longer will you work here?"

"Oh, well, it's hard to say. Things may not have worked out the way I hoped. The idea of running of charming trinket shop is much better than the reality."

"How come?"

"Simply put, I don't sell enough trinkets to pay the bills."

"Will you leave?"

"Probably."

"Where will you go?"

"I don't know. Back to the city. Perhaps put my marketing degree to work."

"That would make me sad."

Ken moved his newspaper from his lap to the table beside him. He stood up.

"Yeah, me too."

Erin pretended to look at a collection of place settings. Some ornate depictions of nature's harmony complete with matching napkins. Ken was pretty sure she had no interest in buying them but that's where her feet stopped moving.

"There's a saying," he continued. "'Man plans and God laughs.' Have you ever heard that before?"

"No."

"What it means is, we all have this vision of how our life will go, and as much as we may plan for it to turn out one way, it rarely does."

Erin nodded. "Yeah, I know about that."

Ken shoved his hands in his pockets and tilted his head down. "You didn't come here to browse, did you, Erin?"

Erin shrugged. "I dunno."

"I can just listen if you want. Or not. Up to you."

"I don't like people talking about me. Looking at me."

Ken nodded. "I know. I wouldn't either. You're a brave girl to push through that and keep your head up."

As if on cue, Erin raised her head and inquired, "What were you reading back there?"

"The newspaper."

"Anything good?"

"Not really."

"Anything about my mom?"

"Not anymore."

"Why do you think that is?"

"There's a lot of tragedy in the world. When people get their fill of one, they generally move on to the next."

"Was it always this way?"

"What way?"

"Tragic."

Ken took off his reading glasses and paused. He motioned to his rocking chair for Erin to sit. She shook her head and replied, "No, thank you."

Ken nodded. "I think as long as human beings look to themselves for guidance, life will be more tragic, yes."

"More?"

"Well, there are two types of tragic. Nature versus human induced. An earthquake versus mass murder, for example. But if there is nothing greater than humans, than everything is just nature. Running its course."

"What do you mean?"

"You wouldn't fault a lion for killing a zebra, would you?"

"No."

"Then if humans are just animals, you can't fault them for anything they do."

"Then what hope is there?"

"People need a moral guide. Something higher than man or government to help their inherently flawed nature."

"Like a Jewish carpenter."

Ken nodded. "Maybe."

"My parents believed in him and they never got along."

"Believing and behaving are two different things. A decent society, or marriage, requires both. Thoughts are nice, but it's actions that matter."

"I don't know what to think anymore."

Ken looked down at a stack of magazines tucked beneath his desk behind the counter. His private collection of various journals, weeklies, and gazettes from the last twenty years. Some in mint condition, others so weathered the whites had faded to saffron. He randomly grabbed a few off the shelf.

"Here. Take a look. The twentieth century has the distinction of being the most godless while also being the most violent. If you still think humans are essentially decent on their own after skimming these, you let me know."

Erin put them on the shelf next to her. She returned to the napkin she was pretending to examine, folding the corners into a triangle and then a crease with her thumb and finger. The forging of a fabric airplane. "Where is your wife?" she finally asked.

"She had to get another job. This wasn't cutting it. So she's doing part-time housekeeping at the Best Western."

"Do you think you'll ever have kids?" Erin asked without looking up.

"Maybe. Window is closing a bit so we'll need to figure that out pretty soon."

Erin put her napkin down and stepped around the row of linens. She eyed a shelf of commonly sold but rarely used kitchen accessories, assuming fake looking at the pottery would be better than fake looking at the napkins and tablecloths.

"How are babies made?" she said finally, holding a mortar and pestle.

Ken paused, not sure if he had heard her correctly. "Say what? Babies? How do they what?"

"I mean, how does it happen?"

"Oh, Erin, I don't think this is a conversation we should be having. It's a little . . . personal." Ken added the hint of a question, not sure if "personal" was the right word.

"Why?"

"Well, it's something better suited for your father, I think."

"He's sad. He doesn't talk to me much anymore. He took me on

a trip for my birthday to Vermont. It was pretty, but there wasn't
a lot of talking."

Ken nodded. He of course knew what transpired at the Cooks'
property up the street. The major details of Helen killing Ian was
common knowledge. The minor details of why were not. Neither was
Erin's visit to the clinic. He was probably the first person to see Erin
outside the confines of her house and school since. Given what this
child had been through, he didn't feel right shoving her out the door.

"I'm so . . . sorry, Erin. For what happened. I don't know what to say."

Erin looked across the glass counter at him and managed a timid
smile. "That's okay. Nobody does. Nobody will talk to me. Not that
anyone really did before, but now nobody will even fake it."

Ken broke. He knew this girl was special. Something told him. So
he needed to get over his own insecurities and focus on her needs.

"Okay, Erin. What do you want to know?"

Erin walked over and pulled the stool up to the counter so that
they were both looking at each other. Their faces reflected in the glass
beneath.

"How does it happen?"

"Babies, you mean?"

"Yes, please, sir."

The fact she was incorporating their past conversation charmed
him. The fact that she was desperate and alone grieved him. He spoke
slowly to keep his emotions in check.

"Well, it, uh, they didn't talk about this in school?"

"They did. But . . . can it happen any other way?"

"What do you mean?" Ken was really hoping for another customer
to walk in the door and save him from the direction the conversation

had taken. What he wouldn't give for a tourist or a power outage. He'd even welcome a robbery right at this point.

"I mean, there's no other way for babies to be made. So like . . . parts need to go in other parts like they said?"

Ken nodded. He had no nephews or nieces or anything to draw on for how to guide him through this. He decided to just pretend he was a doctor and give his best matter-of-fact response. He even lowered his voice slightly, just to keep the performance going.

"Yep, that's the only way. This goes there and that's all there is to it. Your parents never talked about this with you?"

Erin shook her head. "No, I think my dad kinda left that up to my mom. But she's not around anymore."

"Yeah, well, your school or your health class is right. That's how it happens."

Erin nodded and looked around.

"I want to buy something to thank you for talking to me."

Ken shook his head. "Not necessary. You can talk anytime."

"Okay, well, I still want to get something."

"Who is it for?"

"I don't know."

"Well, that makes it tricky."

"I mean, I know, but I don't know her name."

"Then something that would remind you of her."

Erin nodded and looked around the store. She got up and took her short little steps to the first aisle and looked down. She grabbed the periodicals off the shelf and turned back to Ken.

"Do you have anything that can grow?"

thirty-five

Erin walked down the gravel path of the cemetery. Birds and insects joined the sounds of her sneakers crunching over the tiny stones.

In one hand she held a cloth bag. A grape hyacinth bulb. In the other, a trowel. It had been several weeks since she had visited the Nameless Girl's grave. There were far more people, visitors, and grounds keepers alike in the summer months so that served to keep Erin away. Ian was thankfully not buried here. His funeral was easily among the stranger events of her young life. She couldn't imagine anything coming close to the suffocating mix of bitterness and remorse that filled the air that day. No one was sure how they were supposed to feel. Or which people deserved spite and which deserved pity. Most got a mix of both.

Erin walked up the dirt road and passed a small gathering at a new grave site. She couldn't tell if the people attending recognized her. She hated being a local celebrity—and worse still, the reasons for it. When she arrived at the grave site, she saw that her previously well-groomed stone had taken a turn. She kneeled down and began to pull weeds along the edges of the grave.

The first leaves of autumn had started to collect along the tall grass, crisp like paper. Birds chirped randomly and the scratching of Erin's trowel provided the only soundtrack. She worked slowly and methodically. Neither in a rush to finish or to return home. Erin stopped to reach for her bulb and then paused. Sensing that she was no longer alone, she turned. Her knees spinning around in the grass to see Heather standing behind her. She wore a white dress with yellow flowers. The same kind she would often wear to Sunday school.

"How did you know I was here?" Erin asked.

"Your father told me. I stopped by your house first."

Erin nodded.

"How are you getting by, Erin? You don't come to services anymore."

"Would you?"

"I don't know. Not many on earth can relate to what you've been through."

"What is your interest in me?"

"I can't say. I'm not sure I fully know."

Erin looked across to the entrance of the cemetery. An older couple was strolling out together arm in arm. She looked back into the woods behind her and then calmly at Heather.

"I think I know," she delivered with sad confidence.

Heather sat down in the grass. "Can I help you?"

Erin didn't respond but didn't object either.

Heather looked at the tombstone. The date. The inscription. "Why this site?"

"I didn't know at first. Now I think something was pushing me here."

"Calling you?"

"Maybe."

Erin pulled at a few weeds. She began to dig a hole for the flower bulb. "You know the prayer we used to say? The part about how Christ will come again?"

"Of course," Heather responded.

"How will he come again?"

"I guess nobody knows, really."

Erin looked across the graveyard as something caught her eye. Poking its head from the bushes was a weasel. *Her weasel.* It darted its head around. A chipmunk in its mouth. She reached into her pocket and put the plastic ring on top of the gravestone.

"My parents took me to a clinic. I had the baby killed. You know about that?"

Heather closed her eyes and put her hand over her mouth. "I heard rumors about that. Ian, too. But I didn't want to believe them. I'm so sorry."

"They don't bury them, you know. Not like this girl. They just, I don't know. Burn them or something."

Heather watched her, eyes watering.

"There's something about that whole thing you should know."

"Okay, but you only tell me if you want to."

Erin nodded and gave her version of a half-smile. "I think you're the one I'm supposed to tell."

"All right."

"What happened with Ian. It was wrong. And I don't know why I let it happen. Maybe I was lost or something. Needing some kind of attachment. Anything. But it wasn't the kind of wrong that makes a baby. That's what I wanted you to know."

Heather's heart stopped. Her eyes searched Erin for a hint of manipulation.

"Erin, I don't . . . I don't know what you're getting at."

Erin watched the weasel hop out of its hiding place and scamper off into the woods.

"What if Jesus was supposed to come again? Like he did before. To a young girl who wasn't perfect. Who was awkward and lonely but only this time we didn't let him. Our ways and the things we do made it not happen. The way we are now made us say, 'No thanks, we don't need you.' What happens then?"

Heather exhaled and felt her feet go numb as the ambient sounds around her subsided. Her eyes lost focus and the colors became muted like the sepia tone of a silent movie. She felt herself lose her equilibrium, planting her hand on the earth to maintain her balance. She had to inhale methodically to reset her composure. Her mind raced, fluctuating between disbelief and quiet rage. Wanting to scream and mock and shout her down. Laugh at her to shame the notion in her head. Slap her across the face for proposing something so grotesquely fanciful that it should be trampled on and never discussed again.

But she knew it was true.

Heather watched Erin's sad eyes. Those eyes that could not produce tears. Eyes that were so restless, they barely slept. Trapped inside a stoic shell. Feeling the weight of the universe now pressing down on her shoulders. The posture of a ninety-year-old man. Watching this girl, who she now knew in her soul God had chosen to bear the Second Coming. Placing in her in weakness of character and abhorrent behavior. He had surrounded Erin by doubt and pitiable circumstances, all to test the faith of those around her. And they all failed. Each and every one from all specters of wealth and education and influence and age had come up short. Their haste and their wretched human nature all lined up precisely to make a rash, selfish decision and abort the next incarnation of a savior in human form. And the result, the world will have to live with until a time the Lord chose again. If He chose to.

Heather reached out to grab Erin's hand. She laid it in the grass next to her. Erin moved over to take her palm into hers.

Erin closed her eyes and bowed her head.

And felt a tear forthcoming.